I0846735

Hallowed Ground

HALLOWED GROUND

A NOVEL

Nancy Buchewicz

DERBYSHIRE PRESS

To my family,
you are my first and last home.
You gave me time,
and time is the rarest gift one can receive.

One

The Safehouse

"The fire burns low in the cabin's heart, but still it remembers every scream. The hills hold peace like a wound holds blood, never clean, never forgotten."

Esther had never been in the company of a white man who didn't mean her harm. Every white face that she had ever known was a memory of pain; cold eyes, harsh voices, rough hands.

Jacob was different.

His hands were calloused like any farmers, and his voice carried the slow, warm drawl of Kentucky's hill country. But there was kindness behind his eyes, a gentleness she'd never seen in a man with skin the color of his. He didn't look at her like a possession. He looked at her like she was kin. Like she was a child of God.

He glanced often toward the window, fingers tightening slightly around his rifle; a protector watching the shadows beyond. He and his wife, Miriam, kept a simple home tucked deep in the hollows, where mountains rose like old gods and trees pressed in close, keeping long forgotten secrets within their roots. The floorboards creaked with every step and the hearth burned low. A hand-stitch quilt hung over the door to stop the night's chill from creeping in. Under this roof, Jacob and Miriam welcomed all of God's children.

For many years, they had provided a safe haven for weary souls seeking freedom through the Underground Railroad. Jacob knew what happened to men who helped runaways; burned barns, dead livestock, a family strung up from the very tree they planted on the day they wed. Still, he never turned one away.

To Esther, this place felt like stepping into a church. Sacred, silent, and warm with grace.

She did not come here alone. Around the small table sat Nora and Milly, Clem, Solomon, Levi. Candlelight threw quick shadows across their faces, as they gathered in silence, sharing a simple bowl of beans and corn cakes. This was the first sense of peace any of them had tasted since they ran from Broadlawn Plantation.

Nora barely touched her food; her eyes fixed anxiously on Milly. Clem ate quietly, the spoon shaking in his hand, his thoughts far away. Solomon sat watchful and still, flinching toward each sound outside. Only Levi met Esther's gaze, offering a small, tired smile that tried but failed to hide his worry.

Outside, in the chill of the evening, the Kentucky hills stretched wide, shrouded in mist and sorrow. The forest whispered, ancient and restless, as if the trees themselves held the memories of every broken soul that had passed beneath their boughs, every scream swallowed within their twisted branches.

Beautiful and haunted, like Kentucky itself.

Abraham had brought them here. Just as he promised. He had guided them through thickets and creeks, over switchback trails and hollowed-out ravines, the kind only wild creatures knew. For three nights they moved like shadows beneath the moon, breathless with fear, bellies aching from hunger. Surviving on blackberries, pawpaw fruit, and whatever the woods would give. The slave catcher's dogs followed for miles, snarling just out of sight. But Abraham was clever. Careful. He had led many freedom seekers into these mountains. He knew places to shelter from the rain that never ceased. In the daylight hours, they rested in haylofts of abandoned barns, allowing their clothes to dry. Under the cover of darkness, they crossed endless miles of dense wilderness. When they slipped across the narrow creek gurgling behind Jacob's property, and the hounds fell silent, they knew they had arrived.

They ate in silence, tasting nothing.

When they slept, terror haunted their dreams.

They waited for the slave catchers.

None of them trusted freedom yet. But for the first time, Esther could breathe without fear of a whip cracking behind her. She could close her eyes and not feel the Master's unwelcome hands crawling over her skin.

Still, even here, she felt the weight of everything she'd left behind, her mother's kind voice, her sister's tears, Eustace's crooked smile, the rough soil of the fields, soaked with sweat and grief.

The mountains had taken them in. But the sorrow of Kentucky clung like a second skin.

The fire crackled low, casting long shadows along the wooden floorboards. Solomon murmured a soft line of scripture, as he placed another log on the hearth. "We pass through the water, but we do not drown," he breathed, no one dared break the silence that followed.

Outside, the wind moved through the pines and somewhere in the distance a fox cackled, sharp and inhuman. No one was startled; they were fed on fear.

Jacob kept his place by the window, a rifle across his lap, one eye fixed on the dark. Over the years, he and Miriam had hidden many runaways, he knew what to watch for.

"They come at night, mostly," he said, his voice quiet. "Slave catchers, ungodly men. They ride quiet, lanterns low. Looking for fresh tracks."

Levi nodded from his place near the fire. He was chiseling a scrap of pine into a crude spoon, white curls of wood blanketing the floor. "They think we property," he muttered. "And they ain't gon' stop til' they round us up."

"There is a safe place in the cellar. We won't let them take you," Jacob said. "Not while there's breath in my body."

At the far side of the room, Miriam knelt beside a low cot where Milly lay curled under a heavy quilt, her cheeks flushed with fever. Nora hovered nearby, nervously wringing her hands.

"She been poorly nearly a week now," Nora said, voice tight with worry. "Started before we left. Been giving her bitters, cooling her with creek water. But she still burning up."

Miriam pressed the back of her hand to the small girl's brow. She moved gently, dipping a clean cloth into white oak tea. Her hands were steady and practiced. "She's holding on," Miriam whispered, laying the cool cloth across Milly's forehead. "You did right bringing her. We'll keep dosing the tincture, should keep the fever down. This house has healed folks worse off than her."

Nora wanted to believe her, but her eyes kept drifting back to her sister, who did not stir. "Every mile, I thought she was going to stop breathing."

"You're safe here," Miriam said. "And so is she. For now, that's got to be enough."

Across the room, Clem sat hunched on a stool, staring into the fire. His back still ached from the beating he took before they fled, rope burns still raw at his wrists, welts raised along his ribs. But his spirit hadn't broken.

A log popped in the hearth. He looked up, his voice rough. "You think they'll come?"

Jacob didn't answer at once. He looked back out the window; his gaze traced the tree line like he was reading something written in the dark. "They ain't found this place," he said. "Not yet anyhow."

Silence settled again, thick, waiting. The only sound was the distant ticking of the clock.

Solomon leaned back against the wall, arms crossed, voice low. "We won't be safe till we're over the river. That's where freedom starts."

"No," Esther said, her voice quiet but firm. "Freedom starts here." They all looked at her.

She stood near the fire, wrapped in a blanket, her eyes tired but sharp. The flame set a soft glow along the hard weight she carried. "It starts the moment you decide you don't belong to them no more. Even if they still got your name on paper. Even if they hunt you down. Even if they kill you."

Levi looked at her, really looked, and for a long moment, no one spoke.

Jacob cleared his throat. "We'll keep watch tonight. They won't take you, I promise you that."

He rose, patting the rifle. A warm smell lifted from the oven. "We got fresh bread," he added. "Eat while it's hot. Might be the last hot thing you get for a while."

After the others had eaten and the cabin had gone quiet, Esther stepped outside.

The night air was cool; the trees loomed like watchmen under a sky smeared with stars. The wind carried the warbling hoot of a barred owl, and the faint hush of the forest releasing the day's heat.

She sat on the edge of the porch, a worn quilt tight around her shoulders. Levi came out not long after. He didn't speak, he just sat beside her, close enough that their arms brushed.

For a while, they listened to the woods, alive with the steady, rhythmic hum of cicadas. Inside, a fiddle began playing, hauntingly low and melancholy. The notes drifted through the chinks in the logs like old ghosts. It was a hymn her mother had hummed back when hope was still something that rocked you to sleep each night. Esther blinked hard to keep the tears from spilling.

"I can't sleep," she said quietly.

"Me neither."

She turned her head toward him. "You thinking 'bout home?"

"All the time."

"Not sure I know what that is anymore."

Levi picked up a twig and peeled the bark with his thumb. "Back there," he said, nodding toward the dark, "we were ghosts. No names, no choices. Just work and pain."

She nodded.

"But here…," He glanced at her. "We alive."

Esther gave a sad laugh. "Alive ain't the same as free."

"No," Levi agreed. "But it's a start."

The wind tugged at her hair. Somewhere inside, Milly let out a sharp cough. "Every time I close my eyes," Esther whispered, her voice catching, "I see Eustace's sweet smile. I hear Eliza pleading for me to take him with me. Feels like part of me got left in those fields."

Levi took her hand and set it against his chest. "They still here," he said softly. "With us. Always."

"I hate that I left them."

"You didn't leave," Levi said. "You survived. You ran because you had to. You *had* to."

She blinked, trying to swallow the guilt in her throat. "I don't know how to live with it."

He turned toward her. "Then don't live with it. Live *for* it. For all of them."

His hand found hers.

"I see the way you carry people," he said. "You hold them in your soul. And one day, when this is over, maybe we find somewhere. Where we can all be together."

She looked at him, heart caught somewhere between hope and fear. "You still believe that?"

"I have to, Essie," he said, voice barely a whisper. "Or else what's the point?"

A tear slid down her cheek. She didn't wipe it away. She leaned into him, resting her head on his shoulder. In the heavy quiet, surrounded by the mountain's shadow and the weight of all they'd lost, Esther let herself believe, just for a moment, that a life with Levi was possible.

Even here.

Even now.

And yet, even in this refuge of kindness, she felt it, a deep, cold dread. A heaviness beyond mere fear. They all felt it. Something waited, patient and hungry, watching from the shadow of the trees. More terrible than slave catchers or baying hounds. Something older, something far crueler. Wanting not just their bodies, but their souls. Esther knew its eyes were already on them, silently counting their breaths, awaiting their blood.

Two

Into the Hollow

*"Don't stray the path, child.
These woods take more than they give."*

- Appalachian Folk Proverb

They left before first light, while the mist still clung low to the earth and the trees were no more than dark spires in the fog. The air was wet and heavy with the smell of rain-washed soil. Each breath was thick with dew. Somewhere in the gray fog, a wood-pecker drummed, then fell silent.

Jacob stood by the porch steps, Miriam at his side, their arms braced tightly against the morning chill. Her eyes, soft with worry, had the look of someone struggling to find the right words.

Jacob stepped forward, extending his hand to Abraham, who shook it firmly.

"You keep to the hollows, like always, you hear," Jacob said softly. "Stay off the dirt paths."

"Thank you for what you done," Abraham answered, rough with gratitude. "My people won't soon forget your kindness."

Jacob hesitated, his gaze going distant as if seeing something far beyond the trees. "Stay close to one another," he warned gently. "These woods ain't always been kind."

Esther met his eyes. Something heavy settled in her chest, the burden of leaving safety behind pressed sharply into her heart. She reached for Miriam's hand and clasped it, careful and sure. "Thank you," she whispered. "We won't ever forget your kindness."

Miriam gave her hand a gentle squeeze, blinking back tears. "You go with God, child. Find your peace."

Levi stepped up, his hat in his hands. "We'll keep each other safe. You've done enough riskin' for our sake." He paused, his eyes resting on each face, as if memorizing them. Troubled weather lingered in his gaze.

"It's no risk if it's the right thing," Miriam said, sad and certain.

Clem shifted Milly higher in his arms. Miriam moved closer, gently brushing the child's damp hair from her fevered brow. "You're going to be fine, my little lamb. God didn't bring you this far just to leave you now."

Nora bit her lip, reaching out and briefly touching Miriam's sleeve. "Bless you both," she whispered, eyes rimmed with unshed tears.

Jacob stepped back and settled his hand around Miriam's shoulder, his eyes watchful beneath the wide brim of his hat. They stood together, silhouetted against the pale dawn, as Abraham turned and led them away into the fog-shrouded forest.

Esther followed close behind, her footsteps muffled by the fallen pine needles padding the soft earth. Every step felt heavier, as if the land itself resisted their passage. A shiver ran down her spine, deeper than the morning cold. She glanced back at the others, for a heartbeat, their faces seemed too distant, the mist tugging them apart, thread by thread. Esther's mind drifted to thoughts of Eliza and Eustace, to all those she'd left in the fields, she swallowed hard against the rising sorrow.

Single file, the others trailed silently behind her. Their thoughts roaming the possibilities that lay ahead.

The hope of freedom lay far off beyond the next hill. Solomon, Nora, Clem with Milly slumped and burning in his arms, Levi last, eyes on the trace they left behind. No one spoke. Even the chirping of crickets felt cautious, as though the forest had learned to whisper.

The Appalachian wilderness closed around them like a great cathedral, its vaulted limbs overhead, moss and rotting leaves underfoot. The scent of resin and wet earth clung to every surface. The forest breathed in hushed tones, ancient and watchful. But beneath it all, something older lingered. A quiet wrongness, like the bones of old violence buried beneath thin soil, whispering their warnings through the rustling leaves.

They moved along a narrow game path, winding through fern and bramble, careful not to snap a single twig or rustle too loudly. The canopy stitched tight above, letting in little light, casting them in a verdant gloom that turned every shadow into a threat. Even the birds seemed reluctant to sing.

Solomon walked near the middle of the line, his wide shoulders hunched against the weight of fear and hardship. From deep in his chest, he began to hum, low and steady, a spiritual so old it felt like it had been born from the land itself. The sound was neither joyful nor mournful. It was something in between. It was a rhythm to carry tired feet, a call for strength, a balm to soothe trembling hearts. The melody threaded through the trees like smoke, blending with the mist.

Esther heard it and felt it in her bones.

No one spoke.

Abraham never looked back, but he listened. Always listened.

Around them, the forest creaked and moaned, not loudly, but just enough to remind them it was alive. Watching and vigilant. As though it had seen too much blood spilled in these woods to ever forget.

They walked this way for hours, until they reached a small creek that meandered through the valley floor. The water was cool and shallow, its surface spinning with eddies of fallen leaves. Silver minnows quivered within its gentle currents. Above, a shimmer of dawn light was just beginning to pierce the canopy. A breeze stirred the branches, and for a moment everything was still.

They paused to rest. Milly murmured softly, her fevered head leaning against Clem's chest. Nora dipped the corner of her skirt into the creek water, wrung it out, pressed it to her sister's brow, and whispered a low prayer. Clem glanced worriedly toward Nora; his brows knitted in concern but said nothing.

Esther knelt at the edge of the mineral rich water, cupping her hands to drink. The cold bit at her fingertips, tannin and stone salted her tongue.

Across the stream, a stand of black birch trembled in the still air, their bark peeling in curls like old paper.

Levi crouched beside her.

"You hear that?" he whispered.

"What?"

He tilted his head. "Nothin'. That's the problem."

She listened. He was right. No birds chirped. No breeze sang through the branches. Only the set, patient breathing of the forest.

Solomon sat at the roots of a gnarled oak, scanning the trees. "This land ain't empty," he muttered. "It's watching us."

A small shiver ran through Esther. She couldn't tell if it was the cold, or something else.

Abraham raised his hand and waved them forward. "We got to move," he said. " this ain't no place to be stopping."

They pressed on.

Deeper into the forest they went; the trees grew thicker, older. Lightning-split trunks gaped black, their hollow hearts ringed like scars. Esther thought of her mother's stories, spirits nesting in trees, beasts that walked like men but fed like wolves; the ground cursed by all it was made to swallow.

The land of Kentucky had always been cruel to their kind. The old folks called it the Dark and Bloody Ground, said that the soil itself was soured.

Somewhere behind them, far off but drawing closer, a blood-hound howled, the sound cut through the mist like a knife. Esther froze. The hunt had begun again.

Three

Scattered

*"It was not just their bodies that were scattered, but their souls,
flung like seed into the dark."*

The first bark cracked through the trees like a gunshot. Short and sharp, menacingly close. Esther's body tensed before her mind could name the sound. She quickly spun toward Abraham, who had stopped dead in his tracks, his head tilted, straining to listen. Another bark answered from the ridge above them, it was deeper, hungrier. Then came the crash of brush, the whistling commands of patrollers, and the measured thunder of hooves.

They were surrounded. The forest seemed to contract, closing in around them, suffocating and alive with threat.

The air vibrated with motion. Sound ricocheted from trunk to trunk, until direction lost all meaning, echoes folded over themselves, and north traded places with south.

There was no way of telling which path was safe. Esther's pulse boomed in her ears, drowning out thought. Safety felt like a story other people got to keep.

Solomon crouched beside a rotting deadfall, breath high and

fast. "Too many sounds," he rasped. "They everywhere at once."

"Which way?" Levi whispered, the question tight.

Abraham's eyes flicked through the trees. Two fingers raised; *hold*, then a flat palm; *down*. "Stay quiet. We wait."

A savage growl slit his words. Dangerously near.

Nora gasped, eyes wild with fear. Her fingers dug desperately into Milly's wrist, pulling her from Clem's arms. "No, we can't wait! We got to go!" She bolted, dragging the fevered child, crashing through laurel and briar.

The bloodhounds had found them.

"Nora!" Clem roared, panic cracking through his deep voice. He lunged after them, but the thickets erupted. Black shapes surged from the darkness, jaws snapping, white teeth gleaming in the dim. One caught his pant leg and wrenched. He fell hard to his knees. With a snarl, he booted the beast in the snout and staggered back to his feet, lurching after Nora.

"Go!" Abraham shouted, voice gone ragged. "Scatter, now!" He whistled once, sharp as a hawk's cry, *scatter*, and vanished sideways into green shadow.

Solomon broke the other way and disappeared, swallowed by the underbrush. A patroller burst into view, a heavy man riding a hard breathing gelding, his tattered coat flapping behind, "I see 'em! They running southeast!" He piped two shrill whistles and jerked the reins, the dogs leapt to answer.

The woods turned into chaos.

Levi seized Esther's arm, instinctively she tore herself free, her heart pounding too loud to think. The trees became walls, dark and endless, closing tighter with each gasping breath. Whips cracked somewhere up ahead. Men shouted, cruel and triumphant. Hooves thundered like drums of war. The woods narrowed to breath and bark, confusion and terror.

Clem's voice broke through once more, desperately calling out Nora's name, then it was cut off. Silence.

Another howl, closer now, echoed down the slope.

Esther turned and ran. She risked a glance over her shoulder. In the dim half-light of the woods, she saw Clem sprawled on the ground, a lash uncoiling across his back, dark blood already blooming through his shirt. He looked up, pain twisting his features. Their eyes met.

Then, the hounds lunged.

In the madness, she had no direction, no plan, just raw, primal instinct driving her forward. She ran until her breath burned in her chest, until branches scored her skin, until her feet stumbled and nearly betrayed her. She knew only motion and the iron taste rising in her mouth. The others vanished behind a veil of green. Far off, Milly coughed, a tiny spark swallowed by the dark.

Eliza's voice rang in her skull, sharp and steady, *Soak your shoes in turpentine, it'll throw off your scent.* She had; she prayed it would work.

The baying slid past and thinned. The hounds hadn't followed.

She stumbled to a stop, hidden beneath a thicket of laurel, her heart hammering like it was trying to escape her chest. The forest pressed in on all sides, dark and close, with shafts of sunlight slicing through the canopy at sharp angles. Somewhere off to the north, the Ohio River ran murky and wide. It was a ribbon of salvation she couldn't yet see but knew was there.

Behind her, a scream pierced the air, agonized, human, and horribly familiar.

Clem.

They had him.

Esther clamped a hand hard over her mouth to keep from crying out. She could hear the snarling beasts, feral and merciless, as they locked onto their prey. The sound tore through her soul, wrenching it apart.

Footsteps broke close, two patrollers shouldering through the scrub, rifles up, the stink of sweat and beasts moving with them.

"The bitch doubled back," one muttered. "Watch that ridge

over there, she's got a head start, dragging that little one behind her, she won't get far."

"The big buck's done for," the other grunted. "Hounds tore him up good."

"Damn shame. Barrow's gonna be real upset. Dead slave ain't gonna be working no fields."

Esther's stomach turned.

Her fingers curled into the damp earth, jaw clenched.

She held still while their boots passed, so near she could hear stirrups clink together, and fade off downslope.

Only then did she breathe. She rose, shaking, face slick with sweat and smeared with blood from the briars. Tears blurred the tree trunks into columns of water.

She took one faltering step back toward the sound of Clem, then froze, trembling. She couldn't go back.

There was no saving him if that pack still ran.

To go back would only feed the ground another name. The awful helplessness settled over her like chains.

Esther stood alone, powerless, as the darkness deepened all around her.

The forest shifted, shadows braided through the trunks, branches overhead whispered in a sorrowful tongue. The earth underfoot held cool and spongy, moss woven with old needles. This land remembered. The dead waited quietly beneath the leaves.

And now, it had claimed another soul.

Four

The Burning Ground

"I dream of the fields, not for their beauty, but for the pain they remember."

- Anonymous, WPA Slave Narrative

Esther didn't remember lying down.

One moment she was running, tearing through the underbrush, fleeing the whips of the slave catchers. Stumbling, half-blind with exhaustion and shock, the forest folding in on her like a veil. Her legs buckled beneath the shadow of a tall oak, and the earth rose to meet her. The world slipped into blackness.

Then, the nightmare came.

Broadlawn Plantation. The noon heat pressed down with the stench of slop and sunbaked offal. Cicadas screamed from the tobacco fields, louder than reason. Overhead, turkey vultures swung slow circles. The world felt… skewed, like a backward reflection in a cracked mirror. The sky glared, blinding white and merciless.

Everywhere flies swarmed in great black clouds.

Eliza hunched on the cabin steps, her hands red to the wrists, scrubbing blood out of rags in a rusty basin. Her face was slack, eyes sunken and empty. The rags were endless. Each one she rinsed came back bloodier than the last. The water never cleared.

The stench of iron filled the air.

Eustace crouched in the weeds beneath the kitchen stairs. Bits of leaves stuck to his tight curly hair. His skin was powdered in a fine layer of dust. His chest fluttered in shallow, panicked breaths. He silently watched the big house with wide, hollowed eyes. He blinked but did not speak. He held something between his little hands, perhaps a broken bird.

They didn't see her. Esther open her mouth to call their names, but her voice was caged somewhere deep within her ribs, clawing to get out. She lunged forward but the ground gripped her ankles like hands, *no farther*. The land held her fast. She could not move. She could only weep.

You don't belong here anymore, it seemed to say. *You left them.*

She clawed at the ground, trying to pull herself forward. Eliza was so close, her skirt brushing the dry grass within reach, but still, she didn't move. Her eyed held no flicker of recognition. Only that blank, dead stare.

Then came the shadow.

The Overseer, covered in grime, whip uncoiling like a serpent. His shadow stretched far across the yard. Bodies swung from ropes, suspended from the branches of a large oak, moving as the wind told them to.

Behind, John Barrow walked with the ease of a man who had never known fear. He had claimed ownership over everything she knew. His boots were soaked in something too dark to be mud. His smile was slow and smug.

"C'mere girl," he growled, low and vile.

The air thickened. The sky grew dark and angry.

Her mother's voice rose, weak and trembling, as if from underwater. "Protect them, Esther. Even if you can't save them, you must protect them."

Esther screamed, reaching, but the earth pulled her down.

The yard erupted into flames, fire chewed through the walls of the cabins, up tree trunks, towards the blindingly white sky. The screams weren't hers now. They were the shrieks of women and children. A thousand voices howling up through the smoke. Her hands glowed white-hot. She could feel herself burning, but she couldn't wake.

She burned.

They didn't move.

She wrenched out of sleep with a choking gasp, mouth bitter with the taste of ash, cheeks wet with tears.

The forest loomed around her, ancient and still, its trees like towering mourners. They watched her silently, as if they too re-membered. As if they had seen it before. Ferns seemed to edge back from where she lay, as though the dream itself had spilled into the waking world.

No wind. No birds. Only the weight of what had been.

Sorrow burned through her like flame, searing and relentless. But beneath it, something steadier stirred. Not hot, but cold as ice. A second heartbeat. A slow rage.

Rage at the men who had torn her family apart.

Rage at the world that allowed them.

Rage at herself, for surviving, for running.

It rose inside her like something she'd swallowed long ago, something that had waited, patient and coiled, in the pit of her soul.

She stood.

Her legs trembled. Her breath came hard.

But her eyes burned.

Just beyond the tree line, something moved.

Not the slave catchers. Not an animal. Something deeper. The kind of shape that doesn't leave footprints, only silence.

Too tall to be a man. Too still to be a deer.

A dark flicker where the light should be. Gone as soon as it appeared.

Esther froze, her breath catching in her throat. She scanned the woods, searching the underbrush for any sign of what she'd seen.

But there was only mist now, curling low over the ferns. The leaves rustled above her, heavy with dew, as if nothing had disturbed them at all.

She told herself it was nothing. A trick of the light. A shadow slipping through branches.

But the forest had changed. It felt different.

The birds still hadn't returned. The air held its breath again. And the trees, those old Appalachian sentinels, stood like silent witnesses to her terror.

Watching.

Waiting.

Esther backed away slowly, her skin crawling. She didn't dare run. Because something older than instinct was speaking now, low in her gut, sure as a hand on the back of her neck.

If you run, it will follow.

Five

The Hollow Beyond

"I seen good white folks.
But I seen plenty that smile while they cut your throat.
You don't know what they are 'til they show you."

- Inspired by WPA narratives.

In the confusion left behind by the patrollers, they found each other, one by one, mud streaked and torn, beneath the twisted arms of the trees. All except Esther. They called her name in hushed voices, again and again, like a prayer. They combed the bramble, bodies crouched low, listening hard for an answer that never came. They searched until the sun slid lower and the hounds fell farther off. With a single look, Abraham made the call, they had to press on toward the next safehouse.

In the chokehold of dusk, the forest pressed close. Damp and shaded. Only the ragged breath of the runaways broke the strange silence. They moved in a tight line, heads low, shoulders drawn, eyes flicking through shadow and branch. Every snapped twig rang too loudly; every rustle twisted their spines with dread. The weight of what they'd lost slowed their feet, making the ground feel heavier with each step.

Abraham led them.

He was tall and wiry, with sharpness in his eyes, he read what the others could not. He never stopped scanning, not from panic but from habit. A hunter's gaze. A survivor's logic.

He spent his words like rations. Silence was his armor. It had kept him breathing longer than most. His story was written in the weathered lines of his face, the rasp at the edge of his breath. He moved as if he were part of the land, his gait silent, his body lean, curved just enough to make him vanish between the trunks.

Abraham had spent years in the swamps, living among snakes and biting insects, wild as the land itself. A maroon, they called him, one of the slaves who slipped the chains and never looked back. He had vanished into the mud and heat, made a life where white men couldn't reach him, where even the hounds turned back. Up in the moss choked cypress, he hunted and fished, watched his reflection in the eyes of panthers. Abraham fed himself on root and flesh and buried more brothers than he could name. He had learned the old ways. He knew how to disappear. He knew how to survive.

He walked through the forest like a man still part of it, not a guide, but something wiser. Something shaped by the land and hardened by its hunger. The others followed him, because there was no choice. Abraham knew the way.

Behind him, Nora stumbled and Milly's small hand slipped from hers. She caught it quick and squeezed tight, anchoring them both. The child hadn't spoken since the dogs gave chase, since they got Clem. She just clung to her sister, wide brown eyes taking in everything.

"You alright, baby girl?" Nora whispered, bending to adjust Milly's shawl, her voice tight with worry. "You feeling cold?" She brushed a damp curl from Milly's brow, set the back of her hand there, testing the fever that still clung. The girl's skin felt paper thin and too warm. Her eyes stayed unfocused, staring through the trees with a haunted stillness that made Nora's chest ache. Milly didn't answer.

"She's in shock," Solomon said, falling in beside them, his voice low and rough, worn by years of obedience and grief. "Ain't nothin' to do but keep her warm. I can carry her." His arms were already reaching. He gathered the girl as if she were glass.

Nora nodded, though her gaze did not leave Milly's face. Her calloused hand smoothed over her sister's tight plaits with aching tenderness, fingers lingering as if they could press away the pain.

"She saw the hounds take Clem," Nora whispered hoarsely. "Saw them tear him down like he was nothin', he didn't even have time to cry out." She swallowed hard. When she spoke again her voice caught. "That girl's carried too much sorrow for one so little. Watched our daddy go, now Clem. Ain't right. Ain't fair. She jus' a child."

Her shoulders shook; she blinked back tears. "I should have done more. Should have pulled her away. I was right there," she cried, "I don't know what to do. I can't take it out of her head, can't put her pieces back together. All I can do is hold her. Hold her and pray that's enough."

For a moment, no one spoke.

Solomon nodded, adjusting Milly gently in his arms.

"It's enough," he said at last; voice lost in the wind. "You kept her breathing. That's enough."

Levi had fallen behind, lost in thought. He kept looking over his shoulder, jaw clenched tight, fingers twitching at his sides. He had seen Esther in the trees for a beat before she disappeared. She was terrified. He should've gone after her. He had not. Not because he didn't care. Because fear sat in his bones. He hated himself for it. She was all he had.

"Abraham," he called, catching up, his voice low and urgent, "We need to stop. Esther might still be out there."

Abraham did not break stride. "The girl made it. She ain't

stupid."

"She's alone," Levi snapped.

"Alone don't mean dead." Abraham barked back. "She got the turpentine, don't she? Then she got a chance. Only way we help her is by staying alive."

"I'm goin' back." Levi insisted.

"You go back, you dead."

Silence took them.

Branches clawed at their sleeves. Gnarled roots heaved out of the ground. The earth smelled of rot. Off in the distance, a whip-poorwill called, aching and endless.

Ahead, the ridge rose up like a broken tooth. Its silhouette was jagged, as if something had tried to claw its way out of the ground. The moon threw cold, hard shadows over the bedrock.

Abraham paused, raised his hand and dropped low; the others followed without a word.

They reached the ravine as the last light bled from the sky. Below, moonlight silvered the surface of the Ohio, wide and still. The water dancing beneath the stars.

"There it is," Abraham said. "The safehouse is just beyond that ridge. Only a few minutes' walk."

"You sure they'll take us in?" Nora asked.

"Silas and his boy are good people, they took me in," Abraham said. "They'll have plenty of food and dry clothes. We can rest for a few days. Might even have a boat to take us across."

They moved through the forest by moonlight, the trail pale as bone between the trunks.

Levi peered into the dark, brow furrowed. Something about the stillness felt wrong. "Why is it so quiet?" he asked. "Where's the wind? The crickets?"

"It's cause we lost the catchers, jus' seems that way." Abraham said, though even he did not sound sure. They advanced slowly, step by step, the forest watching.

Then the smell fell upon them. Acrid at first, then thick and sweet, the rank stench of rot. Death rolled on the air like fog.

Milly stirred, her nose wrinkling. Solomon turned his head and retched.

"Something's dead," Nora said softly.

They crested the ridge and saw it.

The cabin stood crooked in the hollow, boards warped, a single flame flickering behind the clouded windowpane. Around it, a ring of dead trees leaned outward, gnarled and bent, like they'd tried to crawl away. The front door slowly clapped open and shut in the faint wind. The earth before the steps shone slick and dark.

Under the hush was the low buzzing of flies.

Six

The Weight of Silence

"I hid in the tree all night, watchin' 'em drag my brother like
a hog to slaughter.
I ain't never screamed so loud in my soul."

- WPA Slave Narratives

Esther woke with her heart hammering, her skin damp despite the cold earth pressing against her back. She sat hunched beneath the thicket, arms around her knees, every muscle tight with dread. The forest felt louder now. Branches groaned, leaves whispered, her breath rasped like a warning in her throat.

Her rage had not faded. It had taken root.

It burned low in her chest like a buried coal, fed by grief and guilt, by all she had lost, Mama, Eliza, Eustace, every name etched with pain. And now Clem. Not knowing if he lived hollowed her worse than the truth.

She wiped her face with shaking hands and stood slowly, stiff from the cold. The canopy had swallowed the sun, casting a bruised twilight through the trees. Shadows stretched long and strange.

She turned in a slow circle, trying to find her bearings. The river was gone, consumed by trees and distance.

She was alone.

Still, she moved.

One step, then another. She held to Abraham's counsel: stay low, move quiet, moss runs north. But the moss was patchy here and every trunk looked like the last. The deeper she walked, the less sure she was of any direction at all. The forest felt changed, not only dark but aware, as if it were watching her pass.

Hunger gnawed at her insides. She rummaged through the underbrush, her fingers brushing aside fallen leaves slick with dew. There she found a pawpaw fruit, soft and golden, dropped from its branch. She sniffed, then took a cautious bite. Sweet, like custard. She ate quickly, wiping her mouth with the back of her sleeve. Further on, she pinched a few wild violets and some chickweed, her mother's lessons coming back in the tilt of her fingers. It quieted nothing but gave her legs another mile.

She gathered a few dry twigs and crouched near the shelter of a tree trunk, trying to remember how Levi had sparked a flame with flint and steel. The flint that she carried in her pouch was useless without Levi's blade. All she had were damp hands and frayed nerves. She gave up. Fire would bring warmth, but also attention. If anyone was near, man or beast, it would betray her.

She pulled her shawl close and kept moving, following a faint animal trail. Her steps slower now, the earth threaded with roots and soft loam.

Then she saw it.

A fawn stood in a patch of clover, its coat dappled with the last sift of light. Esther stilled. Her breath caught. For a heartbeat something gentler rose in her, wonder or grief wearing a kinder face. A reminder that the world, for all its brutality, still held the promise of beauty. The young deer lifted its head and met her gaze. For that instant she felt seen, not hunted, not fleeing, simply alive.

The moment held.

Then the fawn bounded away and was gone, a blur between trunks, free and unburdened.

Esther stood rooted, heavy with ghosts, fingers pressed to her trembling lips. She didn't know why she felt like crying. Maybe, the sudden emptiness. Eustace flashed in her mind, that boy charging through tobacco rows, pretending to be a deer, fast as air.

The peace shattered in the next breath.

From deep in the trees came barking, faint and ferocious. Her body went rigid.

The hounds were back.

Snarls carried on a thread of wind. Leaves crisped under heavy steps. The sour stink of musk and old leather drifted near. Slave hunters, coming fast. Instinct told her to run. She ran.

Branches lashed at her face. Thorns tore at her legs. She didn't care. She stumbled through brush and shadow until her foot caught a root, and she went down hard. The breath knocked clean from her chest.

She crawled, dragging herself into the hollow of a rotted oak. Beetles ticked in the dead wood. She pressed her spine to the damp inner bark and forced herself small.

The riders came.

Three men, coats filthy with road dust, thirsty for violence.

One rode with a rifle slung across his back. Another walked beside, a hound straining at the leash, jowls wet, hackles lifted, its breath a hot mist in the cold. Its ears stood erect, listening for the faintest stir. The third led a horse, a man dragging behind on a rope knotted to the saddle horn.

Clem.

Esther's hand flew to her mouth. The world tilted and swam.

His wrists were bound, the rope cutting deep. His shirt hung in rags, lashes stood raw and red upon his back. His chest rose in shallow gasps. His left boot scuffed behind him with each step, leaving a dark drag in the leaves. His eyes were swollen nearly shut, yet they searched the trees as if they might find her there.

The hunters moved slower now. The hound, tired from the chase, nosed the air and whined.

"Damn fool tried to fight back," one said, quiet and pleased. "Ought 'a hang him for the trouble."

"Barrow wants him brought back alive," another muttered. "Says he knows where that girl is. The one he's always dragging to the barn. If it was my say, we'd be done with it."

Clem moaned, small and broken.

Esther bit down on her knuckle, her eyes burning. She wanted to rise, to tear them from their saddles and drag Clem into the dark. But her legs would not answer. Her breath stayed locked inside like a trapped bird.

She saw him again as he had been, humming, Milly perched high on his shoulders, Clem, patient and sure. Now, he stumbled behind a horse, led like an animal.

She stood watching, helpless. Just one woman.

They would kill her before she reached his rope.

The men passed. Their voices thinned. The barking fell away.

The rage pulsed beneath her skin. It whispered of blood. Of fire. Of her mother's lifeless body. Of all the years stolen from her and the people she loved.

Her fingernails dug hard into her palms.

She stayed hidden until only the wind remained. Then, she pulled herself from the tree's black throat, and watched them vanish, Clem's broken body dragged behind like a walking corpse. Her breath hitched. Her heart ached.

She did not move, she was no savior, only a girl with shaking hands and a fire burning in her chest. Clem was gone. She was still breathing. That was her sin.

The wind turned. The forest, once watching, now seemed to be listening. Something had begun in her, cold and certain, and would not stop. In the quiet that followed, the land spoke without words and pulled her backward, toward the night where everything had started.

Seven

The Devil's Refuge

*"They said the devil walked these woods in the skin of men,
grinning with teeth too sharp for mercy."*

-Appalachian folklore

The forest thinned as they neared the ridge. The putrid stench in the air grew heavier with each step. The sun sagged low on the horizon, painting the treetops a deep, iron red. Silence hung like a dense fog. Abraham raised his hand, and they stopped just shy of the clearing.

The cabin slouched beneath a stand of dead oaks; their limbs twisted like grasping fingers. Its unpainted boards had weathered to bone gray, the color of things long dead. The rusted tin roof sagged, hunched like a broken spine beneath the chimney's crumbling weight. The front-porch leaned hard into the earth; boards rotted through as if the place longed to sink and be done.

Behind a cracked pane, a single lantern flickered, a feeble pulse of light inside the darkness. In the corner of the porch, a hornet's nest hung like a relic, its papery shell dry and brittle. A menacing thrum vibrated its warning through the wood. The air was thick with flies, their slow, hungry circles the only movement.

They stepped out of the trees and crossed the clearing. The soil gave underfoot, soft and damp, like a freshly dug grave.

Abraham stared too long. His eyes narrowed as if reading a death notice tacked to the post.

"This ain't right," he said.

Levi edged forward, "What ain't right?"

Abraham didn't answer right away. His nostrils flared.

"There should be smoke," Abraham said. "They always keep the hearth lit. Fire going, food cooking. It's how they signal to travelers, it's how you know it's safe."

"Maybe they out," Nora said, though her voice had no weight. "Helping somebody else."

"Or gone to town," Solomon offered. "Silas got papers. Freeman like him, he might got business."

Abraham shook his head, eyes on the porch. "Not out here. Not this station."

The buzzing gathered. Even the wind seemed to hesitate.

Levi looked at the doorframe. Flies blurred there in a thick cloud. The sweet, cloying reek of decay rolled over them.

Nora covered her mouth. "You smell that?"

"Something's dead," Solomon said.

"You think…?" Levi began and let it die.

Milly tugged Nora's sleeve. "I don't want to go in."

"It's alright, Milly Moon," Nora whispered, but the words wavered. "We just need to rest. There'll be food inside."

Levi felt the same charged stillness. The breathless hush that comes right before a scream.

Abraham did not look away. "Something happened," he said. "Something bad." He took a step, paused. "They might still be inside."

The words hung like a curse.

The door creaked, tapping the frame in the thin wind as if trying to keep time with their footsteps.

They climbed the porch; the boards were dark with mold. Near the base of the door, something black had dried into the grain and trailed outward in ragged strokes, like someone had clawed to get out.

"Don't like this," Solomon muttered, rubbing the back of his neck.

"Neither do I," Abraham said. "But we can't turn back now."

He slid his knife free and closed his hand around it. "Stay close to my side."

Levi came behind, one palm at the small of Milly's back. The girl did not cry. She stared at the door like it might speak her name.

Abraham pushed it open. The rusted hinge groaned like the last breath of a dying man.

Inside, a lantern burned low on the mantle. Its flame trembled, licking soot covered glass like it was fighting to live. Each flicker threw wild shadows that seemed to crawl, as if the darkness wanted out.

The smell swallowed them. A wave, thick and choking, decay and excrement. Beneath the rot, something older and wrong, a cold reek that clutched at the back of the throat and whispered of things that had never lived at all.

Nora gagged. Milly buried her face against her sister.

No voices. No welcome. No fire.

Antlers lined the walls, most broken and jagged. Shards of dishes glittered the floor. A small table had tipped on its side, one leg split clean. Near the hearth, a deer carcass lay twisted and half-covered with a blanket, as if someone had tried to make it decent. An axe sat sunk to the eye in its hide. It's glassy eyes were staring at nothing. Blood pooled black and thick, while maggots writhed in slow white rivers.

Milly let out a choked sob. Nora quickly clapped a hand over her mouth.

"Dear God," Solomon whispered.

God did not answer in that room.

"Silas?" Abraham said, barely sound.

He stepped forward. The floorboards moaned. The lantern's light faltered.

Levi's gaze tracked the room. Dark streaks smeared the floor and walls, not only blood but a tar-thick seep that bled through the cracks, as if the house itself were weeping. Crude symbols were gouged into the timber, some scorched in, vile markings no decent Christian home would abide.

Near the overturned table a darker stain smeared into a trail. It twisted across the planks like a serpent and ended at the cellar's hatch.

"This wasn't a raid," Abraham said. Fear had moved into his voice. "This is evil."

The air grew colder with each step, not a draft, but a chill that seeped into the marrow. It smelled of something that had lived too long and fed too well. The light bent strange, as if unwilling to dwell on what was left behind.

Milly tugged Levi's sleeve. "I hear something," she whispered.

They turned towards the hatch.

It was shut.

From beneath the floorboards, something began to breathe.

Not the breath of a man. But deeper, wetter. A dragging followed, soft at first, like damp limbs sliding across stone. It grew louder. Closer. The wood lifted on its nails and settled again, groaning like it wanted to pull itself free.

The hatch shuddered.

Milly screamed.

Solomon reached for the ring with his fingers shaking. "What if they trapped?" He hauled it up. The iron shrieked.

Silas rose from the darkness.

He was tall, impossibly so, stretched too long for any man.

Rags clung to him like a mockery of the living, bloodstained and soaked through with rot. His skin was parchment pulled tight over a body that was not quite a man. The face was familiar and foreign together, like a mask molded from memory and stitched over something inhuman. The eyes held no whites, no pupils, only black that swallowed the lantern light. The mouth opened and kept opening, a grin split too far. The corners cracked and bled. Teeth glinted like broken glass, small and jagged and endless.

Solomon lunged, brave and furious. Silas moved like smoke. His hand cut the air. Solomon hit the wall with a sickening crack.

The cabin erupted in screams.

Eight

Morning Without Mercy

"Keep your head down, child; the sun can't see your tears."

Before she fled, there was a sunrise where it all began.
That morning came before first light found the ridge.

On Broadlawn Plantation, Esther woke to the hush of breath inside the cabin, then to the light scrape of Eliza's feet finding the floor. The air was sour with old wood smoke and damp cloth. Eustace slept curled tight against her side, boney knees drawn up, his hand still clutching the hem of her skirt like a tether. All night he'd made those small sounds children make when dreams won't let go; his sleep ran broken and fitful. When she touched his shoulder, he startled, then blinked himself awake.

"Hush now," Eliza murmured. "Get up, we got ta' move."

They ate as they walked. Strips of salt pork wrapped in a rag, slick and cold against their fingers. Esther tore hers with her teeth and swallowed without tasting. The salt burned the back of her throat. Eustace chewed slowly, cheeks hollowing, his eyes on the path. The yard was gray as old tin. Smoke bled from the plantation house chimney, a black ribbon against the lightless sky.

"Mind your bag," Eliza said, shifting the strap of her own.

"And keep close."

They passed rows of cabins crouched low in the fog; doors open to the damp. Broadlawn was quiet at that hour, the kind of quiet that made every step sound loud. Cicadas had not yet taken up their screaming, but the day was already heavy, pressing down with the promise of heat.

At the dirt lane a shape came toward them from the Master's house, skirts kicking up the dust. Mama. She moved quickly, a pail on her arm, her yellow head scarf tied neatly. The white children would be up soon. She would be there to feed them, to lift them, to wipe their mouths and gentle their tantrums.

"Morning," she said softly, eyes moving over their faces like hands. She touched Eustace's chin. "You eat?"

"Yes, ma'am," he whispered, mouth shiny with grease.

"Keep your head down today," Mama said, her voice a narrow thread. Her palm lingered at Esther's temple, one heartbeat, then two. To Eliza she gave the smallest nod, and to Eustace she meant to smooth his hair, but he had already turned to look toward the fields, where darkness lifted and the first high-pitched whistle would carry from the Overseer's mouth.

They came to the edge of the tobacco and the earth changed underfoot. Stalks stood shoulder-high, green-black and glossy, the wide leaves already sweating in the warm breath of dawn. The smell drifted, sweet and bitter both, like syrup poured over hot tar. Gum would stain their hands by noon, black crescents under nails that would not scrub out. Mosquitoes stitched at their ankles. Somewhere in the rows a child coughed, then swallowed it back down.

"Lordy," Eliza said, too quiet to be heard, and hitched her sack higher.

Eustace patted his side, then stopped. His hand came up with nothing but air. "My bag," he said, panic sliding into his voice. He looked smaller suddenly; the strap print lay pale across his shirt. "Esther, I forgot my bag."

Eliza's mouth tightened. "Go," she said. "Quick."

He ran the way they had come, thin legs flashing, bare feet a whisper over dust. At the bend he almost collided with Mama again, her pail swinging as she hurried. She steadied him with one hand at his arm.

"Where you flying off to?" she asked.

"Forgot my sack," he panted. "I'm goin' back."

Mama's eyes flicked toward the big house, then to the fields where the first whistle split the morning. She pressed her palm to his cheek. "Run." The word caught like fire. "Run and be fast."

He sprinted on.

In the rows the work began. Hands slipped and tore, the soft snap of stems as they broke the suckers, the leaves lowering into the sag of burlap. Cicadas woke and set the air to a vibrating scream. Heat rose up from the dirt and settled into their backs like a second skin. Esther worked with her head bent, fingers moving in a rhythm set by someone else's profit. Levi was two rows over, his shoulders a hard ridge in the green. Old Amos moved slow and steady, Auntie Bet one plant behind him, both already shining with sweat.

"Where that boy?" Jonas asked, not lifting his face.

"Went for his sack," Eliza said. "He'll be back."

The second whistle blew, now sharper, meaner. Jack's kind of sound. It split the morning air like a blade.

Esther did not let herself look up. She counted the plants, the way Mama taught her. She kept the beat of her hands with the beat of her heart. She told herself Eustace would come around the bend any moment, red-cheeked and breathless, the bag's strap cutting his shoulder like a smile. She told herself to keep moving.

Out on the lane, dust lifted in a small storm around the horse's hooves. Jack sat high in the saddle, the brim of his hat dragging a slice of shadow across his eyes. He looked like a man born to sit and watch others work. He drew the horse up short. Eustace, bag now slung across his chest, skidded to a stop, one foot sliding, one hand lifted in an apology he could not afford to speak.

"You think I don't see you, boy" Jack said, his voice oiled and slow. "Dawdlin'. Late to the rows."

"Please, sir..." Eustace started, breath catching.

Jack did not care for sentences. The rawhide strap lay waiting at his hip. He uncoiled it and did not hurry. The first strike sounded like a clap in a church. Cowbirds in the hedge lifted and scattered. The second found skin. Eustace did not cry out at first. He sucked air and held it like a stone. The third crack sent him to one knee. Dust leapt. The bag slid off his shoulder and hit the road with a soft, forgiving thud.

In the fields the sound carried. It always did. Esther's hands kept working. They had to. Her fingers dug into a leaf and tore it wrong, leaving a ragged edge that would cost somebody something later. Her breath turned shallow, tears welling up.

"Steady," Levi said, so low she felt it more than heard it. Two rows over, his head did not lift. His hands did not slow. The leaf gum shone black on his knuckles like a small, hard truth.

Jack let the whip hang, then stepped down. He took the boy by the back of the neck and set him on his feet with a squeeze meant to do a different kind of hurt. "You run again without asking," he said, "I run you right to the ground." He shoved Eustace toward the fields. "Go on now."

Eustace walked, because running would be a sin against his skin. He kept the bag strap tight to his chest, one hand pressed there as if to hold himself together. Blood had come through his shirt in four thin lines, red as paint. He limped where the road had bit his foot, but he did not limp too much. He had learned that lesson. The cicadas screamed and screamed. The sun pushed its hot hand down on the back of his neck.

At the head of the row, he hesitated. His eyes found Esther's for half a breath, and in that blink, she saw the small boy who sang nonsense to the chickens, who begged for one more story, who curled into her at night when the wind worried the cabin boards. She did not reach for him. To reach was to invite the strap. She looked down instead and took the next leaf, then the next, then the next.

He slipped into the furrow beside her. His fingers shook on the first plant. On the second they were steady. By the third his breath fell into the row's measured rhythm, in and out, in and out, until the sound of it was the same as hers.

Around them the fields went on, green shining, insects gnawing at whatever blood the day could spare. The Overseer's horse shifted and stamped at the lane. The big house windows took the light but gave nothing back. Smoke climbed straight up into the hard blue of a sky that never looked down.

There was nothing to do but make the numbers. Nothing to do but keep their hands moving. Esther bent and broke and loaded, the bag growing heavy against her hip. The weight of it pulled her sideways. The weight of everything did.

Somewhere a laugh rose from the porch of the Master's house, quick and sharp as breaking glass. In the rows, no one laughed. They worked, and the work swallowed the morning and the day after, and the day after that. Tonight, there would be music, a stolen hour with lanterns and feet and breath that belonged to them. For now, there was only heat and the scream of cicadas and the sound a lash makes when it finds a back.

Solomon's voice found the space the cicadas left between their cries, low and rough, more breath than sound. A weary spiritual rose from his chest and moved along the rows like water under rock. He did not lift his head. He kept plucking, kept filling his sack, kept time with the rhythm of the knives.

Auntie Bet's alto slid in, small and steady. Nora followed, barely a whisper. Levi worked the beat with the tug of his bag, the soft scrape of his heel in the dust. One by one the others answered, never looking up, the melody threading leaf to leaf until the whole field seemed to hum.

They sang carefully, close to the teeth. The Overseer's shadow passed and did not linger. Eustace blinked away his tears and reached for the next plant.

The song was their stolen freedom. It did what words could not. It held them in place until the sun inched forward and the day, heavy as a yoke, moved with them. The cicadas thinned for a heartbeat, as if to listen to their sorrow.

Esther kept her head down. She kept her hands moving. She did not let herself weep.

Nine

Before the Storm

*"There is a time to weep, and a time to laugh; a time to
mourn, and a time to dance."*

-Ecclesiastes 3:4

They were bone tired, all of them. Muscles aching. Feet blistered.
Hands rough with calluses that never healed.

But it was Saturday night.

And that meant music. A small rebellion held in the breath
between notes.

They followed the sound like moths to a flame, drawn by the
rhythmic plucking of strings, the heartbeat of a drum, the murmur
of voices gathered close. Sound that promised, for a while, you were
more than John Barrow's property. More than a body to work the
fields. You were human. You were free.

Even if only for a song.

In the clearing behind the quarters, a circle had formed beneath the open sky. Lanterns flickered from stumps driven into the
ground. The moon laid a pale wash across the tobacco. Auntie Bet
had palmed molasses chews from the Master's larder. Eustace lifted
his battered fiddle, the bow hair frayed but still singing sweet. The

rhythm of feet on packed earth answered like a heartbeat. Laughter rose and fell, gentle as wind through the fields. The air smelled of hard labor and the faint sweetness of crushed grass.

Levi stood at the edge, watching Esther dance.

She moved barefoot, skirts flaring at her calves, arms raised as she spun. There was true laughter in her eyes, and when she caught him watching, she smiled like she'd seen the stars and brought one down just for him.

He stepped in without thinking.

"Dance with me," he said, taking her hand.

Esther laughed, "I ain't much good."

"Don't matter," he tugged her gently into the circle. "Ain't nobody watching but God."

Maybe that was a lie, but he didn't care. Her hand was warm. Her timing sure. For a few minutes, the ache in his back loosened its hold. Fieldwork, punishments, fear, it all fell away in the drum's steady talk and the stamp of bare feet. With Esther pressed close, the world remembered how to breathe.

Across the yard, Clem leaned on a barrel and wiped his brow. "You see that chestnut mare Barrow brought in since Sunday?" he asked Solomon, who sat on a low crate, rubbing tallow into the split leather of his boot.

"She sure is fine," Solomon said. "Too fine for that old fool to ride right. He gon' ruin her legs by winter."

Clem chuckled. "That's why I run her before he do. Keep her smart. Keep her strong. Like she belong to me."

"She don't," Solomon said. "But I know what you mean."

That was how it was. Everything they touched belonged to someone else. The horses. The land. Their own bodies.

But this circle? This moment?

This was theirs.

Children darted through the grown folks, sticky with molasses and laughing too loud. Eliza sat on a crate, with Clara's little boy perched on her lap, telling stories low and steady, of gods that lived in rivers and men who turned into animals. Thomas and the other children sat cross-legged, eyes wide. She spoke of the North like a place from a dream, where no one ever raised a whip, and a child could climb trees till supper.

Mama brought a jar of sweet tea from the big house. They passed it hand to hand, and for a moment mint and sugar were enough to sweeten their hunger.

Through it all, the drum kept its beat like a second heart under the skin.

Work began again at four. They'd be in the fields before the stars faded. But tonight, for a little while, they were whole.

Eustace's bow found a quicker tune, and the circle answered. When he shifted his weight, he winced and steadied himself. Jack had found him that morning on the dirt path with his picking bag forgotten, and the lash had done its talking. Eliza had washed the blood at noon and buttoned his collar up high. His shirt still stuck where the cloth had dried to skin. He played anyway, eyes closed, knuckles pale on the neck of the fiddle, pulling sweetness out of pain.

Levi sat with Esther when the music eased, their fingers laced, her head resting against his shoulder, the fire in the circle's center crackling low.

Esther leaned close, her breath brushing Levi's ear.

"You coming to the service in the morning?"

"Wouldn't miss it," he answered.

"Preacher Jonas, say he got a Word," she said. "'bout freedom. Moses and the Red Sea. Says a reckoning's coming like the Good Book promises."

Levi nodded. "That man always preaching freedom."

"Cause it ain't here yet," she said, "But it's coming."

She wiped a streak of dirt from his cheek with her skirt hem. "You always look like you been wrestling pigs."

"And yet," he said, grinning, "you still look at me like I hung the stars."

The music softened as the night deepened, from joyous stomp to slow sway, the kind meant for holding close in the lantern's glow. Children dozed in laps, curls damp, breath in time with the bow.

Off in the shadows, Solomon stepped away from the circle. Clem followed.

"You alright?" Clem asked, careful.

Solomon watched the tree line. "Overseer been giving me extra cornbread and fatback," he said. "Say I earned it keeping the horses sound."

"Ain't that good?"

"He don't give nothing unless he wants something back. That man is stingy as a tick. Been talking on me to the Master. Calls me strong. Says I got fine shoulders." His mouth tightened. "Like I'm livestock. He been watching me too close. Counting money that ain't in his hand yet."

"Jus' ain't right," Clem said.

"Nothing round here ever is," Solomon answered. "But I ain't going quiet."

"You tell Jonas?"

"He said to pray. Said maybe a way be coming."

Under the trees, Nora crushed leaves in a wooden bowl. Milly rested against her, pale and still. She had not danced. She had not even stood.

Nora dipped a cloth and pressed it to Milly's brow. "Drink this, Milly Moon." She lifted a gourd cup. "It'll settle your belly."

"What is it?" Esther asked, stepping over with Levi at her side.

"Wild cherry bark and asafetida," Nora said. "Found it near the stream. Mama used it. Helps with fever."

"She been sick long?"

Nora's eyes flicked to the circle, "Two days now," Nora said. "Stomach. Sweating. Can't keep nothing down."

"Cholera?" Levi asked. "Been going round."

The words fell heavy.

"If Barrow finds out…," Nora's voice slipped. "He don't let sickness linger. Not if he thinks it'll spread."

Esther took Milly's hand. "We'll keep her hid," she said. "Let her rest in your cabin. Mama will bring food from the kitchen."

"I'll help," Levi said.

Nora's eyes shone. "Thank you."

In the circle, the bow's lilting rhythm slowed to a hum. But the warmth remained. The night wasn't over yet, but already the shadows stretched long.

Beyond the trees, Abraham watched. He saw how they leaned toward freedom the way a plant leans to light. Barrow had leased him from a plantation outside Lexington to work the tobacco. Abraham had other plans.

Beyond the quarters a distant coyote's long, mournful howl, unspooled across the fields. Eustace lifted the bow again, and for a few more minutes the night forgot itself and let them dance.

Ten

The Taking

*"They come in the night, take what they want, and leave us
with silence. But I remember. I remember every scream they didn't
hear."*

-WPA *Slave Narratives*

The firelight still clung to her skin as Esther walked back toward
her cabin, fiddle music trailing behind her like the ghost of a
better life. Each note faded into the dark, but its warmth lingered;
Levi's breath at her ear, his palm warm in hers. Her feet ached from
dancing, but her heart felt light.

She let herself dream for a moment.

One day.

A little patch of ground with no eyes on it. Eustace running
barefoot through corn rows. Levi's hand finding hers under a sky
full of stars. Mama tending herbs. Eliza laughing again. A world
where she belonged only to herself.

Sweet liberty.

The moon slipped from between clouds and shone a pale light
across the quarters. Candles guttered low. Jasmine threaded the air.
Katydids kept their steady summer prayer.

Then she saw him.

John Barrow stepped out of shadow, face slick with heat and drink. His shirt hung open; a whip dangled from his right hand. His boots crushed grit as he came on.

His eyes crawled over her like flies.

"Well now," he slurred. "Look at you. Who you been dancing for, girl?"

Esther turned to run.

He caught her fast. His grip twisted her arm, rough and sure. "Don't make me chase you," he hissed. "You know how I hate that."

He dragged her across the yard, past the trough, past the place where laughter still trembled on the wind. The stable swallowed them. Horses stirred, iron rang softly, a chain knocked wood. The door slammed.

No one saw. No one came.

He tied her to the hitch post with the practice of a man who had tied many things. Rope burned her wrists.

"This is what happens," he growled, pulling a switch from the wall, "when you niggers get high notions."

The first strike split her back like lightning. She set her teeth. The second tore a gasp. She would not scream.

Her knees buckled; she stayed standing. She had learned how. Pain was the law here. She spoke its language.

When his arm tired, he stepped close, rank with liquor, and unbuckled his belt with shaking hands. The rest was slower.

Crueler.

She lay still, cheek pressed to wood, the world blurring at its edges. She fixed on the horses; their dark eyes, their breath lifting in the quiet. Her body was not hers. Had never been.

But her soul.

My soul belongs to the Lord; she told herself repeatedly. He can't have that. He can't.

But some nights, even that felt like a lie.

At the far stall, Clem lay in the straw, muscles shaking. He had stabled the new chestnut mare after the dance and stayed to work her legs. He heard everything. Every grunt. Every slap of flesh. The sound of swallowed cries. His fists knotted. Rage burned clean and useless in his chest. He did not move. Not yet.

Barrow finished. Wiped himself, buttoned his trousers, and spat tobacco into the hay.

Lantern light flared at the doorway. Mary Barrow stepped in, hard-faced, the flame carving a blade out of her eyes. She took one look and her mouth thinned.

"Again," she said, flat. "You bring your filthy whore into my stable, again."

"I do as I please, woman," Barrow said without looking at her. "She belongs to me."

"I'm tired of that girl's face."

She snatched the switch and lashed Esther once. Then again.

Clem rose like weather breaking. The word left him, deep and heavy, a rumble that shook the rafters.

"Stop."

Mary turned. "Who's there?"

Clem stepped into the light. "Leave her be."

Barrow's smile spread, slow and poisonous. "Well, well. Now, ain't this a surprise."

He called out into the yard. "Jack! Bring a rope. This boy needs reminding."

Boots thundered. The doors flew wide. Two men seized Clem by the arms. He surged, caught one man in the throat, then went down under fists and heel.

They dragged him outside, kicking and twisting, tearing twin furrows through the hay; straw raked back to darkened earth, heel marks stuttering along the boards, a raw path gouged to the doorway.

Esther was alone again, wrists bleeding. She worked the knots loose with shaking fingers. Pain had gone distant, a dull throb in her bones. Rope-burn flared like fire along her wrists; her cheek was raw with friction, a scrape hot and tender. Straw-seed clung in her hair, burrs and grit threaded through the curls; a smear of hay dust lined her jaw; the musk-stale reek of John Barrow rode her skin.

She did not speak. Did not cry.

She crossed the yard, naked under a torn dress, hem snagging at her shins. The music was gone. The sky showed no stars. She pushed into her cabin and folded to the dirt floor. Debris shook free; husks, chaff, a few sharp needles of straw, spilling from her hair to the packed earth. The silence pressed down like weight. She wept until breath failed.

They strung Clem up, high and tight, from the whipping tree. The strap cracked once. Twice. Three times. Flesh opened. He held on. When the pain cut to bone, he howled into the night.

From the dark the others listened, eyes wet, fists clenched.

Ten.

Twenty.

Thirty.

Blood soaked the roots. The tree drank deep.

In the cabin, Esther lay shaking, her body broken and her spirit frayed. She whispered the only words she had left. I'm sorry. I'm sorry. I'm sorry.

For Clem.

For herself.

For every soul still trapped here with no door out.

And deep beneath the grief a colder thing stirred, clean and merciless, the size of a storm. Something that wanted to set the entire world alight.

Out in the dark, after the last lash struck, a sound found them. Solomon's voice, like sap thickening in winter, carried a line no louder than breath. He did not dare the words at first, only a hum that spoke to their sorrow without waking it. Then, a whisper slipped through his teeth, "Steal away," and the cabins answered with the softest thread of harmony.

Mothers pressed their foreheads to their children's hair and hummed. Men closed their eyes and let the note hold them upright. The song never climbed high enough to call trouble. It moved along the ground, from door to door, like water finding its level.

By the time the yard fell still, the melody had braided them together, a fragile cord no whip could break.

Eleven

Let My People Go

*"The Lord heard the cry of His people, but Pharaoh hardened
his heart and so the river ran red."*

- Adapted from Exodus

Esther woke to the soft shuffle of footsteps and a whisper.
"Esther," Eustace said softly, crouching beside her mat. His
small hand, cracked from working the fields, lay warm over hers.
In the other, he held a tiny white daisy, barely more than a bud.

"Found it by the stream," he piped, gap-toothed and proud.

She drew him into her arms and breathed him in. "Thank you,
my sweet boy."

Eliza appeared at the door, quiet and sullen. "Come on. Jonas
is calling us."

They walked together, arms linked, feet wet with dew. Just before they reached the clearing, Levi fell into step. He did not speak.
He gave Esther a small nod. His eyes held everything.

The fields were still soaked in shadow when they gathered,
heads bowed, shoulders hunched against the bite of morning chill.
The earth underfoot was cold and soft, the kind of damp that crawls
into bone and stays. Dawn had not yet broken, but the horizon bled
a slow red, storm clouds hung low with the threat of rain.

They came barefoot and weary. Their bones aching from too little rest and too many burdens. Every step a labor on stiff knees. Mabel wrapped a threadbare shawl around Flora, who did not say a word, only blinked against the wind, her small hand clutching her mama's apron. Nearby, Clara held baby Ruth to her chest and hummed a tune soft enough to soothe. Old Amos limped at the rear, one eye clouded with age, his face a weathered map of mahogany and sorrow, etched deep by decades beneath the baking sun. Beside him walked his son, Mose, stone-faced, his fingers curled around the last scrap of his wife's apron, tucked into his trouser pocket the day she was sold.

The children carried no words in their mouths, only the silence taught by those who had learned that words could bring the lash. The air was so quiet it hummed.

At the center, beneath the limbs of the great oak, stood Jonas.

The preacher's back was crooked with age. His eyes had seen so much pain, so much sorrow, and still his voice could shake the heavens. He lifted a battered Bible, his hands trembling from conviction, not fear. Wind stirred the thin pages, and with a breath like thunder he began.

Behind him was Clem.

Chained to the whipping tree.

It was no ordinary tree.

It had once been a proud oak, old as the hills, its branches wide enough to shade a field. Bark blackened where lashes split flesh. Roots fed from the wounds of men and women, generation after generation. Screams had echoed through its limbs, soaked into the marrow. Sap wept from the bark like old tears.

It had become a monument to cruelty, reshaped by man's hatred, made monstrous by the pain it had been forced to bear. The slaves called it the *Elder Tree*. They said the tree remembered. That it fed on suffering. That its roots reached towards hell.

Now Clem hung from its branches.

Arms spread, his back a ruin of torn flesh and dark bruises. His eyes were swollen almost shut. Blood dripped slowly from open wounds, slicking his spine like oil. Flies had gathered in a gray hum, drawn to heat and salt and the nearness of rot.

Jonas opened the book.

The thin pages fluttered, the wind whispering like ghosts.

"And the Lord said unto Moses," he began, voice steadying as it rose, "Go unto Pharaoh, and say unto him, thus saith the Lord: Let my people go."

The hush deepened.

"Let my people go," his voice rang out louder. It was no longer only scripture. His words boomed through the morning fog like thunder. It was a verdict.

A few murmured amens moved through the crowd. Tired and broken, but alive.

Esther stood at the edge, arms crossed tight over her bruised ribs. Her dress hung in tatters; sleeves crusted with blood. Her face was swollen at the mouth, her lips split and dry, but she did not cry. Her red-rimmed eyes fixed on the preacher, as if she might will the Word of God into existence.

Jonas lifted his face to the sky. "Let my people…"

Bootsteps, hard and heavy, broke the prayer.

Barrow strode out of the dark like rot from a grave, coat tails flapping, face slick with last night's drink. In his arms, slung like a sack of cornmeal, hung a body.

The music of the sermon fell silent. Even the sparrows went still. But a slow murmuring began to spread.

Barrow stalked to the front of the congregation. He didn't look down when he reached the oak. He let her fall.

She hit the earth with a sickening, wet *thud*.

The smell rose, iron and soap and something already leaving the world.

Barrow looked not at the woman, but at the slaves. His gaze found Esther.

"Get to the fields!" he roared. "Now! Or I'll have every last one of you whipped till your backs look like that!"

He jabbed a finger toward Clem, whose groan was barely audible now.

He lingered a breath, drawing in the pain he had made, feeding on it, then turned and went, boots grinding gravel.

For a heartbeat, no one moved.

Gasps followed.

Then a scream split the morning.

Nora.

Eliza flinched and dropped to her knees beside Eustace, pulling him close.

"Don't look," she whispered, wrapping both arms across his shoulders. "Come away now."

"But who is it? What's wrong with Miss Nora?" Eustace asked, trying to peer around her hands.

Eliza stood and lifted him despite his squirming. "Hush," she said, voice shaking. "It ain't for your eyes." She pressed his face into her shoulder. As she turned, the little white bud he had given Esther slid from her pocket and vanished in the trampled grass.

"Is somebody hurt? Where's Mama? I want to see."

"You hold on to me," Eliza said. "Don't ask no more."

She carried him toward the quarters, steps too quick, arms too tight. Behind them the murmurs rose. Gasps. Weeping. The wind carried whispers of a wordless terror, but Eliza kept on walking, shielding him from the horror.

Eustace clung to her neck, asking questions she could not bear to answer.

Esther pushed forward and staggered. Her knees buckled.

Levi caught her before she struck the ground.

He held her as she wailed, her body shaking. She crawled on her knees to the body. Her hands hovered before they dared touch.

At first, she did not understand. The face was swollen past knowing. But the yellow scarf. The shell ring clutched in bruised fingers. She knew those hands like her own.

Mama.

"No," Esther keened, a sound torn from the deepest place. "No, no, no… Mama."

She gathered her mother close and rocked her, as if she could bring life back into her. Her skin was cold and stiff. Her mouth hung slack. Her eyes were dull and glassy. Her neck bent in a way it shouldn't. Blood had soaked her shift and stained Esther's arms as she held tighter. Her breath shook as she kissed her mother's face.

Jonas fell to his knees beside her. His mouth trembled.

Old Amos stood near, twisting the brim of his cap, tears cutting clean tracks in the dirt on his weathered cheeks. Clara pressed both fists to her mouth and turned away, shoulders shaking. Thomas clung to her skirt, too young to understand, too afraid to let go. Martha, midwife to half the quarters, whispered a prayer through cracked lips. Her clouded eyes swam.

Others wept. Some fell back, wailing in horror. Some reached out to steady those who swayed. They cried, faces turned toward the heavens, their souls crushed beneath the weight of despair.

"She only set a minute," Isaac whispered, his voice rough from tobacco and years bent double. "Said her legs was hurtin'. Jus' wanted to rest a spell."

"They say Miss Mary caught her holdin' that baby of hers too long," Auntie Bet said, low and flat. "Said she stole a biscuit. Said she warn't workin' fast enough."

"No," Elias muttered, hot with rage. "It was Esther. Missus seen how Barrow been lookin' at her, couldn't stomach it. Took it out on her mama. Beat her with a broomstick till there weren't nothing left to break."

Esther could not speak. Her fingers shook as she tried to close her mother's eyes. They would not stay shut. She kissed her cooling brow and whispered a prayer she could not remember how to say.

I will remember your eyes. I will remember your voice. I will remember.

But memory does not return breath. And no prayer could ever bring her back.

"I am sorry," she whispered.

Jonas set a hand on her shoulder. "Dry your tears child, she's with the Lord now."

Esther did not answer.

People drifted away, slow and numb. The service was over. The morning had been torn like flesh under a lash. Only sorrow remained. And labor. And chains.

A wind moved through the clearing. It did not carry with it the warmth of summer. It was colder. Hungrier.

From the Elder Tree, Clem groaned. Agony, guilt, the echo of rage. His swollen head lifted a fraction. Blood tapped from his chin.

His lips cracked. "Esther," he rasped. "Run. Run."

She turned, her eyes wide. There was no corner of this world untouched by cruelty. No place to set down this grief.

Still, she would run.

And she would return with fire.

Esther rose. Blood on her sleeves. Tear tracks drying on her swollen face.

Her eyes did not only mourn. They burned, old and righteous, bright enough to make even Heaven look away.

Twelve

The Weight of the Dead

"To lose the dead is sorrow,
To bury them is agony,
But to forget them is impossible."

- Appalachian Folk Proverb

The fields swallowed them.

Row after row of tobacco waited beneath a sullen morning sky, leaves bowed under dew, cold dirt lay beneath bare feet. Clouds pressed low, rumbling with thunder that refused to break.

Clem was bound to the whipping tree, ropes strung high, turning slowly at the mercy of the wind. His pain displayed as a silent warning to any soul who dared put words to defiance.

With backs bent, the others moved through the rows like shadows, their fingers numb, their eyes dull. The whip cracked now and then, a cruel punctuation, no one spoke. No one sang. No one dared lift their eyes.

Esther and Levi were excused from the fields, Barrow's orders, someone said. Perhaps he wanted them to bury the evidence. Perhaps it was meant as mercy.

But it wasn't mercy.

They cleaned Mama's body in silence, wrapped her in a faded blanket, the same worn cloth that had cradled Eustace the day he came into this world. They carried her behind the quarters, past the cookhouse, past the wash line, to the patch of earth scattered with makeshift markers. A field drenched in sorrow, quiet and humble. Small stones, wooden crosses, torn strips of fabric marking loved ones lost. Graves dug shallow. Lives buried deep.

Esther knew this place. Baby Elijah lay beneath a small dogwood at the edge of the plot, white blossoms shuddering there in the spring, fragile as breath. She could still see Mama digging that tiny grave with her own two hands, tears streaking her face, refusing help from anyone, as if it was her burden to bear alone.

She remembered that day with terrible clarity. She had been eleven, Eliza barely nine. Both of them bent at the washtub, wrists raw from lye, passing wet shirts up to the clothesline. The Overseer rode up, his face a blank mask of cruelty. Without a word, he seized their daddy, Jeremiah, dragging him from Mama's arms and shoving him into the dust. Mama, her belly swollen and heavy with new life, begged and sobbed.

"Please," she cried, falling to her knees in the dirt, gripping his trouser leg. "Don't take him. Don't take Jeremiah. We need him. I beg you, sir. Please…"

"Get off me, woman," the Overseer spat, kicking her away. She fell hard, clutching her stomach, doubled by sudden pain.

Jeremiah fought, shouting his wife's name even as they bound his wrists and tossed him into the wagon. Esther stood helpless, Eliza's small hand gripped in her own, both girls fixed in terror, wet shirts snapping on the line like frightened birds.

That night, Mama screamed for hours, sweat soaking her brow, agony etched deep. Martha gave all she had to save that baby. Women gathered close, whispering prayers, pressing damp cloths to her forehead. Esther hid under the table, watching between the legs of the midwives, too frightened to breathe.

Elijah came small and fragile, heartbreakingly beautiful. He lived just a few short hours, long enough to be held, long enough to be loved, long enough to feel the warmth of his mother's tears.

Afterward, Mama was not the same. Joy drained from her like blood from a wound. She stopped singing, stopped laughing with her daughters. Then John Barrow set his hungry eyes on her, circling like a vulture drawn to grief, and within a year Mama's belly swelled again.

Whispers floated through the quarters, rumors Mama refused to hear, that the baby she carried was the Master's child. She withdrew further, a shadow drifting through days of silence and shame. She spoke rarely, smiled less, but her hands never lost their tenderness when she held her girls.

After Eustace was born, it was Esther and Eliza who raised him, who fed him, who soothed him when he cried. Mama spent long hours at the big house nursing the Master's newborn son, her own baby boy left in her daughters' care. The cloud of sorrow grew thick, creating a fog through which joy rarely broke.

Now, as Esther knelt by the grave she and Levi had just finished digging, something felt different. Mama's pain had ended. At last, she was free.

They lowered her gently into the cold earth. Esther knelt at the edge, her tears spent. The worn blanket clung to Mama's shape, small and still. The ground seemed to sigh beneath her weight. Her mother's face had already begun to blur, not in love, but in clarity, as if her soul had retreated too quickly for flesh to hold.

Esther reached for a clump of earth.

She paused to look for the last time. The curve of her mother's cheek beneath the cloth, the quiet of her brow, the peace death finally brought.

"You rest now, Mama. Go with God," she whispered.

She let the dirt fall.

It struck with a soft, hollow patter.

She scooped again, and again. Her hands moved faster, as if covering her might muffle the pain. She did not stop until her mother's shape was gone, swallowed by shadow and soil.

When the grave was filled, Esther stood in silence.

At the clearing's edge, the dogwood held green shade. She stepped beneath its limbs and gathered what the season offered, Queen Anne's Lace from the fence line, a few wild daisies, a spray of yarrow, white blossoms; summer's small lights. She carried them back to the mound.

One by one, she scattered them.

"For you, Mama," she whispered, laying the last flower. "And for your baby boy."

The petals clung to the soil like blessings.

She believed that the souls of the dead returned each spring in bloom, gentle and bright, like the memory of a laugh. Mama used to say trees remembered everything, that their roots drank sorrow and joy alike, that blossoms were proof that nothing, no love and no pain, was ever truly lost.

Mama was with Elijah now. No longer broken. No longer bound to the pain of this life. Together, where no Master's hand could reach.

Levi set a small wooden cross at the head of the grave.

"Mis' Adeline was a good woman," he said softly. "To everybody. May God, rest her weary soul."

Esther nodded, her voice heavy. "She gave all she had. Even when there was nothing left."

The sky churned darker still, clouds pressing down with silent fury. The air grew heavy, waiting.

A branch cracked behind them.

They turned.

It was Abraham. He stood just beyond the trees, a bundle slung over his shoulder, a long staff in his hand. His hat brim threw his eyes in shadow, but his gaze was steady.

"Time's near," he said, low and sure.

Levi straightened. "You certain?"

"Been watching. Listening," Abraham said. "Patrols thin to the north. Weather's holding. River folks sent word, the safehouses are open. We go tonight."

Esther kept her eyes on the freshly turned earth. "But she ain't even cold yet."

Abraham's face eased, though his voice stayed firm. "I know, but if you stay, you end up under the same dirt. Or worse."

Levi touched Esther's shoulder. "Your mama would want you gone from here."

Esther looked out across the fields, where others bent beneath burdens no human should carry, held to life by hunger, grief, faith, and that frail, trembling thread that freedom might still exist.

She brushed soil from her palms. Somewhere deep beneath the sorrow a heat rose.

"I'll go," she said.

Abraham nodded, respect in it and something near to pride. "Gather who you trust. Sundown." His voice tightening, "We take the stream behind the mill, move quiet through the tobacco. Once we cross the Ohio, we ghosts to them."

He turned and slipped into the trees, leaving only silence and a promise of deliverance behind.

Esther knelt once more, fingers on the newly turned soil.

"I'll carry you with me," she whispered. "I'll carry you all."

A wind moved through the graveyard. The dogwood leaves stirred, and the white petals of lace and daisy trembled where they lay, as if the earth were whispering goodbye.

Thirteen

Last Breath

"Sometimes I feel like a motherless child."

- Traditional spiritual

Morning poured through the plantation windows like a revival; hard light broke into shafts across the scrubbed floors. The freshly polished panes cast a bright edge over the wide wooden boards, every knot and nail head picked clean by it.

Adeline stood at the kitchen hearth holding a long-handled spoon, humming under her breath, the kind of low, holding-on tune a body uses to keep the day from breaking wrong. Steam rose from the pot in soft breaths. Oats swelled and turned, a slow, patient boil. She pinched a bit of salt between finger and thumb and let it fall like snow.

For a blink, the scent of hot grain and lye soap gave way to another morning long ago. She was young again, hand in hand with Jeremiah under a quick sky, kin packed in close, laughter bright as tin. They jumped the broom while Auntie Bet clapped time and the old men thumped their canes, and when their feet touched down together, Jeremiah's grin found hers like it had been waiting his whole life. She felt the brush of his hand on her cheek, the promise in it, and for a breath the kitchen softened.

A sound behind her pulled the memory back by the roots.

Adeline slowly turned, already braced for John Barrow's stink of bourbon and the grab of his hand.

It was not John. It was Mary Barrow, sun-bleached hair pinned hard off her face, jaw tight enough to crack bone. The Mistress's eyes were flat and shining, a kind of misery turned hateful.

"Your girl been tempting my husband," Mary said, each word clipped. "I will have no more of it. You best be putting a stop to it, you hear me?"

Before Adeline could answer, a hand struck the back of her neck. Fingers found her spine and yanked. Surprise took her knees. She went down on the boards, palms splayed, the hot spoon clattering and spinning into the light.

Across the kitchen, Mabel stood at the second hearth, stirring a pot of rabbit and wild onion stew for the evening supper, her ladle moving in small, helpless circles. She turned her face toward the window, then toward the floor. Her mouth pressed into a firm line. Her hands did not stop.

Mary reached for the broom that leaned in the corner.

The first blow landed across Adeline's shoulders. The bristles broke and scattered straw. The second caught the side of her face. The third found her ribs. It went that way, fast at first, then steadier, until the kitchen was filled with the dull thud of wood on flesh and the small, animal sounds a body makes when breath won't come. Adeline scrambled, dragging herself through the blinding beams the windows laid on the floor, fingers finding plank seams, trying for the door, for air, for witness.

"Please," she begged. "Missus, please."

The broom came down again.

Outside a jay shrieked. Inside the oats hissed and spat, then thickened into silence.

Mabel flinched and fixed her eyes on the steam. "Lord, help her," she whispered, so quiet the words never reached the far wall.

Adeline's hand closed on the jamb. She made it half through the doorway, boots catching the sill, then the next strike folded her.

The world became only light and heat and the taste of iron. Somewhere between one breath and the next she felt for the small shell ring and caught it tight in her fist; the one Jeremiah had bought off a Quaker missionary the day they were wed. Her thumb rubbed the smooth edge the way it did when Esther was fevered, and she sat by her counting out the night.

Baby Elijah came to her then, fragile and warm, damp against her chest, as he had been for those few hours he lived. She saw him, not the way he left but the way he arrived, eyes dark and open to heaven. She thought, " I am coming, little angel. I am coming where sorrow can't follow."

Her breath slowed. The pain stepped back. The ring pressed a half-moon into her palm, and she was glad for the hurt because it meant she was still breathing.

"Oh, Eustace," she thought. "Oh, my boy, I should have been softer with you. Your father's sin is not in your bones. Forgive me, child. Girls, my girls. Esther, Eliza. Oh, how I'll miss you. Please, remember how much I loved you. Remember I did my best."

Her chest rose and fell. Then rose once more, shuddering. The sunlight inched across the floor, and Adeline's fingers slackened around the ring, but did not let go.

John Barrow filled the doorway, boots dirty with yard grit, coat unbuttoned, eyes bleary as a storm-blown hog. He took in the room like a man checking a ledger, not a life.

"Who will take care of your brats now, you stupid cow," he said, not to her so much as to the mess.

Mary did not look at him. She stood with the broom in both hands, breath fast and shallow, blonde tresses fallen from their pins in sweat-damp strands. Her face was flushed high, a feverish bloom rising in her cheeks; the broom handle, split and tacky, creaked under her white-knuckled grip. She fed on the hurt she'd made, her eyes wide and frenzied, a terrible exhilaration sparking there. "You keep your hands off that girl," she answered, voice high and sharp. "Or she gets the broom same as the sow that birthed her."

Barrow bent and scooped Adeline like a sack of feed, one arm under her knees, one behind her head. Her ringed hand hung loose against his sleeve; knuckles streaked with flour and blood. He turned toward the yard.

"Green," he barked without looking back, "clean this filth up."

From the butler's pantry Green stepped in, young and tight around the mouth, rag already in his hand. He set his jaw and went for the spilled oats first, because that was how you started, with what would stick if it cooled.

Barrow shouldered through the door into the cold. Behind him, the porch door banged once, shivered on its hinges, then settled. Morning lay hard and gray across the yard. From the quarters came the first hum of voices and the whisper of a Bible opening. He walked toward that sound with Adeline in his arms. Her fingers still cradled the shell ring; its white curve showed the palest gleam, like bone rinsed clean.

Fourteen

The Leaving

*"And they fled by night, guided only by whispers and
prayers.
For behind them was bondage, and ahead lay freedom or
death."*

-Adapted from oral histories of the Underground Railroad.

Night fell without stars.
A hush settled over the quarters, thicker than fog. Their low
roofs and lean-to porches pressed flat under a sky that would not
show its teeth. Even the dogs were quiet, as if they sensed something dark moving in the air. The moon hid behind swollen clouds,
unwilling to witness what was about to unfold.

Esther stood in her doorway and held Mama's yellow scarf,
tied into a small pouch against her chest. It held almost nothing, a
scrap of cornbread, a nub of flint, Mama's shell ring that Daddy had
set on her finger before he was sold. Her shoes, sharp with turpentine, waited for the long road ahead. She felt hollowed out, grief had
scraped her raw. There had been no time for mourning. There was
only movement now.

She waited.

Levi slipped out from the shadow of the toolshed and took her hand. His touch was firm, but careful.

Crickets trilled their fine chorus through the grass, while the night made small sounds around them.

"You sure 'bout this?" he whispered.

Her breath left her in a narrow thread. She nodded.

They moved carefully in the dark, crouching low, past sleeping cabins where exhaustion held others fast. Every footfall echoed too loudly, and the shadows along the path seemed crowded with danger.

Behind the stables the Elder Tree waited with its dark history. Clem hung broken there, wrists chained high, dried blood crusting at his swollen eyes. Flies crept slowly through his torn wounds. His breath was shallow. The wind turned him like a warning toward every soul who passed. At the scrape of their feet he stirred, barely conscious.

"Lord Jesus," Levi said, barely sound.

They worked at the buckles with shaking fingers. When they eased him down, the rusty iron bit into his skin. Clem groaned, raw and low.

"You good to walk?" Levi whispered, taking his weight.

Clem set his jaw. "I ain't dyin' in this hell. Not tonight."

Esther felt her throat tighten but said nothing.

From the behind the women's quarters came Solomon with Milly gathered to his chest, her head lolling against his shoulder. Nora followed close, clutching rags and bitter roots, fear sharp on her breath.

"She burnin' up," Nora whispered. "But I ain't gon' leave her. I won't."

Esther touched her arm. "Don't you worry, we'll get her across. We jus' got to keep moving."

They gathered behind the cookhouse where the yard turned into trees. Abraham stood waiting like a ghost. His eyes moved face to face, counting in silence.

"This everyone?" Abraham asked, voice low and sharp.

Dread rose in Esther's chest. "First, I need to see Eliza."

Levi caught her wrist. "Make it fast. We got to be quick."

Eliza was already at the drying barn, worn shawl pulled tight around her thin shoulders. Tears glistened on her cheeks, but her eyes were set in quiet determination.

"I can't come," she said before Esther spoke. "Somebody got to keep their eyes off you."

"They'll punish you," Esther whispered, hands firm on her shoulders.

"Nothing I ain't had before," Eliza said, steady. "You get Eustace out of here. Find better. Give him a life we never had."

"I'll come back," Esther promised.

Eliza gave a small, sad smile, and shook her head. "Essie, don't promise what the world won't give. Just run."

They held each other a breath longer, counting heartbeats. Esther kissed her cheek and turned away before the tears could blind her.

Eustace waited in the yard, eyes wide and brave.

"I'm coming with you, Essie. I'm slow, but I'll keep up."

"You ain't staying here," she said, gripping his shoulders. "We'll carry you if we must."

He nodded and gave her a soft, frightened smile, then drew Mama's worn Bible from his pocket and pressed it into Esther's palm. "Take it. Mama would want you to have it. Promise you'll keep it safe"

"I promise," she said, pulling him close.

A hound's bay cut through the night. Distant, then nearer. Men shouted. Horses whinnied, their hooves clomping over the hard packed earth.

"Run," Abraham said, voice flat and fierce. "Run and don't stop."

They scattered like leaves in a gust of wind.

Esther hauled Eustace by the hand, Levi close behind. Branches whipped at their faces. Thorns took skin. Terror pushed them forward.

Eustace slipped on the slick ground and went down.

"Eustace!" Esther turned, reaching, but the dark swallowed him whole. She called his name repeatedly until her voice frayed. Only shadows answered.

Gunshots cracked. Abraham seized her arm. "You can't help him by dying here."

She fought him, wild with panic. Levi locked his hands around her shoulders. "We got to go, Esther. We got to!"

Agony tore her throat as they pulled her forward. She let herself be taken, stumbling, eyes burning, Mama's Bible clutched hard in her hand.

They ran until the woods swallowed the sound of men. When the noise at last thinned to wind and their own ragged breathing, they sank beneath a stand of sycamore. Esther knelt, shaking.

"He'll make it," Levi said. "He's clever. He'll hide till morning, wait it out."

She felt emptied, a body moving without a soul. The thought of Eustace alone in the dark kept knocking against her ribs like a bird that could not find the door.

Abraham led them along a faint path with a trickling stream to their right. The trees arched over them like hands in prayer, branches interlaced, begging mercy. They moved single file, the ground cold and damp underfoot, turpentine stung the air.

Esther walked because there was nowhere else to go. Mama screaming as they dragged Daddy away. Baby Elijah's small grave. Eustace's morning daisy pressed into her hand at dawn. The yellow scarf against her heart. So much sorrow, and still the night asked for more.

Ahead, the dark lifted to a colorless dawn. Somewhere beyond the ridge, the river held its secret.

She kept on. Not because faith was easy. Not because hope was close. But because the road ran one way now.

Somewhere beyond the pain, beyond the chains, the Promised Land waited and the sweet mercy of never seeing another sunrise in bondage again.

Fifteen

Atchen the Tearer of Corpses

"Not all demons come from Hell. Some are born of hunger."

-Old Appalachian Folk Proverb

Long before the blood of slaves was spilled onto the soil, long before the name Kentucky was carved into maps by white men's hands, the land remembered. It remembered the dark cloud the old ones spoke of, a season when blood seemed to have a will, when the hills took everything and gave little back. They called it, *Katentateh*, the dark and bloody ground.

But the Cree held faith in *Nekawaya*, the land between waters. A place of winter refuge and summer plenty. Here the rivers ran silver and thick with fish. Herds moved like weather through oak and chestnut. The mountains whispered to those who knew how to listen. Atchen was one of those.

Kentucky, the winter of 1659. Snow came early and did not merely fall. It descended with a mind, poured out of the high saddles, as if from the mouth of a great wolf and set its teeth in the valleys. What should have been a season of quiet preparation became a season of panic. Before the elders could give warning, trails that had carried families and sleds for generations vanished in a white breath. Ice swallowed the forest paths. The wind hunted the hollows and made a flute of every crack in the trees. Cold laid its hand on the camps and would not lift.

By the third day, the people turned south, the strong bent double beneath heavy bundles and the old ones leaning into staffs that had been carved by the hands of their fathers. Children cried until their throats rasped and then cried no more. What could not be carried was left behind. The world turned small and bitter.

In that white, trackless hush, Atchen disappeared.

She was not yet twenty winters. Laughter had lived in her throat. Her fingers had been quick with pelt and bead. Her songs were the kind that smoothed a child's brow. Her children clung to her skirts like shadows, and her husband, Tewanit, spoke her name as one would speak of the moon, something distant and sacred.

When the tribe realized she was missing, it was too late.

Somewhere in the drift of bodies and wind she lost the line of her people. The snow took away voices. The sky never cleared. For days she wandered, her third child still strapped to her chest. She walked until her milk dried and her tongue turned to leather. The baby's cry thinned and then went out like a flame. She prayed to the ones who had always answered, but the storm kept its own counsel. Her feet, wrapped in good moccasin, filled with ice. Her breath crackled in the air and was stolen by the wind.

On the fourth day, she was found by white fur traders from the North. They spoke to her in a tongue like frozen creek water. She, weak and starving, thought they were her salvation. Atchen wept with joy. They smiled and tied her to a tree.

Naked but for her deerskin dress, she was too weak to fight. They said she was a savage. They beat her with belts and laughed when she cried for her children. They lashed her wrists to the cold bark and left her for the weather when they slept. She became their dog, fed scraps of raw, gristly meat tossed into the snow at her feet. In the mornings the beating came with the gray light. In the darkness came the other thing, the taking which has no word that makes it smaller. Her breath rattled like old leaves. The snow beneath her grew slick with blood.

They took turns.

Day and night. For weeks.

At first, she screamed. Then she learned that screaming had no shape in the frozen wind. Her baby was gone. She could not remember if he had died in the storm or if they had taken him. Time bled together. Days did not measure the way they used to. By the time the moon showed itself again as a yellow bruise hidden behind cloud, prayer had gone out of her. Language went next. Hunger stayed.

On a night when the wind screamed hard enough to cover any cry, she chewed through her own wrist. Skin gave. Muscle parted. She tore through tendon, snapping like stiff sinew when you pull it. Her hand dropped into the snow, a small, dark thing steaming in the cold. She ran, clutching the ruined stump to her chest, staggering between black trunks like a wounded bear.

Somehow, she survived.

They assumed the wolves would finish what they'd started. But the wolves knew better.

She lived because hunger took hold of her and would not let her lay down. She drank meltwater. She ate roots that fought in her mouth. She licked the blood from her own arm because it brought warmth. Her black hair turned to tangled ropes of ice. Fingers blackened and fell. Her mind, which had once been a bright house, fractured into rooms she could not find again. Still her legs moved. Still the thing inside her wanted.

When she finally reached the winter camp she came like a shadow between trees. Women ran to her with furs, weeping. Elders spoke the old prayers and pressed hands to her brow. Children gathered, wide-eyed, peering at the stump of her arm, then hid their faces. Tewanit held her like a man who had been drowning and found ground. Her daughter climbed into her lap and fell asleep against her ribs.

That night, she lay down to sleep in the heat of bodies and cedar smoke.

In the morning, the camp woke to screams.

Tewanit lay with his throat opened to the bone. Their little girl lay beside him, belly turned out, the small pouch of her life emptied on the skins. Her baby boy, Elu, rested across Atchen's knees. His chest was folded in. His tiny bones were ragged where teeth had worried them. Blood made dark streaks in the fur. Bits of flesh clung to her lips. Atchen crouched near the fire pit, giggling like a girl hearing a crude joke, and gnawed at what had been part of her son. His bones cracking between her teeth.

There was no word in that language for what had happened. The people bound her without speaking. They took her to the wedding tree, the one Tewanit had carved with her name and his when they married. They tied her there and built a small, perfect fire at her feet. She cursed them in a voice that belonged to no one they had ever known. No one wept when the flame reached for her. They watched as she burned, her screams splitting the dawn. Snow fell without a sound and the smoke rose into a sky that refused to cry.

They slept that night believing the fire had ended the horror. But death had not claimed Atchen, something older had. She came again. By dawn the guards lay with their bellies torn out and the creek below the camp ran slow and red around a necklace of ice. Her spirit had taken root in the blackened heart of the tree. She breathed where there was no breath. She learned the paths between lodges and the way children smell when their mothers are sleeping. The prayer smoke did not rise. The warriors' arrows struck nothing that could die.

By the second morning, not a soul was left breathing to bury the dead.

In the years that followed, the hills carried a new caution. Graves that had been mounded with care rose up, clawed and open.

Bones stripped of flesh showed white as winter moons. Year after year, the snow came earlier. Trees grew wrong, twisting against a sky that would not ease. Animal tracks around water holes turned shallow and then ceased. When hunters talked low over their fires, they gave the thing a name that kept them company and warned their children, Atchen was no more, something else walked. Not ghost. Not woman. Not a creature you could meet with spear or treaty. She was vengeance. Hunger given shape.

Atchen the Tearer of Corpses. The Mother of Hunger. Witiko.

She became legend.

For two hundred years Atchen wandered, through graveyards and battlefields. Feeding through the mouths of cannibals. She learned the smell of slaughter the way a river learns its bed. Wherever men made other men into beasts, she came. She did not ride the strong, she nested in the cracked places. Drawn to sorrow like a buzzard to rot. Hell had no use for her. She was made on this earth, born from torture and starvation, from black hunger that only grows when mercy dies. She had no memory of the woman she once was, only that she moved, she ate. She was the hunger that woke after death.

Time turned. Forests burned and grew back. New roads were cut with iron. The old trails became whisper and rumor.

Still, she moved. Still, she listened.

Then the lash carved a tree in a new country and named it with blood. Men were counted as animals and sold. Women were taken where the hay smelled sweet and the doors were bolted shut. Hounds hunted. Whips spoke. The ground drank and did not protest. The air around those places had the old taste.

She came.

She found a house that was meant for mercy and stood in filth. Lantern smoke smeared the rafters. A good man's name lay on a mouth that no longer knew how to pray. Loss had split him down to where the light used to live and left the door wide open.

Silas breathed, but the breathing had no music. Grief had made a hollow of him long before the blade and the cellar did their work.

He was a vessel that trembled and did not shatter. He was a cup waiting to be filled.

Atchen leaned in close and listened to the answers the bones make when they are asked a question. The river outside turned in its sleep. The hills held their breath.

A tree that remembers screams will welcome any wind. A man who has been emptied will hold whatever comes.

She entered as cold enters a room when someone forgets to shut the door. No trumpet. No sign. Only the small, sure settling of hunger into a place made ready for it.

In the fields that lay beyond the plantation, work went on under a sky the color of iron. The whipping tree lifted its black limbs and the wind moved through them and made no sound. Where blood runs like sap, the old stories find their shape again. Where the ground is taught to drink sorrow, it will grow a root that knows the way back to the mouth.

Atchen walked the rows. She tasted the air. She turned her face toward the tree. When night came, she did what hunger always does. She fed.

Sixteen

The Hunger Below

"There are hungers deeper than the belly.
Some claw at the soul."

Before Silas ever pulled the cellar latch, before the first runaway's cry ever echoed off of stone, the land had already been made ready. The curse did not sprout like a weed in one night. It had rooted itself in the nail-holes of history, in the damp between river and ridge. Atchen's sorrow did not live only in the soil. It lived in what the soil fed. It did not ride only the wind. It spoke to the ears that the wind whispered into.

Battle had salted these hills. Floods had sown them again. Trees grew over places where men had been made to kneel. Atchen watched the seasons turn and fed where the ground remembered. The lash drew her nearer. The rattle of chains made her listen. But it was Silas's grief that spoke her name.

Once, he had been a quiet man whose eyes knew patterns of the night sky. He held star-maps in his head and routes in his bones. The cabin he raised was a true thing, squared and plumbed by his own hands. He ringed it with stones carried from the creek. A quilt hung in the back room with a pattern that meant salvation. His larder held flour sacks that hid extra shoes. A false board under the bed gave room for a breath and a prayer. Many had lived because his lantern had been left burning in the window. His cabin was a beacon of protection in the shadow of the South.

Then his boy took fever. Joshua burned for three days. On the fourth he was weightless in Silas's arms. The ground accepted him without argument.

Silas dug with a spade until blisters opened, then with his hands. He filled the grave when the sun had already left the fence rails, tamped it flat with the heel of his palm, and sat beside it long into the cold dark. Morning broke as he screamed into the trees. That week he forgot to eat. The next week he could not remember how.

The voice came when the world had gone quiet enough to hear her cruel lies.

Daddy, I am cold. Come get me.

It floated through the pines as if the needles were a mouth. It rattled in the eaves even when the air was still. He rose in the gray before dawn with bare feet and followed a sound that no other creature spoke. Snow lay over everything like sifted ash. The creek steamed where it met with a pocket of warm stone. The mouth of the cave was a black cavity pressed into the hillside. Breath misted there as if the mountain itself were a living, breathing creature.

Daddy. Trembling and full of need.

He stepped inside. Darkness closed like a door that had been waiting to swing. The cold was a shroud in that place. It placed a hand on his chest. He went forward anyway, one palm on the wall where the rock was slick and grooved by ages of water.

What came to meet him did not come with claws. It rose without breath, carved from hunger, gaunt and emaciated. Its mouth was a raw crevice that held too many edges. The eyes were hollows where light climbed in and could not climb back out. It did not tear him. It studied him and found him already open. She climbed into the wounds he never let heal. Into the ache behind his ribs. He tried to scream, but the sound turned useless in his throat. He felt her laughter like ice poured down his spine. Her rage was ragged in his breath. His heart did not stop beating, it merely began obeying a different master.

When he opened his eyes, he could not remember how long he had been on his knees. The cave said nothing. The dark said nothing. But his belly spoke. It called for flesh and would not be bargained with.

The cabin waited on sour ground at the forest edge. The chimney leaned with a witch's crook. Tin rattled when the wind shook the rafters. No birds came to nest. No deer took the path by the well. Even the flies behaved like clergymen in that place, solemn and many. Inside, ash lay in the hearth like gray snow. The air had the sweetness of rot under it. The thought of bread meant nothing to the thing that dwelt behind Silas's eyes.

Beneath the floor, the stones kept the bodies cold. Drips counted minutes in the dark. There were empty shelves where jars of preserves should have been. Hooks where hams should have hung, now held fouler things instead. They murmured through torn lips and vacant eyes. Some were still clothed in the tattered remnants of freedom, shoes worn thin from the long journey. Their hands lay folded as if in church. Bones, cleaned more carefully than a butcher would have taken a hog, lay stacked ceiling high. The dead did not speak. The room gave them voices anyway. When the wind worked under the sill, the whispering began. It spoke of stolen dreams.

Silas sat at the long table and looked almost human. His skin held a color borrowed from the firelight of winters' past. His hands lay still, but the tendons stood under the skin like wire. Only his eyes told the truth. They were deep and without reflection, two wells full of night. He did not blink. He did not pray, his mouth remembered the shape of a blessing, his tongue did not.

A deer lay by the door with its throat opened. Steam rose from the pool that had settled under its jaw. The meat was sweet and without sin. He had thought it could be enough. It was not. The hunger that lived in him now spoke only the language of human flesh.

He had tried to keep his station at first. He had taken a man in and fed him bread that cracked into good crumb. He had shown him the North Star between clouds. He had set him to rest on a pallet and kept the lamp trimmed. When sleep came, Atchen raked the inside of his ribs. When morning broke, the bed was empty. The prints in the dooryard ran for twenty strides and then were just a long, dark drag.

The second traveler did not leave. The third died with a prayer in his mouth and a question on his face. After that, he could not remember how many had come through that door. Time lost its edge. Nights stacked upon one another like cordwood. Memory kept the sound of a bone cracking under his teeth. It kept the heat of blood spilling down his chin on a winter's night. Of screams ending too quickly. But it let the names drift away.

He buried those he could not stand to look at. He shoved what could not be consumed under the floor. He told himself it was only for now. Eventually, he stopped telling himself anything at all.

The cellar took on its own atmosphere. The stones sweated. Spores floated on stray drafts. Mold crept in thin veins along the mortar. A pink hair ribbon drifted in a pan of water, as if someone had just stepped away.

Above, the house leaned a little more each day. The hornets' nest in the porch corner turned to paper lace. The quilt in the back room kept its pattern, meaning remained, but all mercy had gone out of it.

Silas waited. Sometimes he sat so long that a fine coating of dust would settle over his skin. Sometimes he stood and listened to the world. He could tell by the way crows called over the sycamores if men were on the ridge. He could tell by the taste of the wind when rain would come. He could tell by the pull in his belly when a mouth he had never seen formed the word freedom.

There were nights when the thing in him slept like a cat in the sun. He would feel the shape of his own name again. He would stand on the stoop and look at the stars as if they still arranged themselves for him. Those moments did not last. Atchen woke hungry and the stars winked out like a row of candles pinched between her fingers. She gnawed at his belly. Scraped at the back of his eyes. She screamed from within his walls.

The dead under the floor did not accuse him. That would have been mercy. They rustled in their places. They turned the house hotter in July than it had any right to be. They made a sound like the settling of a grain bin, soft and relentless. Every so often, the floor gave a small sigh. It could have been timber settling. It could have been breath.

He learned to wait as a hunter waits, with his body silent and unmoving. The lantern on the mantle burned low because that small, trembling light could be seen from the ridge. It said to the night what smoke from the chimney would have said. Come. There is bread. There is rest.

The river swelled after a thaw and then laid itself down. In that pause, the trail from the south became plain again. Men and women who had been counting days by the ache in their feet began counting breaths by the smell of cedar smoke from the house ahead. They were hungry for kindness. He was hungry for them.

Silas did not rise when the first foot touched the yard. He did not call out. He did not reach for his shotgun. He sat with his fingers curled on the scarred table and listened to the latch consider its work. The floorboards waited with him. The stones below waited. The thing in him smiled without lips.

Above ground the night carried the small sounds of hope. Below, another kind of hunger turned over and settled itself. The cabin drew one long breath through every crack and then held it.

When the door opened, the house welcomed them in.

Seventeen

The Hunger Waits

*"The mountains don't lie, but they don't forgive either.
They remember every footstep; every soul lost in the dark."*

-Lucy Bell, born into bondage, Kentucky, 1840

Silas knew they were near.

He could smell them, the warm pulsing tang of blood, still locked inside living bodies. It called him like a bell in the fog. Sweet. Terrible. Even before they stepped into the clearing, he felt them as a shiver along the thick roots of the mountain, a pulse beneath the floorboards, where he crouched in the dark.

He waited.

Still as stone, he pressed his body to the dirt beneath the cabin, where cold seeped through the timbers and the corpses whispered. They were louder now, the dead. Hungrier. Clamoring with teeth they no longer owned.

Above him, footsteps crossed warped planks. The floor let out a deep groan.

A small voice, soft and trembling, "I hear a noise."

A grin stretched across his torn face where lips had once been. He did not answer. Not yet.

Boot-scrape rang loud. The door dragged cold in behind them. He listened.

Ragged, choking breaths. Quiet prayers, whispered fervently in a tongue older than the lash.

So many footsteps, he thought.

So many beating hearts.

The last runaways. Esther's kin, the ones who still believed that freedom was possible. They brought the outside world with them, mud, sweat, woodsmoke. Hope.

A lantern swayed from a low rafter, casting a jaundiced glow. Shadows climbed and widened with the flicker. Old scrawls and desperate carvings crawled along the boards like scars, rough marks he had scratched in the earliest days, when he still believed prayers could quiet the thing living inside him.

They hadn't. Atchen's hunger was never satisfied.

The cellar hatch creaked.

A hush fell like new snow.

Solomon, broad-shouldered, dark-eyed and steady, reached for the iron ring in the trapdoor. His fingers shook.

He lifted.

The darkness breathed.

A sound rose from the pit, not a growl, not a snarl, but a long, tired sigh, as if something had waited a very long time to be seen.

Then, he rose. Slow. Towering.

Silas.

Or what remained of him.

Unnaturally tall, he peered with enormous black eyes that reflected their horror. His back bowed in a slow, swaying curve, like a corpse left too long on a noose. What the maggots had not taken clung in sickly patches, as if death had rooted under his skin. His mouth was a wet, raw maw pulled over yellowing teeth, chewed ragged by hunger. He moved like a thing that had once been a man but no longer remembered.

Solomon moved first. With fire in him, blade drawn, a shout climbing his throat.

Silas barely shifted.

He swept Solomon aside with a motion so fast it might have seemed gentle.

That was all.

The blow carried him across the room. He struck the far wall with a dull crack and dropped boneless. Blood smeared where he hit. The knife clattered uselessly across the floor.

Silence shattered.

Milly screamed, sharp and piercing. Nora quickly hauled her back, shielding her with her body in the corner.

Abraham drew his knife, teeth gritted, face pale but set.

Levi stood frozen, eyes locked to Silas. "You don't have to do this," he said, a breath of sound. "You're not this."

Silas tilted his head. He studied their faces, and for one heartbeat, the monster blinked. Something in his eyes flickered, regret, maybe memory. It vanished. His voice came like dry leaves blowing across a grave.

"Silas is not here."

Wind shouldered the plank door, banging it open on its leather latch. Dust lifted. The lantern guttered, shadows wheeling. A storm was gathering. Inside and out.

"You come seeking freedom," the voice spat. "But the land remembers your pain. And it is starving."

He stepped forward.

Boards creaked underfoot like ribs breaking.

Nora's arms cinched around Milly. Levi's hand found them. "Go," he mouthed. "Go now."

"I have watched you," Silas whispered. "Watched your blood water this ground."

"The hunger is not mine alone."

He raised a hand, not to strike, but almost in benediction.

"The mountains demand tribute."

Then he moved.

Not like a man. Like a shadow unpinned from a wall.

He crossed the room, too fast to track, too wrong to look away from. Bones and rot and hunger in a blur. He did not tear. He didn't need to. Terror did its work; hunger did the rest.

Deep in him, Atchen hummed, content as a mother rocking a newborn babe.

Abraham roared and charged. Silas struck him open-handed. Abraham folded, choking on his own blood.

Levi grabbed Milly, shoved Nora toward the door, turned and Silas was there already.

His hand closed on Nora's throat.

She did not scream.

Her lips mouthed an old prayer. Tears glassed her eyes. Milly sobbed into Levi's shoulder, too fevered to understand.

"Don't," Levi said. His voice broke. "Please."

Silas paused.

He leaned, and breathed a word into Nora's ear, a memory only she would know.

She shivered.

Then went still.

He let her down gently, as if he pitied her, as if his were not the hands that stole her breath.

Levi howled and swung a hatchet he had ripped from the deer hide that lay by the door. The haft splintered across Silas's chest.

Silas did not flinch.

Milly ran.

Levi lurched to follow, but Silas caught him and drove him to the boards with a strength that was not strength so much as an absence of mercy, of restraint, of anything human.

There was no fight left to win.

He stood over them; Levi bleeding, Milly keening beside her sister's body, Abraham twitching in dying spasms.

"I have carried you all," Silas rasped. "I bled for you. Still the hunger comes."

His voice changed, layered now. A second voice, female, more ancient than the trees, slid beneath his own.

"Freedom," she said, "is a dream meant only for the dying. The old gods await your arrival."

He sank to his knees. Not in pain. But in pleasure.

His mouth opened wider than it should. A ragged split slowly climbed his cheek.

Sound tore out of him; scream, wail, howl braided into a single, bestial note. Something in the rafters answered.

The lantern chimney burst. Flame gulped and went out.

Darkness took the room.

Milly's hand searched the floorboards toward the door, tiny fingers feeling for a way that wasn't there. Levi tried to crawl to her, but his body failed. His breath ran thin and rasping. He closed his eyes. The dark behind his lids was terrible and it was also an ending, a place that belonged to no master.

Silas stood among the bodies. His hollow gaze passed from one still form to the next. It had ended too quickly. Whatever satisfaction hunger gave had already waned, leaving only the old emptiness behind.

He lifted his eyes to the crack in the ceiling, as if the mountain could be seen through the wood. A tremor crossed him, and for a moment, the man he had been, tried to rise in the ruin.

Outside, wind tore the trees.

Inside, nothing moved. Silence screamed against the walls.

He whispered, "You are free now. No more chains. No more men to claim you."

He sat in the dark.

Alone.

Among the dead.

Outside, the wind spoke of ghosts. In the shadows, the mountain watched. And somewhere far beyond the trees, morning began to lift, but not for this place.

Eighteen

The Distant Shore

"They say freedom lives beyond the river.
But I seen her once, sitting by the fire in the woods,
Quiet as the stars, waiting for us to come home."

-Spiritual Collected by Moses Blue, 1867

Levi drifted. No overseer. No hounds. No Master. Only peace. Pain went out of him like a tide pulling away from the shore, leaving only a hush in its wake. His ruined body floated beneath him now, distant and unimportant.

The darkness no longer clutched with claws.

It cradled him gently.

And then, there was light.

He stood on a riverbank.

Water ran wide and slow as a held breath, a mirror lifting the horizon. Clouds drifted lazily across a sky so blue it hurt to look at. White butterflies, some tipped with amber, trembled like leaves on windless trees.

He looked down.

His hands were clean. Unscarred. No rope burns. No calluses. Only skin, whole again.

A warm breeze combed the tall grass at his ankles, carrying with it the fresh scent of honeysuckle, damp earth, and sun-warmed stone. It felt like spring. A spring untouched by sorrow.

Then he heard it.

Laughter.

He turned.

Nora stood in a quilt of wildflowers, her apron crisp and white, her arms open. Beside her, Solomon stood, tall and proud, no longer stooped from labor. Abraham lifted a steady hand, his eyes kind and unburdened. And Milly, sweet Milly Moon, ran barefoot and laughing through the bloom, kicking up a flurry of white petals. She turned to him, grinning wide, a daisy tucked behind one ear.

Joy rose hot in his throat.

He stepped, and the ground answered, sure-footed, not the red clay of the South that dragged hard at his heels, but something that welcomed him. Something pure and true.

And then, Esther.

She waited at the water's edge. Her dress caught the light like lilac haze. Braids spilled down her back. Her eyes, deep and knowing, found his. There was strength in her, not only the kind born of surviving, but the kind born of becoming.

She lifted her hand, smiling softly. "Come on," she said. "It's time, freedom waits across the water."

Words weren't needed.

He went to her, and the river took him in.

Cool water lifted his feet, his calves, his knees, not pulling down but bearing him weightless. This river bore two names, to the world it was the Ohio; to the faithful, Jordan. It answered to both.

With each step, burdens unlatched: chains, fear, nights listening for dogs. The cabin's horror thinned behind him like mist.

Ahead, the others waited in a golden field of buttercups and wheatgrass. Faces turned toward the sun, with the quiet knowing of those that are free.

Before them lay only sky and song and the warmth of what is unbroken.

He reached for Esther's hand.

The last veil unfastened from his shoulders like a shawl caught by the wind.

The river carried him gently.

And on the distant shore, he was home.

Nineteen

The Night Hollow

"She lay with her grief in the hollow, and the land laid its grief beside hers."

-Old Mountain Prayer

Esther moved like a ghost through the trees; her breath ragged in her throat. She didn't know how long she'd walked, only that if she stopped, the fear would catch up to her. Her legs carried her forward without thought, numb and trembling, driven by something deeper than will.

Clem's cries still echoed behind her. His body jerking when the hounds lunged. The wet snap of flesh. His arms stretched, wrists bloodied and bitten by rope. The way his feet had drug against the earth, as if the soil might show him mercy.

She bit her lip until the taste of blood steadied her.

The forest deepened. Dark and endless, each step took her farther away from any world she knew. The path narrowed, then vanished completely, swallowed by thickets and low hanging branches that clawed at her face and hair. Still, she pushed on.

Somewhere ahead lay the river. The others had spoken of it like scripture. The River Jordan, freedom lived across that river. She held to that thought, fragile as breath.

Dusk thickened and the woods changed.

The air went colder, heavy with damp moss and rotting leaves. Trees pressed close, gnarled limbs like clenched fists that held painful memories. Birds fell silent. Even the insects stilled.

She stumbled, then folded down onto her hands and knees, shaking with hunger and bone-deep weariness. She wrapped her arms around herself. Sobs came, raw and unstoppable.

At the base of a hill, a small hollow opened in the root-woven slope, shallow as a handprint. Shelter enough. She crawled inside and drew her knees to her chest.

Her fingers worked at her pouch and found the worn bit of flint Levi had given her days ago. Twice she dropped it, hands shaking so hard she could scarcely close them.

Keep moving, Abraham's voice murmured in her mind. No matter what. No matter what.

Not now, not tonight.

She struck flint to a sharp stone. Sparks lit. Then fire.

A thin flame caught in dry moss. She fed it carefully, spindly twigs, curled bark, dead leaves, until a shivering light licked the hollow walls and threw long shadows into the dark.

With her back to the earth, she cradled the flame as if it might hold her heart together. It hissed and danced. Cold pressed in from every side. The trees stood motionless, black against the deeper black of the sky. A hush fell over the hollow, eerie and still.

When the whispers began, she thought she imagined them.

Then, soft. Familiar.

"Esther."

Her spine went rigid. She turned, eyes wide.

Nothing.

Her breath snagged. She pressed a palm to her chest, as if she could push the fear down.

Again, closer, "Esther…"

Her mother's soft voice. Warm as hands at a washbasin. Crueler than any dream.

Tears blurred her sight.

"Mama?" her voice was frail.

No reply. Only wind sliding through branches.

Wanting made her chest ache.

Her face crumpled. She bit her sleeve to muffle the sobs. But they broke anyway, hard and raw, shaking her small frame. Each one tore something deeper loose, grief with nowhere left to hide.

She saw Mama's hands, cracked, blistered, gentle when they needed to be. Heard the low humming while she scrubbed, old spirituals so worn no one remembered where they started. Esther had learned them before her own name.

She saw that morning. The sermon.

The sky burned red as an open wound. The congregation gathered, their heads bowed, while Preacher Jonas spoke of Moses, of deliverance, of a Promised Land they might never see.

Then John Barrow swaggered through the fields, smiling. Dropping her mother's limp body onto the dirt like a sack of spoiled grain.

Bruises, black and purple. Blood-stained skirt. Gasps rising from around her. The scream tearing up her throat.

Levi's hands steady on her shoulders when her knees gave out. Catching her as she fell. The weight of her mother as they carried her behind the cabins, to the poor soil where the others rested. The shallow grave. Earth clinging to her fingers when she tried to cover Mama's face one last time.

No songs. No prayers. Only that burning sky and the sound of her heart breaking.

Her tears ran quieter now, spent like a passing storm. She stared into the flame until it swam. The fire flickered, as if it fed on her pain.

Beyond the light, the trees slowly shifted, whispering secrets she could not make out.

"I should have stayed," she breathed, voice cracked and dry.

She did not know if she meant the plantation, the cabin, the graves. She did not know where "home" had ever been.

Levi's voice, calm in the dark, returned, " You didn't leave. You survived."

Then, from somewhere in the timber, a second voice rose, soft as breath through cloth.

"Esther."

Not the whistling of wind. Not the talk of dry leaves. Not her mother's voice, it did not hold the same gentleness. This voice was worn thin at the edges, sharp and ragged.

Her head snapped up. Firelight licked the hollow and died against the trees. At the edge of the dark stood a shape she had not seen a heartbeat before, a length of shadow separated from the trunk, too tall for any person, too still for anything living. No plume of breath. No sway.

"Esther," it said again, from no mouth she could see.

The little fire crackled and popped. Between two trees, a darkness gathered itself into the idea of a figure. She thought, God help her, she saw its eyes move. Not a blink, but a shuttering, the way black water will take a reflection and let it go. It remained unnaturally still, eyes pointed towards her, studying.

She could not make her legs move. Her name came once more, nearer, and not in her ear so much as inside the bones of her face.

An owl let loose from somewhere above, one long, rich note, and she flinched so hard the flint cut into her palm. When she looked back, the thing had changed its distance without moving, as if the woods had folded the ground between them.

"Esther."

Her body rose before her mind agreed. She stepped out of the hollow, fire close at her heels, and went toward it, knees watery, her breath uneven. The night took the sound of her footfall. Three paces. Five. Bark showed, ordinary, ridged, damp with cold, and the place where the figure had been, was only a seam of shadow where two trunks met.

She stood there, shaking, with nothing looking back at her but a forest of trees.

From the dark came one final whisper of her name, stretched thin as thread drawn through a needle's eye. Then the woods closed their mouth and breathed only silence.

Tonight, survival felt like betrayal. Sorrow pressed down until it seemed her ribs might crack open. Her body lay still, but something inside twisted tight and cold.

She did not sleep, not fully. She drifted.

And in that hollow between waking and sleep, face wet with tears and heart splintered, she felt the land begin to stir.

Roots shifted beneath the soil, old and impatient. Slowly, almost imperceptibly, as if the forest exhaled.

Dark spaces between the trees drank in the night. Trunks stood watch, tall and black, leaves rustling with secrets.

Stones slick with moss and time remembered every footstep that had pressed them down.

This place hungered.

For centuries, pain had been sown into the earth so deep it took root. It swallowed screams like rain. Blood spilled from men and women who never saw another dawn. Rusty chains dragged across clearing and creek bed. Babies torn from their mothers' breasts to be sold, their cries swallowed by the hills. Their agony seeped into lichen, into streambeds, into the marrow of the mountains.

It was a sorrow as broad and uneven as the terrain itself, valley floors etched deep like open palms, waiting for more offerings. Ridges rising like ribs beneath the skin of the world.

The mountains of Kentucky sang their own elegies, low and mournful, along the traces carved by the hunted and the hanged.

It sang of lashes striking bare backs, of lives called out like prices, of bodies buried in unmarked ground, of mothers screaming into the night.

And the trees listened. They drank it in. They held it, season after season, until even the sap carried the memories.

The land remembered.

It had no words, no eyes. But it knew her. It felt her coming. Another broken heart. Another lost soul, cracked open like a seed.

Now, it reached.

Not to harm.

But to offer.

As Esther drifted in and out of sleep in her shallow cave, old sorrows coiled around her like smoke. They whispered through the leaves. They pressed against her heart.

She did not wake, but something in her soul heard the song. Somewhere in the dark, part of her began to change, slowly, inexorably, just as the land had changed.

Deep in her chest, something opened.

Something ancient.

Something terrible.

Something patient.

If there was a power that could break the chains and burn the Master's house to the ground, she would take it. Even if it meant losing herself forever.

Twenty

The Road to the Devil's Door

*"Some roads lead toward freedom. Some walk you straight
into the Devil's mouth."*

-Old Appalachian Saying

Esther woke to the smell of rain on damp earth. Her chest felt heavy, as if something large and unseen had nested inside her rib cage during the night. For a moment she didn't know where she was. The woods around her were so dark, she could see nothing but the warm throb of her heartbeat behind her eyelids.

The fire had burned low, it held no flame, only a scatter of ash and the ghost of heat. The air tasted bitter. The cave felt smaller in the gray dawn, as if the ground had crept closer while she slept, breathing against her skin.

She sat very still and listened.

When she slowly pushed herself up, her palms came away gritty with soot. Hunger gnawed at her belly. Her limbs ached with weariness; but that was not what lifted her to her feet.

Something was pulling her.

Not hunger.

Not hope.

Something colder.

It moved through her bones like river water in winter, slow, deep, sure, as if she had stepped into a current she had not chosen.

She stumbled out into the gray morning. A bead of water fell from the lip of the cave and burst cold on her neck. The rain smell was strong; stone, damp bark, a faint iron in the air like lightning getting ready to speak.

The forest stood waiting. Cold and certain. Pressing in on all sides. Thick mist pooled between the trunks like low-lying smoke. The sky sagged with clouds. Thunder rolled loudly, like something massive turning in its sleep. The air hung heavy with the promise of a coming storm. She shivered and wrapped her arms tightly around herself.

She did not know where she was going. The trail was gone, or maybe it had never been there. It felt as if the trees were guiding her. Their trunks rose like columns in a great, ruined cathedral; roots braided through the soil like veins, unseen and everywhere. The growth parted beneath her feet, as if it had been waiting, bending back with a kind of reverence, guiding her north.

She moved like someone dreaming. The pull in her chest tightening with each step, not painful but sure, as if something ancient had claimed her and watched from the dark.

Above, the canopy knit a ceiling of limb and leaf. Light barely touched the ground. Shadows stretched long and thin, flickering just outside her sight.

Crows called from the high branches, one, then two, then a chorus, harsh cries that might be warning. Or welcome.

She could not tell.

As she walked, sounds came through the trees; a hound, sharp and vicious; a man's voice calling; another answering, farther off.

Slave catchers.

She dropped low into a laurel thicket slick with dew. Rain tapped her shoulders in slow, heavy drops, chilling her to the bone. She held firm, hardly breathing, muscles drawn tight as wire.

Minutes lengthened. The men's voices thinned and finally fell away. The forest did not quiet.

Leaves rustled without wind. Trunks creaked without moving, seeming to lean in closer. Something watched and listened. Not the men. Not the dogs.

The trees.

Memory lived here.

She moved again, slower. The ground underfoot felt spongy with decay. Roots bulged and caught at her heels. The deeper she walked, the thicker the air became, as if she pushed through breath rather than fog. Though the late-day sun should have been climbing, the leaves above wove themselves tight and blotted out what little light remained.

The pull around her ribs had become a rope, tugging, tightening, drawing her forward.

With every step her bare feet sank into soft, deep earth.

She pressed on in a low crouch. Wet soil blackened her palms. Tall, thin shapes flickered at the edges of her vision, standing in the hollows between trees, gone when she turned.

Whispers trailed behind.

"Esther."

Don't look back, she told herself. Don't you dare.

Thunder rumbled nearer. A white vein of lightning split the sky and showed the woods all at once; every twisted branch, every broken stump, every path that led nowhere.

The smell reached her first, sweet rot edged with iron.

The storm light went thin and colorless.

Then she saw it.

A figure hanging from a tree just ahead.

She stopped. Her stomach turned to stone.

Please, God. Don't be Clem.

She crept closer, her heart breaking with every step. One step. Then another.

The man was a runaway.

Newly dead, his skin waxen, feet bare. His trousers dark with blood and urine. Hands bound behind his back. Hemp cut deep at the neck; his weight had done its work. His head lolled forward, chin resting on his chest. The wind turned him gently, side to side. The branch creaked under the strain. A warning left for any who dared the road to freedom.

Not Clem.

It did not matter. He was someone's son. Someone's brother. Someone who fled north and did not make it.

His toes brushed earth. The dirt beneath him was churned, as if others had died here too.

Esther clapped a shaking hand over her mouth, swallowing the hot bile. She wanted to look away. The forest would not let her.

Lightning broke again. The clearing flared white.

Darkness folded back.

The body swayed. Side to side.

She stepped beneath the dead man's tree and whispered an old prayer her mama had taught her. Rain swallowed the words.

She walked on.

The pull was too strong, like the woods themselves ushered her toward something waiting and terrible.

Behind her, the forest swallowed the man again.

She still felt him.

Felt all of them, alone in the dark.

Her foot slid at the edge of a shallow depression, round, sunken, freshly packed earth. A grave.

Then another.

And another.

A whole field, unmarked. No names.

Her foot sank up to the ankle. The soil there was darker, richer, turned too often. Wormcast and clay gleamed where rain had started to work the mounds into small, sad slides.

Only mounds of dirt and the knowledge that something had been here long before her, burying, watching, waiting.

The trees crowded tight.

Crows screamed overhead.

In her bones, the pull twisted.

She set her forehead to the nearest trunk; her breath shuddered in and out. The moss was cold against her skin, cold like something long dead.

The whisper came again.

"Esther."

Not her mother.

Older.

Hungrier. Vile.

It did not come from behind so much as through the trunk beneath her brow, traveling through the wet channels of sap.

She turned slowly. No one stood behind her. Only shadows. Only trees. Her fingers curled, not from fear but from resolve.

She was not lost.

She was being led.

Whatever waited ahead wanted her.

And some part of her, dark, grief-wrecked, full of rage, wanted it too. She kept walking.

Not toward safety.

Not toward freedom.

Toward something worse.

Something deeper.

Roots arched like ribs. Rhododendron closed in, their glossy leaves like a thousand tongues. The air grew warm and breathy, a damp exhale rose from the ground.

The forest opened like a mouth, and Esther stepped willingly into its throat.

Twenty-One

The Devil's Bonfire

"They thought the fire would be my end. But I rose with the smoke and fed my hunger."

-Atchen the Tearer of Corpses

Esther followed the river in darkness.

Water flowed black beside her, muttering noisily over stones she could not see. She kept one hand to each trunk she passed, guiding herself by touch more than sight. Storm clouds packed the sky, leaving no stars to mark her path.

The deeper she went, the colder the air grew. It smelled of wet ash and moss.

The pull tightened, an invisible force tugging at the center of her chest. Every step felt inevitable, as if she were walking into a choice already made.

When the cabin came into view, she stopped.

It squatted at the clearing's edge; roof bowed inward beneath the years. But it wasn't the cabin that held her.

Beyond it, a great bonfire blazed. Flames leapt high, painting the trees in a blood-tinged red. Oily black smoke rose and smeared the sky. Sparks drifted upward like fleeing souls, then fell back as ash.

Silas moved within the glow.

At first she saw him in slices, a long shadow pacing between the pyre and a heap on the ground, a burden slung over one boney shoulder. His body looked tall and gaunt, stretched thin by something that did not belong in human skin.

He stepped close to the fire and cast down what he carried.

It struck the coals with hollow weight. Fat hissed. Sparks scattered like startled birds.

A body.

Esther's breath caught. She pressed behind the trunk of a tree, her heart hammering so hard it seemed louder than the crackle of burning flesh.

Silas turned back to the pile. Shapes lay there heaped together, limbs tangled, faces turned toward the flickering orange glare. The smell hit her next; hair and fat and iron, the sweet-sickly stench of rot braided into smoke.

She pressed her fist to her mouth to stop herself from retching.

One by one, Silas dragged bodies to the fire. Methodical. Patient. As if keeping a rite older than the shale under his feet. His voice rose on the wind, sharp and bitter, like a man locked in argument. Esther crept closer through the trees and listened. There was no one else moving in the yard, yet a second voice threaded his, rasping and female, winding through his fury like smoke through branches, answering word for word.

He wasn't talking to himself.

He was speaking with something.

Something inside him.

When he bent to lift the smallest form, she knew before she saw the face.

Milly.

Her little legs limp. A small hand trailing the dirt.

A sound tore out of her, low and animal, not her own.

Silas paused.

Slowly, he turned.

Fire threw his face into shifting planes, skin pale as old parchment, eyes black as a starless sky. Ruined as he was, she knew he had been waiting for her.

He straightened, still cradling Milly.

In a voice calm as any preacher's, he called across the clearing, "You came at last. We have been waiting."

Flames climbed, painting the clearing red.

There was no going back.

Her mouth worked; no words came. Her body felt too small to hold what broke loose inside.

Dread came first, cold and suffocating, rooting her where she crouched. The fire flickered across his sallowed face; looking upon him felt like madness.

But she could not turn away.

Then loss struck her heart. Milly's body limp in that creature's arms. Nora and Solomon somewhere in the heap. All who had fled Barrow Plantation with her, all who dared to imagine one sunrise of freedom, gone.

A keening started in her chest. She pressed a hand to her gut, as if she could keep herself from spilling apart. Grief swelled, filling her mouth, lungs, skull.

Under the grief, something darker rose.

Fury.

Fury at this thing that wore Silas like a mask. At whatever had hollowed him out and slipped inside his skin. At the land itself for drinking so much pain it birthed a new monster to carry the old torments forward. At herself for daring to hope.

Thunder rolled down the ridge like an angry god's breath. Rain began to spit, and when the drops struck the fire they hissed, lifting a thin veil of steam.

Silas watched from the light, the rasping voice murmuring in his ear. He set Milly down beside the flames, as if the gentleness mattered. "You feel it, don't you?" The words moved through the trees, soft as wind through grass. "The hunger. The sorrow."

"A ground that drinks this much blood can never grow clean," he went on, voice deepening, layered now, no longer only his. "Roots have tasted grief. Stones remember the screams. And now they will remember you."

He stepped closer to the blaze. Bodies crackled behind him like dry leaves. "I was like you once, when the old gods walked among the trees and vengeance was a song sung low beneath the stars."

His eyes found hers through the dark, and something ancient looked out, feral and feminine, carved of agony and fire.

"I have known torment," the other voice said. "My chains were forged by wicked hands. My flesh torn and fed upon, thrown aside to rot." The flames surged; fat popped; smoke folded low. "I rose, and the earth embraced me."

The wind whipped through the clearing. The fire flared, red and savage.

A beat of silence passed, "And now… so will you."

Esther shook her head, though the air itself felt thick, alive with a presence that had waited generations to be answered. The forest pressed close, listening.

Her fists clenched.

She didn't know whether to run, fight, or fall to her knees.

The rage in her rose vast and unstoppable as a storm.

Silas turned back to the heap and began again, lifting, placing each body with ritual care. Steam breathed where rain met flame.

He reached for the last form, tall, familiar, limbs loose with death. The firelight brushed a face she knew like her own heartbeat.

Levi.

Her breath caught.

No. Not him. Please, not him.

His jaw slack. Eyes half open, filmed with the haze of leaving. Blood spread dark across his shirt like a night-bloom. His arm dangled; his hand, the same hand that had once tucked a flower behind her ear, brushed the mud.

He looked peaceful. That was worst of all. No fear. No fight. As if he had simply slipped away.

The world held its breath. The wind died. Even the fire settled to a low, greedy hum.

Her heart twisted slow and sharp.

She saw Levi's shy smile. The way he listened like every word mattered. The gentleness in his hands. The quiet beside her when silence was the answer.

He was kind.

Too kind for this cruel world. And now gone from it.

Tears warmed her cheeks. Her palm pressed to her mouth did nothing to dampen the pain.

She had not told him she loved him.

Not with words.

But she had. Oh God, she had.

No more quiet mornings. No steady hands. No dreams of tomorrow. Only this. This awful moment.

Levi's weight in the monster's arms. The fire waiting.

Her knees gave. She sank to the wet ground, a cry folding in on itself, small and broken.

If she could have taken his place, she would have.

If only she could have seen him once more.

She set her forehead to the earth, not only to pray, but to touch something solid that could not be taken.

Thunder grumbled. The pyre cracked. Fat spit on coals.

Inside her, something bright and tender went dark.

All the fear, grief, guilt she had carried since the night she ran, tightened to a single burning point behind her ribs.

Her mouth opened.

The scream tore loose, raw, splitting.

Not her voice alone, it was every voice this place had swallowed. Women held down under unwelcome hands. Men dying with freedom on their tongues.

Silas turned, Levi hanging limp in his arms.

She was already moving.

Feet pounded the wet ground. Mud slapped her calves. The storm crashed overhead, and she did not hear it. She saw only the axe handle jutting from a stump at the fire's edge.

She seized it in both hands.

The weight shocked her arms. She did not slow.

Silas waited, black eyes bottomless. "Come."

Her scream climbed higher, wilder, nearly inhuman.

She swung.

The blade sank deep into his shoulder. Bone cracked. Hot dark blood flecked her cheek and sizzled where it struck coals.

Silas lurched, dropping Levi into the mud. His mouth opened on a sound that had no shape.

She wrenched the axe free, panting, hair plastered to her face by rain and heat.

In that instant, she felt no fear, no doubt.

Only the fury of every life this land had stolen.

She stood in the rain, breath tearing in and out. Blinded by rage. The world leaned toward her, listening.

Atchen waited, silent and patient, as if she already knew the answer.

Oily black smoke climbed up the trunks; sparks whirled like prayers. Steam rose where rain met fire and wrapped the branches in breath.

Her mother's face. Eustace's crooked smile. Levi, who dared to believe.

The children still on the plantation, still dreaming of freedom.

Her heart felt too big for her chest, overfull with loss, with rage, with a love so fierce it curled toward hatred.

Silas's hollow voice drifted near, soft as a prayer, "All you have lost… all that was stolen… can be avenged."

Lightning flared, carving his ruinous face into sharp relief. His arms opened, not mercy, but invitation.

She understood.

This was the price.

Salvation and damnation in the same breath.

She would never see her mother's face in Heaven. Would never walk beside Levi in the fields of the Promised Land.

But she would end this.

If she must be a monster, she would be the monster her people needed. Their merciless angel.

She stepped toward him.

Rain streamed from her hair. Thunder cracked close enough to rattle her bones. She lifted her face.

"I will be your vessel. Your blade," she whispered.

Silas's black eyes gleamed.

Atchen moved.

She climbed in like a storm, cold and endless, filling every hollow inside her with something vast and ancient. Esther's heartbeat stuttered. Hunger coiled within her soul.

Head thrown back, her body rigid, she stood under the torrent. Braids tore loose in the wind. Her knees bent; she did not fall.

Visions flooded her mind,

Roots threading old bones.

Chains rusting in the earth.

The mountain rising, crowned in fire.

The sovereigns of the forest bowed, not to weather, but to witness. The pyre cracked loudly; embers burst like far flung seeds. Deep in the mountain's belly a sound like laughter rolled, ancient, sorrowed.

She gasped; no air came.

The last shred of her old self, Esther the daughter, Esther the freedom seeker, unhooked and went like breath.

What rose was beautiful and ghastly at once.

She opened her black eyes.

The world sharpened, not brighter, but deeper, as if a shroud had lifted. The land itself quivered with hidden current. She felt it moving through her the way a river feels its banks.

Trees breathed, sentinels, vast and ancient, roots twined in a great communion underfoot. They whispered a song as old as the land. They sang of sap and silence, memory and mourning. She heard them, low murmurs echoing through the soil.

Beneath the moss, the stains remained, centuries of blood, wounds that would never heal. Spirits drifted, shadows of men, women, children, beasts, each bearing the lore of sorrow.

Even the birds carried it in their wings. Animals held it in their eyes. Grass in its trembling blades. Everything that breathed had borne witness to the pain man had inflicted over generations.

Her senses sharpened. A deer's heartbeat thudded in a thicket. Iron-smell of buried chains rose wet from the ground. The wind carried the frayed ends of a hundred dying prayers.

Under all of it, deeper, something turned.

Hunger.

Not only for flesh.

For reckoning.

The forest watched.

She belonged to it.

Finally, the land would have its retribution.

Twenty-Two

The Angel of the Hollow

*"And lo, the angel descended with fire in her mouth and
sorrow in her wings,
and the land trembled beneath her feet."*

- Folk Gospel

The rain eased to a soft drizzle as Esther straightened.
Atchen had nested deep inside her. She felt her curled within
her core, cold and primal, breathing through her lungs.

But she was not lost.

Esther would not surrender as Silas did.

She faced him where he crouched near the bonfire, one hand
clamped to the cleft in his shoulder. For the first time he looked unsure, a child who had broken something that could not be mended.

His hollow voice quavered. "You feel her. The hunger, it burns
within you."

She looked past him to where Levi lay the mud, Milly's small
body still burning in the cruel light.

She understood. But not as Silas hoped.

"You are small," she said, voice raw and older than her own.
"Hateful, like all the others who poisoned this land."

Something faltered in him. He blinked hard, staring at his hands, turning them like a man waking from a fever and finding them stained. His mouth worked.

"I...remember the cellar," he whispered. "So many names," His breath hitched. "Lord help me, what have I done?"

For a heartbeat the rain sounded louder than fire.

Silas's black eyes flickered, already fading. "I am the hunger," he rasped, but the words came thin now, unsure of themselves.

She stepped and the ground seemed to move with her, roots shifting under the sodden grass. "No," she said. "You are a wicked man. The dead do not need your sorrow."

She turned from him. He was already less than a shadow.

She turned toward the bodies.

One by one, she lifted them from the fire. Pain did not reach her, the spirit lent strength as inexhaustible as the forest. Milly, first. Then, Nora. Solomon. Abraham. The others whose names she did not know, though she knew the hope they had carried over these ridges.

She laid them on the high ground beyond the flames. Rain matted what hair remained; water washed blood and soot from charred skin. Where the drops struck the pyre, they hissed.

Kneeling beside Levi, something in her chest tightened, a last ache for the girl she had been. She set her hand on his brow. A heavy tear slid down her cheek.

"Go," she whispered. "You are free now."

The earth seemed to listen. Roots shifted. Grass bowed. The quiet gathered, sudden and complete.

Esther dug. Hands wet with ash and loam, she clawed back the soil and covered scorched bones and splintered cloth, giving them to the ground, not as sacrifice, but as kin returning home. The mountain would hold them now, cradle them in root and loam, where no whip would crack, no hound would bay, no child go hungry. A place where their souls would finally know peace.

This would be their homeland now.

A memory opened, Saturday night by the tobacco rows, stars high, cicadas humming. Fiddle music rising like laughter in the warm dark. Lanterns swinging halos on the dirt. Nora clapping along, her cheeks flushed with joy. Milly twirling, a blur of braids and bare feet. Levi's fingers laced with hers, his other hand steady at her waist. They stumbled and laughed. He had looked at her like she was the whole sky.

She felt his palm at the small of her back; the safety in his smile; heard his low voice promising better days. For a little while, there had been.

She pressed the last handful of dirt in place.

She had given everything; body, soul, her future, not for vengeance alone, but for love. Love so deep that she would burn the world to keep what remained safe.

When the last body was laid to rest, Esther rose.

Rain slid over her skin, as if it dared not touch her. Cold and weariness no longer gnawed her bones; such things belonged to the world she'd left behind. She was something else now, a force made flesh.

She seemed taller. Her limbs were long and spare, corded with a strength older than her blood. Her skin had taken on a strange pallor, bound to neither the living nor the dead. Her braids had unraveled into loose black curls, tangled with moss and streaked with soot; a dark halo framing a face no longer hers alone.

But her eyes told the truth, wide and bottomless, black as river silt, drinking the last light from the clearing. In them burned an intelligence as old as the hills and a hunger no man could hold.

Her ragged dress clung like old bark, streaked with blood and earth. Shame had no place here. Softness had been put away.

Where Silas was a hollow vessel, blind in his fury, she was something different.

Purpose; perfect and brutal.

Atchen did not demand indiscriminate slaughter. She only demanded justice. The innocent would not die. The weak had suffered enough. Reckoning would fall on those who twisted this land into a graveyard for her people's dreams.

And it would be merciless.

Esther turned to the cabin, warped and rotting, the last monument to Silas's ruin. She felt the land's hunger around her, her purpose was clear. "You will not remain," she said into the cabin's dark throat. "You will not stain these hills any longer."

She stepped inside. The air stank of rot and blood. When her fingers brushed the jamb, the grain seemed to tremble, as if the wood remembered what had been done within its walls. In the dim, she gathered what was left; fragments of bone, scorched cloth, brittle remnants of lives stolen and silenced. She bore them as one carries the fallen from a field, and at the fire's rim fed them, one by one, to the flame. Embers surged like prayers made of ash.

It was not enough. This house, this shrine to suffering, could not be left standing.

She turned back to the threshold. The darkness yawned like a wound that refused to heal. She worked with purpose, splintered chairs, dry bundles of thatch; eaves soaked with years; beams thirsty for spark. She fed the blaze with the cabin's blood-soaked bones.

When she stepped out again the flames began to lick the walls, catching fast. Smoke rolled through the roof. The door sagged open, exhaling heat and ghosts.

The cabin burned.

Not only a fire, but a reckoning.

She watched in the rain. Pitch popped; rafters groaned; rain hissed and turned to steam. Smoke threaded the trees and climbed the sky. It smelled of endings. Of cleansing.

Silas lay in the glow, broken and slack-jawed, firelight dancing in the black pits of his ruined eyes. He looked up, perhaps seeing at last what she had become, what Atchen had made of her. In the fading hollow of his black gaze something flickered, recognition, surrender.

She did not look again.

Flames climbed higher. A final beam fell with a roar of cinders.

She turned away, tall and strange against the fire's glow, and stepped into the trees. The demon within her hungered, silent, waiting. Darkness opened before her like a road.

She was not afraid.

The land was quiet.

She was the forest's own child now, sharing its fury, its sorrow, its relentless will. And she was going home.

Twenty-Three

The March Home

*"She did not walk alone, death walked with her, hand in
hand, cloaked in love and fury."*

-Appalachian Folklore

The land welcomed her.

She moved beneath the boughs as if she had never belonged anywhere else. Moss underfoot recognized her steps. Low fog parted to let her pass. She was not a trespasser here, she was kin.

The mighty Ohio River drew her west, a current she felt in her bones as surely as she felt her own heartbeat. She did not question where it would take her. Instinct had become her compass, and it was true.

Esther traveled beneath the veil of darkness. She moved like wind through tall grass, gliding between towering sycamores without sound, her tattered skirts whispering through fern and bramble. Moonlight fell in broken slivers that fought to reach the forest floor. Her bare feet pressed into soil thick with fallen needles and the bones of old leaves. Fireflies drifted in her wake like sparks from a guiding spirit.

When she scented the blood of travelers she stepped into the arms of shadow. The trees closed around her like old friends. She was gone from sight. But, when the slave catchers rode past with lanterns swinging and hounds straining at their leashes, Esther did not vanish. She stepped into the road. Horses tossed their heads, ears flicking, hooves drumming worried time. The dogs, trained on terror and the salt of human skin, lowered their heads and snarled.

It always began with silence. The forest drew tight around the path, tree trunks shouldering inward, briars knitting the margins. Moonlight laid a pale bar across the rutted dirt. Esther stood in it, tall and still, hair whipping in the night wind, black eyes catching the lantern-glow and throwing it back like wet stone.

The men always advanced.

Pride and stupidity drove their boots. In their bones they felt something was wrong and still they came on. Esther invited them.

Atchen moved.

Reins went slack; girths parted as if chewed by night. Esther's hands flashed, not with steel but with certainty, cutting leads, turning bits from mouths. "Go," she breathed, and the horses bolted into the dark. Wild and unowned.

The hounds lunged.

They were not innocent. They served the lash.

She caught them as they came, by the collar she stilled them with swift, sure twists. She laid their muzzles to earth. The forest accepted the offering.

Men reached for rifles with trembling hands. Esther crossed the distance like weather. Lanterns shattered, night swallowed their shouts. Roots rose, clutching boots; stone met skull and breath left with a wet grunt. She drove them down until the earth took their air. The horses continued on; the men did not. Silence folded in again, save for the rain ticking on leaves.

At times, when the path felt uncertain, she would climb into the crook of a great oak, folding her long limbs against the bark like a creature born for the boughs. From her high perch, she watched the world grow still. The forest below whispered its old secrets, of things buried, souls forgotten, roots drinking blood spilled long ago.

The Kentucky twilight was something she could taste on her tongue, bitter and damp, touched with coal smoke and honeysuckle. The air was rich with life and mourning. Moths beat their wings against the dusk. Cicadas buzzed like ghosts caught in sap.

She marveled at the slow surrender of day to night, the bruised sky deepening to lush velvet, the trees holding their breath before the stars emerged.

When the whippoorwill called, its lonesome cry flowing like amber through the hush, she heard her name in its voice. It welcomed her home.

She knew the language of the land now. The rustle of leaves was speech. The hush of fog was thought. Every living thing was kin to her, each bird, branch, and beetle part of the great, aching song of the earth.

She was the guardian of her people, the vessel of reckoning. And the land understood.

Atchen stirred within her, a quiet presence. She marveled at the calm inside Esther, the ease with which she folded into the natural world. It was something Atchen had once known, long before pain and hunger, when her people still spoke of *Nekawaya*, the land between waters. It was a place of plenty, where her people were at one with the land. There, the great mountains embraced her people.

Then hunger came. Fire remade her. What once spoke in leaves and current, spoke only in pain. Kin turned their faces away; rage took the place of breath. The demon was born of flame and agony; her rage had scorched everything it touched. That was why Esther steadied her. The girl carried her grief the way a bird carries its song, held, not devoured. Esther had wings that carried her.

Atchen had been wildfire, but Esther would be a storm, inevitable, slow-moving, and final.

[117]

When dawn approached, Esther slipped down the banks of the river. The silt was cool as she sank into it, letting the soft mud swallow her limbs until she was just another shape among the roots and driftwood. Atchen watched her with a start of recognition, this becoming part of water and earth, this vanishing into the old cradle. The smell of fern and mineral and wet bark rose up, the very tongue of *Nekawaya*.

There Esther lay motionless, dreaming of long-ago days, her mother's hands in her hair, the sweet hum of lullabies beneath the croaking of bullfrogs, the songs that rose from the fields at dusk, the rhythm of footfalls on worn dirt paths after supper. Atchen listened, and the memories did not burn; they settled, clear as stones at the bottom of a cool stream. They were not wounds. They were stories, old friends meant to soothe. And for the first time in a long while, the ancient one felt something like kinship, not with fire, but with the world that had once claimed her, and with the woman who belonged to it still.

This was their freedom.

No pain. No fear. No master.

Esther answered only to Atchen.

Atchen did not command. She understood. And she demanded only what Esther had already burned to give.

A malevolent spirit, yes, but also a sister shaped by the same cruel hands. A woman scorned, brutalized, left to rot and reborn in fire. Their grief carried the same weight. Their fury sang in the same key. And now they walked the same path, and vengeance braided between them like a shared heart.

As Esther rested, water flowing gently over her, she stared up toward the hollowed sky, listening to the confessions of the trees. Their branches groaned and swayed in the dawn wind, creaking like old bones, whispering truths kept hidden beneath their bark.

They told her what they had witnessed. Lynchings and lost children. Blood soaked into roots. Prayers never answered, sent up by mouths too bruised to speak.

The trees did not lie. They remembered everything.

And now, so did she.

Small creatures passed her hiding place. A fox sniffed her foot and moved on. A doe stepped delicately around her half-buried form. Even the fish slid past in the current without fear.

She was not here for them.

She hungered.

That need, cold, fierce, righteous, drew her back to the place where her chains had first been forged.

The land demanded tribute.

And she had come to provide it.

Twenty-Four

The River Tribute

"And the waters shall rise up in judgment, and the earth shall not hide the blood of the slain."

- Adapted from Isaiah 26:21

Esther followed the river until it bent southward, a black vein cutting through the wilderness. The banks were steep in places, overgrown with reeds and twisted vines, roots clutching the muddy earth like fingers. Limbs stooped low above the water, gnarled and moss-draped, their outstretched arms like sorrowful guardians. The current spoke in low murmurs, babbling it's secrets to the stones, with the patience of centuries.

In the mornings, mist clung to the river's surface, rising in pale sheets like breath from an unseen mouth. Days turned hot and thick with insects; the air hummed with the song of wings. The sun baked the scent of moss, mud, and decay into the world. At night, bullfrogs croaked mournfully, while bats flitted above the canopy in silence.

Time meant nothing. It meandered like the river, slipping over rocks, winding through hollows, vanishing behind her. She followed unhurried, unbound. Shadows guided her. Water sang her forward.

The day broke blindingly white. Sunlight glanced off the river in hard silver flashes that stung the eyes. The sky above lay wide and empty, bleached with heat.

Half-submerged along the bank, she lay with skin caked in silt, hair drifting like black weed in the shallows. Her bottomless eyes remained open, unblinking. She did not sleep. She required no rest. Instead, she quietly fed on the world's small sounds, the groan of old trees, the hush of the current, the tireless elegy of insects in the rising heat. It was enough. It made her whole.

Hunger flared. Sharp and alive.

Atchen stirred like a fire catching wind.

She tasted them before she heard them.

Men.

Cruel men.

Esther's body hummed with knowing. Every nerve came alive.

She slowly lifted her head from the cool water, droplets sliding from her chin like falling glass.

A flatboat crept downstream, its broad deck sagging under the weight of chained souls, men slumped in silence, women clutching crying children, elders too weary to lift their heads. Pain radiated off them like heat. She knew that hunger, the slow, hollow gnawing that wears a body thin and cracks the mind. She had worn it like a second skin.

What rose in her was not pity, but wrath. Behind it, Atchen pulsed in dark assent. This was an offering. This was a sacrament.

Worse than the sorrow of the captives, was the stench of hatred that clung to the five slavers who walked the deck. Their boots rang against the planks. Their laughter splintered the air.

They spoke of prices, not people.

They spoke of flesh.

"Ain't nothing like a fresh catch," one man said, spitting black tar into the river.

Another slapped the back of a gaunt captive who flinched hard from the blow. "We'll get good coin for this buck. Strong back, just needs fattening up."

Laughter rang loud amongst the men.

Esther's hunger curled inward, tight, measured, holy. There was no trembling. No visible rage. Only certainty.

This was why she had been called; this was her purpose.

Within her, Atchen shivered with dark pleasure.

She slid from her hiding place and let the current claim her. Soundlessly, she drifted beneath the hull, fingers skimming the worn boards. She rose at the stern, hands catching the rail, her face veiled in shadow.

They never saw her.

She listened and marked the timbre of their voices, the same voices that had echoed over the bodies of her kin, had poisoned bark and soil and air.

They were still laughing when she came over the rail.

No words.

No warning.

She moved amongst them like a wraith.

The first man died before he could find breath. The second, managed a strangled cry. Blood streamed warm across her skin. The captives watched, eyes wide and emptied, while she passed among them, ragged and towering, black hair tangled with river reeds, eyes fathomless and dark. She did not touch the chained. She was not there for them.

She was there for the wicked.

One by one, she broke them.

The last crawled on his knees, sobbing. She bent, voice soft as prayer. "The land remembers."

Then he was gone.

When it was done, the river ran red. It swallowed their remains without protest, as if reclaiming what was owed.

She turned to the captives. They stared, too stunned to speak, too weak to flee, unsure whether she might be a ghost or a god conjured from the river's shadowy depths.

Their eyes did not beg; they only bore witness.

She reached for the chains.

Iron groaned under her touch, softening like wet clay. Shackle after shackle broke, the sound not unlike bones snapping. Some flinched at it, expecting pain. Others wept without sound. A young mother held her child tightly, her tears silently cutting clean tracks through soot. An old man fell to his knees when the last ring clattered to the deck, his wide eyes caught somewhere between reverence and terror.

When the final link fell, she stepped back. Her voice was quiet, carrying over the hush like a commandment, "Go."

No one questioned.

They climbed over into the shallows, some limping, some carrying those who could not walk. A few risked a looked back at her, half-woman, half-wraith.

She led them north, up the bank, and into the green cradle of the mountains. Cedar, oak, and poplar parted to receive them, tall and watching. Branches whispered an ancient language the forest shared with her alone.

Atchen lay quiet. Her hunger did not flare for the innocent. Only the wicked. Only for what deserved to burn.

As the last soul stepped beneath the trees, the woods closed behind them. They vanished into the hush she called home.

At dawn, a flatboat lay aground on the north bank of the Ohio. It was empty. Not a single soul aboard. Only blood on the deck and chains that had been crushed like dead vines. Not a trace of the enslaved.

Days later, five bodies washed ashore miles downstream, they were twisted and broken, half-consumed. The river's verdict written clear upon their flesh.

Esther was already gone, moving through the verdant hills, drawn by the last flicker of grief left inside her, toward her final purpose, toward the place where all reckonings waited.

Twenty-Five

Dangerous Hope

"Even a whispered dream can set the forest alight."

-Old Appalachian Saying

Eliza and Eustace's days in the fields were long and punishing. They rose before the sun, breath hanging pale in the cold dawn, their bodies already aching before their feet touched the frigid earth. The late fall chill bit through thin cotton, turned their breath to smoke, and worked into their bones before the picking even began. Frost rimmed the edges of the tobacco leaves but there was no pause, no mercy. The harvest did not ease with the cold, it worsened. Fingers split and bled in the brittle air. Backs bent beneath sacks that grew heavier each row.

The rows themselves held absences. A gap where Esther's basket used to rasp the dirt. The slice of Levi's laugh gone from the wind. Worst was the silence where Solomon's voice had stood, no low hum to catch the first note, no call to lift their chins, no answer rolling down the line to carry a soul from one end of the field to the other. Someone would try to start a hymn under their breath, and it would fray to nothing before the second line. The days felt longer, sadder, without the song.

As the days shortened and winter crept closer, the Overseer's voice carried like a lash across the fields, his words sharper than the whip that followed them. And the whip, Lord, that whip sang out through the fall air like a hawk's cry, circling again and again until it found flesh. Without Solomon's spirituals to lean on, the blows seemed louder. The silence after each crack was a hole they had to step around, and there was no safe way through it.

Hunger deepened. It was not just a feeling but a sickness, a slow, devouring ache that hollowed them out from within. Bellies gnawed with emptiness. Mouths went dry from thirst. The world swam before their eyes, and still they worked the rows. The hurting in their bodies became a constant thing, a shroud they could not escape.

At night, when the fields emptied, darkness brought no peace. The cabins offered little shelter, just damp earth and thin walls that could not keep out the cold. They curled close in the dark, bruised and trembling, listening to neighbors' muffled sobs, to coughs that would not stop, to prayers that had long ago thinned to silence.

In those long nights, the longing for freedom pressed against their hearts until it hurt to breathe. It felt like a lie too cruel to believe in.

And still, they did.

That aching hope was the heaviest burden of all.

In the quiet between dusk and dawn, the stories came. They traveled on the wind, carried in whispers too soft for the overseers to catch. From one cabin to the next, from one field hand's lips to another's cupped ear, they passed like contraband, stories of the one who freed the enslaved.

Some spoke of a great winged creature, black-feathered and silent, sweeping down from the clouds to carry the stolen people north to the Promised Land. Other folk swore it was no angel but a monstrous beast, tall as the trees, eyes burning like coals, risen from the mountain to devour slave owners whole and salt the earth behind them.

No one knew what to believe.

But the hope was there, flickering like a candle in the dark.

That hope was the most dangerous thing of all.

When word reached John Barrow of murmurs in the quarters, he was swift.

The Overseer was summoned to the big house.

By morning, a hard rime silvered the yard. Puddles wore a skin of ice that crackled under boots. The sun had not yet cleared the dark line of trees; maple and sycamore leaves hung dull copper, stiff with cold. Woodsmoke from the chimney drifted thin and sweet, hanging low over the fields. Crows argued from the tree line. Behind the sheds, the field hands were driven to stand shoulder to shoulder, breath lifting in pale plumes.

Jack stepped forward, leather creaking, the whip dark and stiff in his fist. He set his boots on the brittle grass and let his voice carry along the frozen ground, flat and cruel.

"Any tongue that dares speak of freedom will be cut out."

The frost did not melt. It only glittered while the whippings began. Each day the blood flowed thicker. The Elder Tree at the clearing's edge took more weight. Men were hoisted by their wrists to its low limb, toes scraping the brittle ground, backs opened in ragged slashes. The whip cracked like splitting ice; the sound ran the rows. Welts rose, then split; shirts stuck and froze; steam lifted off bloody flesh struck in the cold. Women and boys were made to watch. The Overseer barked curses into the air, spit freezing at the corners of his mouth, while crows bickered through the branches.

Each night the moans of the wounded braided with the wind. In the cabins, blankets glued to scabbed wounds; the smell of iron and liniment hung heavy; prayers faded to breath.

But the stories did not die. If anything, they smoldered hotter, passed hand to hand like coals, fed by the very brutality meant to snuff them out.

Eustace lay awake on a bed of burlap, his frail body shivering beneath a blanket more hole than thread. His back was a ruin of scars, some still bleeding. His ribs pressed sharp against skin that barely held him together. In the dark, he nestled close to Eliza, their shared warmth the only comfort left. He listened to the slow rise and fall of her breath.

And in that breath, he dreamed.

He dreamed of the Angel that would come.

Of a place where no whip cracked.

Where no man owned their names.

Where children ran barefoot and laughing, through grass that had never known blood.

Sometimes, when sleep finally took him, he saw Esther's face, older now, fiercer, eyes black and endless as the river. She did not speak in those dreams. She only reached out her hand.

Eustace woke with tears on his cheeks, whispering her name into the dark.

Twenty-Six

Merciful Death

"Some sins are paid in blood. Others in sorrow."

From the high branches, Esther heard the haunting melody.
It rose, dark and beautiful through the leaves, a low soliloquy of dragging chains and the snapping of the whip, a song made from iron and breath. She followed it, as the mournful requiem called, branch to branch, until it led her to a coal of fire glowing like a heartbeat in the dark.

He sat on a rotten log by a low blaze; his face and forearms were mapped with bondage's savage script. Around his neck hung a punishment collar, an iron band thick as a thumb, riveted shut, three uprights arcing like ribs, a ring at his throat to take a chain. Rust had eaten the edges jagged; the metal had rubbed his skin raw. Each small movement answered with a dull clink.

The fiddle he played threw a warm flicker through her, memory quickening of a small boy with dirt on his face and sadness pooled in his eyes.

Esther settled across the fire, the flames casting long shadows that climbed and fell along her ragged form.

William Byrd had accepted that the Devil had finally caught up to him.

He meant to play for her his confession.

She listened, and the tune told truths she already knew. She saw him in the big house, broad-shouldered under another man's roof, carrying a life that was never his. The collar's weight bowed his head while the Mistress whipped his boy. Day after day, she unleashed her wrath on that innocent child, while keeping a steady eye on William, certain he dared not speak against her.

His misery was a room that never emptied.

One evening the Master said to his wife, "If you beat this boy anymore, he'll be no good for the fields."

The beatings grew worse.

Until the day when she struck him so hard the child did not get back up.

The last note of that memory shivered in Esther's chest.

Then another refrain braided through the tune, bitter and precise; William in the yard, his fingers moving among the oleanders. In the kitchen, pinched leaves were ground into stew; a touch in the tea; a dusting in the porridge. Day after day, until the planter's family paid its debt.

As his final act of defiance under that roof, William set the big house alight.

He fled in the dark with onion rubbed into every crease of skin, barefoot over furrows and creek stones while the bloodhounds raged behind. He found a stone well no wider than a man's shoulders and slid inside, standing cramped, knees bent, ribs scraping rock. Seven days he crouched there, fear hanging on him like wet cloth, rats nosing his ankles until the skin bled. He climbed out only when he could no longer bear the gnawing.

Now, he was traveling north along the old roads toward Camp Nelson, hoping to secure freedom with a musket and a blue coat if the Lord allowed.

Esther took his story into her, eyes half-closed, senses open. She tasted the violence in him, the sharp bite of it, but beneath lay grief and something sturdier; a will that refused to break, a father's love turned hard and exact.

Slowly, she stood.

William bowed his head; certain the end had come. The iron collar at his throat knocked softly against the uprights, a bell for the condemned.

Esther reached. Her long fingers cupped the collar, feeling the cold bite, the heat of skin beneath, the pulse that would not submit. With a swift turn, clean, final, the rivet gave. Iron fell to the leaves with a flat, stunned sound.

In the hush that followed, she offered absolution, wordless, complete.

Her shadow eased back from the firelight. She turned and walked on, steady and deliberate, toward the prayers of her people.

William Byrd folded over his fiddle and wept.

Twenty-Seven

Fields of Sorrow

*"There are ghosts in the furrows.
And they are hungry."*

Esther could smell the violence.

The plantations outside Lexington unrolled before her, vast fields of cane and tobacco, laid in straight, orderly rows glinting silver under the Hunter's Moon. From a distance, it looked almost beautiful.

Beneath that thin veneer, the land seethed. These fields were a scourge laid on the earth, a wound carved deep that still wept.

She felt it in the soil clinging to her bare feet, damp and heavy with bloodshed. She tasted it on the wind rolling down from the ridgelines. The ghosts stirred at her passing, an unseen congregation gathering to witness the great unraveling.

Their voices rose in a chorus only she could hear.

Remember us.

Men hung from trees, their faces slack, ropes creaking in the night breeze.

Remember.

Bodies lay half-buried in the rows, rotting beneath the watchful eyes of hungry crows, left as a warning to any who dared dream of freedom.

Remember.

Esther did.

And in the eerie stillness, Atchen began to stir, not with fury, but with something deeper.

Sorrow.

The demon's presence rose in her like smoke from a long-dead fire, curling through bone, tightening behind her eyes. Memory layered beneath memory, from a time before chains, before fields were carved deep into the land's flesh. A time when trees had not yet witnessed such cruelty.

Together, they saw it all.

Blood pooling at a whipping post.

Iron brands heated until the air reeked of flesh.

Women forced to scream in silence.

Children sold and lost forever.

Atchen's hunger swelled, not mindless, not wanton, but exact. She demanded not only vengeance.

But balance.

Memory made flesh.

They will know us, Atchen breathed, her voice a whisper that moved through marrow. *They will see what they have brought forth.*

Esther nodded once, her face pale in the moonlight, her eyes bottomless. She stepped forward, and the ghosts followed.

Her people's suffering lay thick over the fields, heavier than the fog pooling in the furrows. The cries of the long dead rode the wind and braided with the dark hymn in her heart. Their only sin had been to want what all men claim by birth, to stand unchained, faces warmed by the sun. To call their children their own.

As she walked, the land opened itself to her senses.

She smelled old blood ground into the dirt. Felt the echo of blows struck a hundred years before. Heard the rattle of chains, the slap of a whip, the low moan of a mother burying her child in secret.

Esther did not flinch. In each shadow she read the shape of her purpose.

The patrollers had come in force. Their camp lay where the trees thinned into open hills. A low fire threw long tongues of light across sleeping bodies. Tents slouched like crooked teeth. Rough voices muttered in uneasy dreams. Rifles glinted beside bedrolls; threadbare blankets twitched over sweat-sheened brows despite the cold.

They'd chained the hounds to a sapling at the edge of camp, iron collars biting their necks, links run short so the dogs could only circle and fret. They smelled her before any man did. Lips peeled. Nostrils flared. Growls rose, ragged, frenzied, the sound of animals who knew what walked in the dark. Then, they broke off mid-rise. Esther turned her head and looked at them. Nothing but black water in her eyes. The dogs dropped to their haunches, ears plastered, throats working soundlessly. Chains rattled then went still, as if a hand had been laid over every muzzle.

The horses sensed her next. Muscles ticked under their sweat-slick hides. Tethers creaked. Hooves tapped frost-bitten ground. A young gelding let out a strangled whinny that split the stillness. The men did not wake.

A wind passed through the trees, dry and whispering, though it carried with it no leaves. Only her scent.

Like a demon risen from the darkest nightmare, Esther moved among them unseen. Her bare feet left no mark. Her breath did not stir the air. She paused at the edge of the firelight, then she stepped in.

The first sentry slumped against a stump, rifle across his lap. His eyes opened as she passed, just long enough to see a tall, gaunt silhouette haloed in black coils, before her hand pressed through his chest and his life went out, as swift as a candle in a sudden wind.

She did not stop.

One after another, they died soundlessly. Some in sleep; some with eyes wide, mouths shaping pleas that never formed. One man managed a strangled, "God, help..." before she stilled him with a hand on his throat.

By dawn their bodies lay stacked. Blood darkened the frost-bitten grass; steam lifted from the ground. Atchen paced within her.

Her ravenous teeth pressed to Esther's heart, not for cruelty but for justice. For the reaping of wicked men. She left the corpses half-consumed, a throat missing here, a chest hollowed there, not as trophies, as warnings.

Let the overseers come.

Let them see what the forest had birthed to answer their sins.

She did not count the dead. Numbers were the white man's vanity, used to tally profit and measure loss.

To Esther, this was only debt repaid.

She turned to the woods. The trees parted like kin. Behind her, spilled lamp oil found spark; flames licked canvas and flesh.

And still, she moved on.

Twenty-Eight

House of Ash

"The angel comes on quiet feet."

-Spiritual by Moses Blue, 1867

She reached the first plantation house in the blue hour before dawn, when night loosens but the day has not yet taken hold.

Two stories of gleaming white brick rose before her; grande columns laced with ivy blackened by frost. Once, she would have been required to enter through the back door, gaze lowered. Now, she climbed the sweeping front stairs.

She moved like something summoned from the oldest night, tall and spare, bare feet silent on the broad boards. Her black hair hung in coils crusted with river silt and leaves. Atchen lay quietly beneath her scalp, curled like a shadow serpent, watching through her eyes. Moonlight shone bright across her blood-lacquered skin, stretched tight over long, strong limbs. But it was her eyes, vast and lightless, that would have stopped any heart. They were the eyes of a creature that had known all suffering and found it wanting.

The house dazzled, columns tall as trees, clapboard luminous as pearl in the lamplight. The veranda was swept clean each day by enslaved hands. Lanterns burned behind lace-curtained windows, throwing warm squares of light across floors laid for generations on stolen backs. Here stood the white man's pride, what he imagined would last forever.

Esther's bare feet crossed the threshold, tracking blood and sludge from the tobacco fields.

Down the wide center hall, gilt-framed portraits watched, men in starched collars, women in silk gowns, children with spaniels and riding crops. Their painted gazes judged her trespass.

Somewhere within the house a grandfather clock kept time with a slow, solemn tick, as if measuring out the last moments these walls would be allowed to remember.

She paused in the parlor doorway. Velvet drapes sagged in the gloom; beeswax and roses clung to the air. On pressed linen, a silver tea service waited; on the desk, an open ledger, its ink still wet, tallied harvest yields and human bodies side by side. The clock went on counting behind it all. She did not bow her head. She was no longer a woman belonging to the shadows. She was the reckoning come to claim the price.

Her black gaze swept the room. Every inch of polish was wrung from broken backs. Every shine reeked of the same sickness that had devoured the land.

She set her hand on the banister. The wood flinched, and in the marrow of the house she felt the dawning knowledge that its very foundation was already ash.

Above, bedsheets rustled. A small child began to cry. A woman's voice answered, ragged with sleep.

Esther tilted her head. Her hair spilled over her shoulders. She had the calm beauty of a storm about to break.

She felt no pity. She was what they had borne with every lash, every chain, every child stolen and every mother left screaming. To become this creature, she had buried her own soul within the earth. She had given up tenderness. There was no room inside her now for anything but fire.

Tonight, she had come to deliver the answer they had earned.

At the landing, she lifted the latch on the nursery door. Inside, the sash eased, letting a slip of cold air move like a path through the room. A small sound answered; soft, hiccupping cries. In the cradle a baby turned, wrists sweet and dimpled, mouth rooting in sleep. Something in her eased back from the edge; for a breath she saw only Eustace, the weight of him, the milk-warm sighs, the way his tiny fingers had once caught her thumb and would not let go. Her voice, when it came, was barely more than breath. "Run," she said into the stairwell, not loud, but a pitch only the innocent could hear. Small feet pattered. A nursemaid woke with a gasp, gathered the child, and fled. Below, the servants door swung wide; the night took them in.

The house seemed to be tightening around her; floorboards braced against the inevitable. She could feel it in every beam and nail, the slow dawning that all its stolen safety was a lie.

She passed the ledger. One fingertip brushing its open page, smearing the fresh ink. For a heartbeat, she could hear the voices of the dead whispering up from between the neat black columns.

Here, we were counted.

Then, Esther walked to the hearth.

A low fire glowed, little more than embers under the grate. She knelt, ragged skirts pooling around her feet. Dried blood lay on her skin like varnish. The flame's glow threw sharp shadows across her features; for an instant her eyes caught the light and gave it back, red as coals. She breathed, and the embers brightened, recognizing her purpose.

Slowly, she set both palms to the iron grate.

The coals flared white. Heat rolled out and scorched the velvet drapes. Shadows grew long and frantic, the air shivered with a dry crackle.

She rose; her face washed in an orange flush.

Flame leapt higher, hungry, answering the demon braided to her breath. Atchen rose, too, no longer separate, but seam to seam. This was their sacrament.

Atchen whispered, *"Let these walls drink smoke as we have drank sorrow. Let them burn for every name they never learned, for every life stolen."*

Room to room she went, trailing a palm along every wooden surface. Where her hand passed, paneling blackened; tongues of fire licked up in her wake. The house moaned, timbers shifting, plaster cracking as heat found every hidden seam. On the paneled wall above the hearth, a gentleman's portrait caught, riding crop clenched and blistered; painted eyes peeled back like skin.

She did not pause. Let the house remember itself.

She returned to the wide front door and stepped onto the veranda. Behind her, smoke boiled through the rafters into a paling sky. Windows glowed orange and gold.

She descended the steps, leaving sooty prints in her wake.

At the edge of the long drive, she turned one last time. Fire burst the upper windows in banners; the roof buckled, groaning. Sparks whirled into the dark and scattered toward the cane.

Esther stood motionless. Her black eyes reflecting the inferno.

She felt no triumph, no sorrow.

Only the certainty of justice.

When the roof finally fell with a roar that shook the ground, she turned away. She continued her march through the fields, a dark silhouette wavering in the glow.

Behind her, the land feasted.

Ahead, the night opened wide to receive her.

Twenty-Nine

The Crumbling House

"They built their homes on the backs of the broken,
but the bones have begun to shift beneath them."

On Broadlawn Plantation, John Barrow was coming apart.
It began as a tightness in his chest, a gnawing unease he could not name. He told himself it was only the rumors, nonsense spread by idle tongues. But as the days passed and the countryside burned, that unease grew into a cold, unreasoning dread.

In the fields, the enslaved whispered.

They whispered of a dark angel moving through the canebrakes, of a woman with eyes black as pitch and hair tangled with riverweed, who left nothing but cinders in her wake.

They whispered of freedom.

Barrow knew better than to dismiss it.

Hope was more dangerous than any torch. Once it took root in the quarters, it spread like wildfire.

Every morning, he found new signs that his grip was weakening; a tool left deliberately broken, a gate unlatched in the night, a look in the eyes of men who no longer cared if he saw their hatred.

At supper he sat across from his wife, Mary, while she dabbed delicately at her lips with a linen napkin and told him to get hold of himself. The scent of lye clung to her fingers; her rings flashed in the lamplight, the same rings that had boxed a girl's ear in the pantry that afternoon.

"You're letting them see your fear," she said crisply. "You must control them. They only understand the whip."

Mary had never carried a whip. She preferred small, private remedies; the back of a hairbrush, a kettle tipped close enough to scald, pins and salt and sleepless nights on her knees in the kitchen. The house had its own punishments, and she administered them like prayer.

John reached for his glass. His hand trembled; the ice clinked.

"Woman, you ought to mind your tongue," he muttered. "You forget yourself in my house."

"In your house?" She laughed without mirth. "Daddy's money laid these bricks. My name bought your tobacco, your slaves, your overseers. You wear my dowry like a frock coat and still manage to look cold." She set the napkin down with neat precision. "You've squandered what was placed in your hands like a child with sugar. Debts in Lexington. Notes past due in town. I should have rid myself of you years ago."

His mouth tightened. "Watch yourself."

"I've watched you," she said, voice low and sharp as a knife. "Watched you shrink. Watched you slop bourbon down your shirt-front while these fields go ragged. Watched you let the quarters whisper until even the pickaninnies stare you down." She tilted her head, rings chiming against the stem of her glass. "Do you know who does as they're told in this house? Your bastard slaves. They are very attentive, grateful for direction. They serve better in every respect than you ever have."

Color climbed his throat. "You filthy bitch."

"Truth sits ill on a weak stomach." She smiled, small and pitiless. "You were only ever handsome standing beside my fortune. Without it, you're nothing but a clerk with a temper."

His hand moved before he thought. The slap cracked across her cheek, sharp as a pistol in the quiet dining room.

Mary's head turned with the blow. She touched the corner of her mouth; a ruby red bead welled and caught the light. Then she laughed, soft, delighted, like a woman surprised with a gift. "There he is," she whispered. "A little heat under all that ash. Pity it never amounts to anything."

He pushed back from the table so fast the chair scraped. "You'll hold your tongue."

"Or what?" She leaned in, voice soft as silk. "You'll go down to the women's quarters and remind them you're a man? You and I both know you haven't darkened that door in months." Her eyes glittered. "You can't even look them in the face."

John stared at the empty plate until the pattern blurred. He could not bring himself to visit the women's cabins anymore. His body would not answer when he sunk his fingers into unwilling flesh. The very thought turned his stomach to water. It wasn't their bodies he feared. It was their eyes, eyes that now saw he was no longer in control. Eyes that measured him and found him small.

Mary reached for her wine, unbothered. "Eat," she said, as if to a child. "In the morning you will stand in the yard and make a show of being Master. And I will speak with the Overseer about the rest." She lifted the glass in a tiny, mocking toast. "To hope, John. The most dangerous thing on this land and the one thing you never learned to govern."

He sent the Overseer to the quarters instead.

The whippings grew more frequent. Punishments harsher.

Men were separated from their families, locked in the smoke-house overnight.

Children were beaten for speaking the wrong word.

At dusk, Jack made rounds with a lantern and a musket, locking the cabin doors from the outside.

It did no good.

The sense of something coming, something vast and merciless, thickened the air until no one could draw breath.

Mary had carpenters up from Lexington on a pretense, a new hasp on the attic door, a length of chain, iron rings set into rafters "for drying herbs." The maids kept their eyes on the floor. John did not ask.

With Mary no longer sharing his bedchamber, Barrow lay awake at night, listening to the sounds drifting in through the windows; the wind in the tobacco, the rustle of bare feet moving where no feet should be. Sometimes he thought he heard a woman singing, her voice low and mournful, carrying across the fields to settle in the rafters of his house.

The patrollers he had hired to watch the quarters grew restless, glancing over their shoulders as they walked their circuits. One by one, they began to leave, citing sick wives or old debts to collect.

Barrow understood with a hollow certainty that none of his precautions would save him.

The dark was coming.

It was only a matter of time.

He could feel it at the edges of his vision, brushing against his skin in the still hours before dawn.

So, he did the only thing a frightened man of power knows how to do, he reached for others like him. He sent riders with letters sealed in beeswax, dispatched to the neighboring plantations. The messages were terse, veiled in formal language, but the meaning was clear.

There is unrest. We must act.

At week's end, before first light, he left the house. Behind him, Mary's ring of keys chimed on the landing. The sound ran up his spine; he told himself it was only the cold.

The planters of the region gathered in the grande parlor of Roseloe Hall, a place built for opulence, now reeking of cigar smoke and expensive liquor. They arrived with the rattle of carriages and the clopping of hooves. Their boots clean; their wives left at home.

They clutched silver-topped canes and spoke with slow southern drawls, sharpened by years of harsh command.

Barrow sat among them, stiff-backed and hollow-eyed. He saw the same worry etched in the lines of their faces, though no one would admit it aloud.

"We are not under siege," scoffed Major Harlow, whose plantation sat just beyond the pine ridge. "It's only fearmongering. The fire at the Whitlock Plantation was a catastrophe. Three people died that night, worse off, God only knows how much value was lost on all those slaves fleeing into the hills. But, for Christ's sake, John, it was an accident. This is only a few foolish slaves telling stories in the dark."

"But they are telling them," Barrow replied quietly. "They say there were human footprints left in the soot of the front stairs. And the slaves believe this."

"Listen to me, John, they always believe nonsense, spreading tales of hoodoos and the like," insisted George Scott. "We've dealt with it all before."

Thomas Lee, a portly man with red cheeks framing a perfectly groomed handle-bar mustache, leaned forward. "Then we must remind them who holds the lash."

There were nods. Murmured assent. The scent of pipe smoke thickened the air.

They spoke of stronger patrols. Night raids. An increase in public punishments to reassert control. One planter suggested importing bloodhounds from the Carolinas, bred to track runaways. Another proposed reviving the old slave codes that outlawed organized prayer gatherings.

Their solutions were old tools drawn up from bloodstained hands. Not one of them imagined that something had changed. Not one of them understood that it was not just fear they were facing. It was hope.

And hope, once born, does not die quietly.

Barrow watched them, his heart thudding like a funeral drum. They saw themselves as gods still, cloaked in vanity, clutching their ledgers, weighing life in coin and tobacco. He said nothing when they laughed.

But he knew. He had seen it in the fields, in the steady gaze of those he once called property.

They no longer flinched.

They no longer feared him.

A tide was rising, and these men, for all their power, could not stop it. The meeting ended in cigars and false confidence.

They made their plans.

And they never saw her coming.

Thirty

Justice Delivered

"And the light of the wicked shall be put out."

-Job 18:5

The men poured out of Roseloe Hall in good spirits, frock coats shrugged up against the late-autumn chill, breath blooming white over cigar smoke. Laughter rang under the portico's grande columns. Silver-headed canes clicked. Spurs chimed. The gravel drive crunched with hooves and wheels as coachmen brought the carriages round.

The moon rode the sky, high and cold, a coin hammered thin. Dry leaves scudded across the lawn in quick, rustling herds. Somewhere beyond the tall oaks, a hoot owl traded question for answer.

Major Harlow clapped George Scott on the shoulder, gave Barrow a smile too loose at the edges, and lurched for his carriage. He misjudged the step, boot skidding on the iron step, and grabbed the doorframe with both hands, chuckling at himself. "Too much of Roseloe's hospitality," he muttered, breath sour with bourbon. He hauled his weight inside and dropped onto the velvet bench with a grunt, relieved to be off his feet, stories of angels and devils all but forgotten.

The door thudded closed. Outside, the driver's whip cracked, polite as a tap on a parlor door. The harness jingled; the team leaned hard into the traces. The carriage rocked and started down the long, raked curve of the drive.

Within, the dim was soft as a bullfrog's throat. Lamp glass in the corner threw only a smear of glow, not enough to make sense of the dark. Harlow blinked repeatedly, trying to will the cabin to sit still. The bench opposite held a shape, nothing definite, only a seam of deeper shadow, tall and wrong, like a coat hung from a nail too high.

He squinted. "Who the hell are you?" he said, half-turning toward the speaking tube, "Driver..?" The shape did not move.

The horses' shoes rang hollow on the wooden bridge planks. In the pause between clatters, he heard it; breath not his own, slow as a bellows pulled by a careful hand.

His mouth went dry. "Who…who's there?" he stuttered, softer now, as if a whisper could convince the dark to be reasonable.

The figure tilted its head. Slowly. As if listening.

Moonlight slipped through the curtained slit of a window and slid across the cabin like a blade. It cut the shadow's edge and found a cheek, a spill of tangled hair, the suggestion of a mouth set in a patience far older than him. The eyes lifted last, catching the light so they seemed to hold it, black made liquid for an instant.

He forgot breath. Forgot speech. Thought, absurdly, of stories told in quarters he did not enter, of a woman with river silt in her hair and ashes for footprints.

The carriage jolted over a rut. The lamp-flame guttered and steadied. She was no longer across from him.

She was nearer.

He tried to shout. What left him was small and animal, swallowed by the creaking of leather and clomp of hooves. The carriage banged over the next rise; the moon went ghostly white, and the world shrank to two hands closing the space between.

Outside, the driver hunched against the cold, thinking of his bed and the coin promised at the end of the road. He did not look back. He did not see the horses throw their ears or the way the roof-springs began to creak in an odd, condensed rhythm, like a dance taught to the unwilling. The coach rocked hard on its axle. Then settled into an ordinary sway.

At the gate, a wind came off the fields and set the dead leaves running ahead of them, fast and low. The driver clicked his tongue, and the team trotted down the long, moonlit road.

Thirty-One

Bloody Mary

"Woe to her who builds her rooms with blood."

-Jeremiah 22:13

John Barrow's carriage had not yet vanished around the bend when Mary slipped the brass key into the attic lock.

Mabel had the boys for the night. The house, at last, belonged to her.

She dressed for the climb, silk the color of cream, long tresses pinned hard and high, a dusting of powder and the cool bite of perfume at her throat. The little bell on her key ring chimed with each step. The fire inside her rose with every stair.

The attic breathed heat. Dust motes hung in a pale corridor of light that fell from the far gable vent, a bright, narrow seam shone across the floorboards. The rest was only shadow, thick and close.

Mary paused in the doorway and drew the air in through her nose. She could smell them.

The shapes resolved as her eyes adjusted; two bodies hung from the braces, their weight borne by iron and rope. One head was hooded; the other turned toward her, swollen features mottled and still, his stare unfocused and afraid. They were stripped naked from the waist down. Bare feet found nothing to stand on. A slick, dark sheen colored their thighs, pooling thick where the boards met beneath them.

In the corner, a small crate crouched under the eaves, barely large enough to hold a person. Something inside breathed shallowly. The crate's slats were crosshatched by broken fingernails.

The room had been prepared. She had seen to it herself. On a narrow table, wrapped in linen, lay her implements: irons and pokers, lengths of cord, clamps, a kettle blackened at the lip. A dish of coarse salt waited beside a sponge. Along the rafters, new iron rings gleamed where the carpenter's hands had worked that afternoon, "for drying herbs." He knew better than to inquire.

Mary moved among the shadows and began to set the candles alight, one after another, her breath steady, the small flames catching and multiplying until the faces she had come to see took on depth and shine. The silk of her dress whispered as she walked. The floor answered with a low, tired groan. From outside came the chirping song of crickets and the far-off creak of the well.

"This will be orderly," she said, not raising her voice.

"Neatness in all things."

The hooded man shifted; the rope creaked. Muffled sobs came from the small crate. Mary tilted her head, as if listening to a piece of chamber music only she could hear. She set the brass basin beneath the table and aligned it with care.

A candle sputtered and caught again.

"You will be quiet when I am speaking," she added, almost pleasantly, as though scolding a child for crumbs.

She took up a length of linen and wiped a clean path down the handle of the copper kettle. In the candlelight, she could see herself in the warm metal, an oval of pale face, the fixed blue of her eyes, a smear of lamplight riding her cheek like blush. She smiled at her reflection and let it fade.

The house listened.

From below drifted the grandfather clock's slow counting, the faint rattle of a window in its sash. The attic air trembled with small, human sounds, faint throatings, the scrape of a heel on a board, a dry swallow, and with Mary's own measured preparations; the gentle clink of metal on wood, the soft tear of linen into strips, the wet sigh as water met heat.

She stepped to the line of light and stood where they could see her. Silk, pins, the press of rings at her fingers, every inch of her considered. She looked at the men the way a seamstress looks at cloth.

"You are here to be useful," she said. "Do not make a lesson of yourselves."

The hooded head nodded quickly, a frantic, clumsy motion. The other man watched her with a steady, exhausted hatred that did not please her. She stepped closer until her shadow swallowed his face. His eyes dropped then, and the balance of the room returned.

The crate knocked softly against the wall. Mary rested her hand on its top rail, feeling the breath within it, the quick, shallow flutter. She leaned down, not to peer but to be certain the small, contained shape heard her.

"You will do as you are told," she chimed, crisp as porcelain. "If you bite, you will regret it."

She straightened, smoothing her skirts, and crossed back to the table. She placed each implement in its place, cloth, water, iron, until the surface was as precise as a dressing table before a ball. She preferred it like this; clean, arranged, unhurried. The night was long. She had been given the gift of time.

"Look at me," she told them, and waited until all eyes, hooded or not, turned toward the sound of her voice.

"Good," she said, pleased. "We will begin."

The attic door swung inward a finger's breadth on a draft, then settled shut again. Down in the yard a hound barked. Mary lifted the kettle and tested the weight of it in her hand, as if gauging a teapot before pouring for guests.

When she turned, the candles made a ring of gold around her, and for a heartbeat she looked every inch the mistress of a grand table, hostess, patroness, queen, until the light slid along the copper and changed her.

From the rafters a rope creaked.

From the crate came a small, swallowed choke.

Mary's rings clicked together as she reached for the first tool.

The house flinched.

Outside, the night listened…and did not interfere.

Thirty-Two

Stolen Innocence

"Even the smallest bird remembers the sky it was never allowed to touch."

From the moment Eustace drew breath; he belonged to somebody else. He was born in a shack behind the big house, his first cry rising under the shadow of the ledger where John Barrow tallied every life he owned. Born to a mama who turned her face from the lamplight; the pale of his skin shamed her and told a truth they could not name.

He learned early on what bondage felt like, how he could be sold away any day, how nothing he loved was really his. The knowledge sat in his belly like a stone and never moved.

He never got to be a child, not really. He carried the weight of injustice on shoulders too small to bear it. The white children rolled through the grass, while Eustace headed off to the rows.

He had no daddy. Deep down, though, he knew. He heard it in whispers, saw it in the way folks looked away when he passed, read it in the skin he couldn't hide. It made no difference. If anything, Barrow's hand fell harder to prove a point, reminding him he wasn't special, he wasn't anything but property.

"Get to work," the Master said the first time he pushed the boy into the rows and cuffed him hard enough to take his air. He picked until his little hands curled into claws, until his fingertips split and bled on the dry stems.

On Sunday morning, when their clothes were boiled and beaten with lye and every soul wore a gunny sack, Barrow sent Eustace to the big house to clean up after the white children. He scrubbed their footprints off polished floors and emptied their chamber pots while Mary watched from a high-backed chair to be sure he did not dawdle. When backs were turned, Barrow's oldest boy, John Junior, tugged his ears and told him he looked like a ghost with mud for blood. He bowed his head and kept moving. He learned to carry his silence like a bucket he didn't dare spill.

Eustace didn't have many words. Some days none at all. The quiet inside him was a well with no rope. Only Esther could lower a cup into it. When she looked at him, it felt like a patch of warm sky opened above him.

His mama wasn't there for any of it. Most days, she was kept in the big house tending to the Master's real children. Eustace spent long, lonely afternoons sitting on the backsteps, waiting for her to come home.

But, from the first time he could remember, there was Esther. Her smile was the only bit of sunshine in that sorrowful place. She would find him. Sit him on her lap, tuck a curl behind his ear and sing, sweet and gentle, old songs, older than the rows, songs of freedom and better days. She told him about the land beyond the river where little boys could run through tall grass and splash in creeks, their laughter floating on the breeze. For a little while, he believed her.

But hope died with his mama. It died again when Esther was gone.

Eliza did her best to fill his hollowed heart, but the fields had pared her down to the necessary. Long before, on a thin-moon night behind the kitchens, she and Martha had chosen, between themselves and God, that she would never carry the Master's seed. There were old ways, bitter teas and quiet remedies handed down in whispers; Martha kept the watch, and Eliza bore the choice like a weight she could not set down. It saved a part of her, and it scarred her too. She told herself she was made for work, not for rocking cradles. Her hands blistered and her spirit became broken. The brightness she'd once had felt like a story somebody else told.

At night, after Eliza turned her face to the wall, Eustace lay on his pallet of rags and let the dark press close. When sadness grew too heavy to breathe, he took up his fiddle and went to the hickory tree by the cabins. No one taught him. He listened to wind rustle through the tobacco and pulled the bow until the wood spoke the truth for him. The sound was small and aching, the kind that never quite climbs to joy. Children from the quarters sat quietly on their heels to hear it, like it was sacred. The white children laughed and called it slave crying. Said it sounded like a dying cat. He played anyway.

Some nights he stayed awake long after lamps in the big house died. The wind moved through the leaves, and he pretended it was Esther's hum at the door. He pictured the dimple on her cheek and the way her hand smoothed his hair when he couldn't reach the wash bucket.

"You're my sweet, brave boy," she'd whisper. "You hold on. Remember who you are."

He tried. But the rows took so much from him it was hard to keep the rest. The overseers' shouts. The crack of the whip. Stems and stems and stems. By dusk, he felt hollow-boned, light enough to blow away.

But in the deep dark, when everyone else had fallen silent, the sadness would creep back up his throat. He missed her so badly, it might split him in two. The aching in his heart never went away.

He'd press his face into his thin blanket and whisper her name, soft as breath.

"Esther."

He didn't know where she'd gone.

On the night they ran, he and Esther slipped past the smoke-house, breath held, feet learning the softest path. Her hand found his. He thought he could hold on forever.

Then, the dogs opened the sky with their howling.

The shouting scattered them. He ran until his lungs burned, until roots tore his feet. He climbed the tallest tree he could find and wedged himself into the branches, a sparrow of a boy shivering a-gainst the trunk. He prayed the only prayer he knew, *"Please, Lord, keep Esther safe. Let her find that Promised Land,"* until the words turned to rhythm and the rhythm turned to breath. He hoped if he said it enough times, it might be true. Sitting up in that tree, whispering Esther's prayer, he was free. If only for a few hours.

At gray light, the fields flashed with dew, he climbed down, stiff and nearly numb. He slipped into the cabin before the rooster lied about the sun and lay still, as if he had never left. He picked tobacco leaves beside Eliza all day with grit in his eyes and a secret heat in his ribs. He told himself Esther had made it. He told himself she was somewhere under a big sky, belonging only to herself.

He didn't see her again. But he never stopped feeling her hand on his shoulder when the wind blew in from the river. Hearing her voice when the breeze shifted and the tobacco leaves rustled. Sometimes he'd feel a spark deep in his chest, a flickering hope the world had failed to smother.

Maybe, she was out there.

Maybe, she was coming back.

Maybe, he wouldn't be alone forever.

Thirty-Three

The Coming Storm

"The earth does not forget the blood that fed it. In time, it will rise to remember."

The sky smoldered crimson as the sun slipped behind the trees, a line of fire laid across the horizon. The world had been set ablaze, already burning in the ruin she intended to unleash.

Esther stood on the ridge without fear. This was the moment she'd been called to, the purpose whispered into her bones the night she first met Atchen's gaze and felt, marrow-deep, the sorrow of every man, woman, and child; beaten, broken, and buried without name.

What moved her now was not only fury, but mercy. Mercy for the enslaved. Mercy for the children waiting behind locked doors. Mercy for the women forced to carry a shame that was never theirs. She had become the answer to generations of prayers spoken into the dark.

She was the fire.

She was the flood.

She was the guardian of her people.

Below, Broadlawn Plantation lay quiet, whitewashed and proud, arrogant in its silence. Windows polished. Silk-upholstered rooms breathing in lamplight. Fields stretched in every direction, orderly and cruel, planted over the bones of those who were never meant to rise.

She could feel the hearts beating there, taste them on the wind. The Overseer pacing, fingers tight on the rifle stock he no longer believed could save him. Patrollers stiff in their saddles, eyes flicking, murmuring prayers that were already useless. John Barrow sitting alone in his study, bourbon-sick and shrinking from the silence pressing in at every pane. And the enslaved, her people, huddled in their cabins, eyes lifted toward the night, asking God for deliverance.

A cold, wet wind brushed her bare arms like the breath of the forgotten. She closed her eyes and let the scent of tobacco resin and old blood wash over her. This place had been fed on suffering so long it had forgotten any other way to live.

Tonight, she would remind it.

Esther's eyes opened, bottomless and black, reflecting the last flames of sunset. They will be free, she thought. And if the price was the last scrap of her humanity, a price Atchen had already begun to consume, she would pay it.

She stepped down from the ridge, and the land exhaled. Esther moved toward Broadlawn, her bare feet silent on the damp earth; the dew parted at each step, leaving a ribbon of darkened prints trailing in the silvered grass behind her.

John Barrow sat behind his desk with a decanter of bourbon clutched in his trembling hand. The porcelain clock on the mantle ticked too fast, each second screaming in his thoughts. His ledgers lay before him, rows of tidy figures blurring in his gaze. He tried to focus on the yields, to be the man of order he'd always claimed to be. But none of it mattered anymore.

No amount of bourbon could steady the sickness rising in his belly. The dread would not release him.

Out there in the dark was the thing that had set half the county to flame. Stories came faster now, plantations burned in the night, men disappeared from their posts. Some were found with their hearts torn out. Others were not found at all. Always, the same whisper, a woman with black eyes who walked through fire.

He ordered tighter patrols, harsher punishments. It made no difference. He hadn't unlatched the front door in three days. He no longer rode the fields or prowled the quarters by lantern light. The air itself felt wrong, thick and quivering, as if the land had eyes on him.

"John. Come away from that window."

He hadn't realized he'd risen, the decanter dangling at his side. Mary stood in the doorway, lace dressing gown cinched tight at the waist, her hair loose, face tight with fear she no longer cared to hide.

"You look like a fool," she said, voice sharp and shaking. "Sick with superstition. Get hold of yourself."

He meant to answer, but the words died. Something was coming. Pressure pooled in the air, dense and unnatural, like the moment before a storm breaks. The wind had stopped. The crickets were silent. Even the fire behind him crouched and shrank.

From the kennels at the far edge of the fields the hounds lifted their muzzles as one. A howl rose, agitated and frenzied, shivering along the fence rails. Chains rattled. Boards thudded under their paws. Then, the noise fell away, leaving only low squealing whines. They cowered; bellies pressed to the straw. The beasts knew their reckoning was near.

He pushed the curtain aside. For a heartbeat the rows lay empty, silver fields of tobacco stretching still beneath the moon. The last watch fires guttered low, the patrollers' shadows slumped beside them.

In the tobacco, leaves stirred.

Esther stepped out of the darkness without hurry, as if she belonged to this land in a way he never could. Tall and gaunt, beneath a ragged dress that clung like burnt skin. Bare feet sinking into soft earth. Her limbs caked in ash and blood. Her tangled hair spilling in a torrent down her back, snarled with briar. It moved when the wind did not.

She came the way of storms, quiet at first, then far too late to stop. When she raised her head, John Barrow saw her eyes. Eyes that knew the faces of the dead buried under his fields. Eyes that re-membered. Two pits of darkness that swallowed the last shred of his sanity.

The decanter slipped from his hand and shattered onto the hardwood floor.

Still, she came.

Up the center road.

Straight toward the house he had built with the blood of her people.

He gripped the sill, his breath wheezed, and his knees buckled. And then, recognition struck. Not in her face, which had been hol-lowed by fire and fury. Not in her body, which bore the marks of the world she meant to unmake.

But in something deeper.

A memory.

He remembered her eyes, defiant, even then.

He remembered the sound of the whip.

And the silence she held afterward.

Esther.

In the stables he had forced himself on her in the dark, bourbon on his breath and hate in his hands. So many times. He took what he wanted because no one would stop him, because the law said she was his. Now she stood at his gate, wrapped in ash and shadow, eyes lit with the memory of everything he had done.

She had come back for him.

Esther.

The name ripped through him. She had belonged to him. Now she had returned, no longer a girl, no longer anything human. She was what he had made her. What all of them had made her. She had brought the darkness with her. He stumbled back from the window, his mouth gapping in a voiceless scream.

Mary called out again, but it did not reach him. All he could see was Esther standing before the gate, the earth rising to answer crimes he thought were buried.

She did not stop.

For a moment, the whole plantation held its breath.

She stepped to the iron latch.

The gate swung open without a sound.

And Broadlawn began to burn.

Thirty-Four

Breaking the Master

*"The sins of the fathers shall return with flame, and the house
of the wicked shall fall into ash."*

John Barrow pressed his palm flat against the windowpane, his
breath clouding the glass. Terror showed in his eyes.

Below, the fields glowed with watchfires. The patrols moved
in uneasy circuits, rifles cradled tight against their chests.

The Overseer stood near the drying barn, a lantern swinging
from his fist. From this distance, Jack looked small, just another man
quaking in the dark.

Barrow told himself that if the fires burned and the men stood
watch, nothing could touch him. But the instant he thought it; the
lantern went out. He blinked. It hadn't been snuffed or dropped. It
had simply ceased. The dark around Jack thickened and swallowed
him whole.

His mouth went dry. He strained to see, one hand fumbled for
the pistol on the sideboard, sending Mary's silver tray skittering
along the floor; china leapt, cups toppled, and porcelain shattered
across the boards.

Then something moved in the darkness.

Long and pale.

A shape gliding beside the tobacco.

The Overseer's scream came sudden and shrill. It was cut off so cleanly it might have been a bird crying in the night.

Barrow clutched the pistol, his knuckles white. He pressed closer to the window, heart slamming against his ribs.

The patroller nearest the portico raised his rifle. He shouted something Barrow couldn't hear. Esther turned toward him, pale and emaciated. In the fire's glow he finally saw her face. His mind refused to accept it. He hadn't really believed it could be her.

Esther.

And in the same instant, he knew it was.

The rifle cracked. The ball struck her square in the chest.

She did not stagger.

She did not bleed.

She only tilted her head, questioning.

Then she raised her hand and caught him by the neck. Her fingers pressed deep, tearing his flesh. The patroller convulsed where he stood, a strangled cry escaping as his body arched backward. His boots left the earth, and for one breathless moment he hung suspended like a man crucified. When she let him fall, he did not rise.

The others broke, bolting into the fields. Their lanterns bobbed like fireflies as they fled.

Esther moved across the lawn without haste.

The wind caught her skirts, whipping the ragged cloth around her legs. Sparks danced in the darkness, carried on the same wind that had once carried the cries of the beaten across these fields.

Behind her, the bodies of the patrollers lay twisted in the dirt.

Ahead, Broadlawn rose, white columns gleaming in the moonlight, the front door standing ajar as if to welcome her in.

Barrow's vision blurred. His pulse roared in his ears. The gun slipped from his fingers to the floor.

She turned her black gaze toward the house.

Toward him.

He stumbled back, hands groping along the edge of the desk. Mary was calling his name from somewhere behind him, her voice thin and distant. He could not look away from the window.

She was coming.

The creature he had made with every lash, every cruelty.

All the stories, all the warnings, he'd dismissed them as superstition. But as her bare feet ascended the porch steps, silent as a grave, Barrow felt the last fragile scaffolding of his mind collapse. He sobbed, not for salvation, but from knowing none would come.

She glided across the porch.

With one quick movement she crossed the threshold and brushed a candelabrum with the back of her hand. It toppled, flame kissing velvet, sending fire crawling up the drapes, finding the varnish on the walls. Smoke unfurled across the ceiling in slow, sinuous patterns.

John Barrow crouched behind his desk, his face pale and wet with tears. Mary cowered against the far wall, clutching a Bible to her chest, as if it could shield her.

Esther paused in the foyer.

The plantation house drew one long breath around her, timbers tightening, velvet lifting with the draft, as if it understood at last what had come to claim it.

She turned toward the staircase.

Mary made a small animal sound in her throat. Esther did not look at her. The long-case clock counted off a final, patient measure as she climbed, bare feet soundless on the treads.

At the landing the air changed, it was hotter, salted with lye and fear. Children's breath. Milk. Camphor. Esther crossed to the nursery door and laid her palm to the latch. It opened as if it had been waiting.

Mabel started from the rocker; the two boys clutched against her apron. Their eyes were wide and wet with tears; one still held a toy horse by its broken leg. Hot air pushed past Esther, belling the curtains. "Run," Esther said, voice low and even. "Do not stop."

Mabel didn't ask why. She bundled the boys, quilt over their shoulders, small bare feet tucked in and hurried them down the back stair into the service hall. The door yielded at her hand and opened wide; the winter night inhaled them. Behind them, the bolt clicked back on its own, as if the house were glad to let them go.

Smoke licked along the ceiling. Esther lifted her head. Above the nursery something else breathed, shallow, frightened, threaded with iron.

The attic.

She followed the heat up the narrow back stair, past the linen press and the locked storeroom. The new hasp on the upper door glinted in the dim. Esther set two fingers to it. Metal softened like wax; the hinge sighed from the wood.

Inside, the attic was hot and thick. The air sweet with rotting wounds and singed flesh. Shadows hung from the high rafters, their weight held by rope and ring. A small crate crouched under the eaves. The room's long bar of moonlight cut across the floor like a blade.

"Not them," Atchen hummed in her bones.

Esther crossed the boards. The first man's head sagged under the hood. She set a hand to the rope; the fibers slackened. He came down into her arms like a child falling out of fever. The second stared without blinking. His bonds gave at a touch. She eased them to the floor, put their backs to the wall, and turned to the crate.

Fingertips showed between the slats, raw crescents, patient and small. Esther set her palm to the lid. The nails drew themselves out with tiny squeals. The woman inside unfolded an inch at a time, breath catching high in her chest. Twine crossed her mouth in tight stitches. "Be still," Esther murmured. The twine loosened under her fingers and fell away like cobwebs.

The woman's first sound was not a cry but a long, shaking inhale, revealing a ragged, charred stump.

"Leave," Esther told them all, the words a path in the dark. "The trees will open."

The men nodded. The woman touched her own throat, then Esther's arm, and rose. They moved together into the hall, into the cooler strip of night that ran along the baseboards, and were gone, ghosts released back into the world.

Esther stood alone in the attic one heartbeat more. The rings in the rafters glowed dull as old brass; the ropes blackened and parted, dropping harmless lengths to the floor. She turned and went down through the heat.

Portraits blistered along the corridor; eyes ran from painted faces and pooled in the gilt. Near the nursery door a small wooden horse lay on its side, its broken leg pointing toward the back stair. Esther stepped over it and descended.

Mary still crouched at the study threshold, Bible clutched to her chest, lips working around a prayer that would not come. John Barrow huddled behind his desk, white as paper, fingers pressed into the leather edge, as if it could save him.

Esther crossed the burning foyer; the fire bowed in her wake. She turned toward the room where he cowered.

She did not hurry. For one long moment, she studied him, the man who had called her property; who violated her; who built this house on the backs and bones of her people; the man who stole her mother's life.

She stepped forward.

Barrow tried to speak, but his voice broke on a sob. He scrabbled backward, his boots slipping on the polished boards. Mary shrieked as the flames climbed higher.

Esther reached across the desk. Her hand closed on his shirt-front. The placket tore, brass buttons snapped and pinged off the wainscot like buckshot. With one effortless motion she hauled him upright. Pleas, apologies; nonsense spilling from a mouth that had only ever known commands.

She turned and walked back through the doorway, dragging him through the fire like a rag doll.

The night sky had blackened. The moon slid behind cloud and the stars turned their bright faces away. Wind rose in a long dirge through the trees, lifting ash from the tobacco fields where blood still steamed beneath the crust of earth.

At the center of the smoldering field, Esther dropped him to his knees. The ground under her feet pulsed, thick with ancient hunger. It remembered; the cries, the lash, the lives swallowed whole and nameless. The earth breathed shallow and slow, waiting.

Barrow looked up at her, his face raw with terror, his cheeks slick with tears. Moonlight gleamed in his wet eyes. His mouth trembled open. "Please," he gasped. "Please, don't."

Esther bent and closed her hand on his throat. Atchen climbed. Centuries of pain and rage gathering into a single point of fury. The demon surged through her limbs, coiling into muscle and bone, lending strength carved from generations of pain. Her eyes shone like two orbs carved into the world's first night.

The clouds churned.

Lightning flared and died without thunder.

The land leaned close.

When she spoke, it was not her voice alone.

"These fields drank the blood of my people," she said, low and final. "Tonight, the earth takes its due."

Her long fingers knotted in Barrow's matted hair. With a single, terrible wrench, his scalp tore free. Blood sang across her chest, bright against ash.

His body convulsed, mouth opened to a wet, broken scream. The raw bone of his skull flashed pale in the moonlight. His shrieks were swallowed by the trees.

All the cruelty he had sown rose up to claim him.

The women. The children. The mothers who died weeping for babies ripped from their arms. The men beaten to dust. The daughters defiled in the dark.

Esther bore it all in her hands.

His blood poured out in steaming waves, seeping into the scorched earth, where the roots drank deep.

And through it all, Atchen howled.

The sound ripped from Esther's throat; a banshee wail, made from every scream that had ever been stifled, every prayer that had gone unanswered.

Inside the burning house, Mary Barrow stood at the head of the stairs. Smoke rolled around her like the hem of a funeral gown. Flames licked up the wallpaper, devouring years of stolen comfort. Portraits crackled and peeled, their eyes blackening in the heat.

She did not run.

She did not call out.

She stood still in her white dressing gown, hair tousled, eyes wide with a knowing that went bone deep. This was the end she had earned. She had watched her husband defile his slaves and done nothing. She had beaten them herself when they displeased her. She had struck the children when they spoke too loudly. She had found Esther's mother humming in the pantry and beaten her until the humming stopped.

So many lives extinguished by her hand.

And now, she was its final offering.

The banister beneath her hand was searing. Her lungs burned. But she did not move. She watched through the front window as the man who had called himself Master was unmade in the field; watched the creature he had called forth by his cruelties stride out of smoke and ruin.

Her lips parted as if to pray.

But there was no God to answer the prayers of the wicked.

Mary Barrow closed her eyes, lifted her chin and let the flames take her.

Esther turned from the field.

John Barrow's soul, black and rotting, was swallowed whole. The land shuddered beneath her. Then fell still.

Silence returned like a blessing, dense and sacred.

When it was done, nothing of John Barrow remained; only a bloodied mass returned to the dirt he had poisoned with his cruelty.

Esther stood, breath slow and even, blood drying on her skin. She faced the house. The porch was already a skeleton of flame. The roof groaned. Windows burst in jeweled showers. The whole of Broadlawn folded inward, a whitewashed mausoleum collapsing on its sins.

She watched as the flames devoured the walls that had once caged her. When the last of the screams were consumed by the fire, she turned her face to the wind, black eyes shining. Behind her the fields smoldered. Above, the clouds cracked open, and the first drops of freezing rain began to fall, not to cleanse, only to mark the end.

Her work was not yet finished.

But Broadlawn Plantation was no more.

The land had been fed.

Thirty-Five

The Angel's Return

"They cried out in the fields, and the voice that rose was not the Lord's, but the daughter of sorrow, come to gather the lost."

Esther turned, steps measured and sure. She crossed the wide lawn, grass bending beneath her bare feet. The slave quarters rose ahead, a line of squat cabins cut dark against the burning glow of the plantation house. She knew this place, every doorway, every sagging porch board. She had been shaped here, and in some secret way, she still belonged to it.

The night air was sharp with the promise of winter.

Above, stars glimmered cold and watchful as the sky opened. Snowflakes drifted silently in an endless dance. They settled on her hair and shoulders, along the torn hem of her dress. The soft, cold weight steadied her.

She had become the hand of Atchen, and through her, justice had come. In return, Atchen had brought her home, back to her kin, back to soil that remembered their sorrow when no one else would.

Their cries reached her, almost lost in the wind. Prayers, rising soft from the cabins where the enslaved gathered in the dark. She heard the rustle of bare feet on packed earth, the trembling hands clasped tight in supplication.

Voices low and urgent.

"Lord, send us an angel."

"Deliver us from this suffering."

"Take us home."

They called to something they could not name, to the darkness, to the stars. In that space between hope and terror, they called her.

She crossed the last stretch of yard, snow laying on her cold skin. Her shadow fell long across the doorways, and the night stood in awe.

She paused near the field's edge, where the rows gave way to hard-packed earth and wild grass. The dogwood waited, winter-bare, stripped of leaf and blossom, its branches reaching toward the sky like pleading hands. No bloom would come this year. Perhaps, never again.

Here, she and Levi had laid her mama to rest, folding her gently into the arms of the land. No name marked the grave, only the small cross Levi had carved. She was held by the rich soil, the wide watching sky, and Esther's trembling hands pressing earth over the body that once cradled her aching soul.

Esther stood beneath the gnarled tree and let the silence take her. Memories came without mercy. Her mama's humming in the morning light, callused hands braiding her hair. The way she stopped to touch Esther's cheek before rising for work. Her voice, gentle, telling stories passed from mother to daughter, like roots of a tree, forever entwined. Then, Eliza's fierce eyes saying goodbye. Eustace's thin arms around her neck, breath warm against her skin, whispering, "Don't let go."

Her breath hitched.

She had let go.

Of all of them.

For the first time since taking Atchen into herself, something within her gave. Grief rose slow and deep, not rage, not vengeance, but the quiet fire that hollows a soul without sound.

She sank to her knees, fingers digging into the dark soil that had swallowed her mother, her girlhood, and so many lives. Her shoulders went rigid. No tears came. She lifted her face toward the falling snow. It drifted down in slow spirals, blanketing the world in white. Flakes caught in her hair and on her lashes, weighted her shoulders. She let it cover her, and the world grew very still.

Esther wavered.

For the innocence of childhood lost.

For the warmth of her family, stolen and scattered.

For the woman she might have been, if the world had not been so cruel. She was still, but inside, she felt a quiet splintering in the storm. *Am I still myself? Or only what they feared?*

The wind moved through the tobacco like breath in a chapel. The fields seemed to wait for her answer.

In the hush beneath the tree, something stirred, not a voice, not a vision, but a presence. Her mama's love lived here, braided into roots and loam. She felt it in the quiet the land offered back.

Esther touched the trunk and closed her eyes. One lonely tear slid down her cheek. "I'm still yours," she whispered.

Above the whispered prayers, drifting from the slave quarters, a voice rose that stopped her heart. Thin and wavering, familiar as her own heartbeat.

"Esther."

Her name.

Her knees nearly buckled. She turned toward the cabins.

She could see him without seeing; Eustace, small and hollow-eyed, kneeling beside his makeshift bed. Her sweet boy. His hands clasped so tight his knuckles shone.

"Esther… Please come back for me."

The boy she had loved with her entire soul.

The wind took his prayer and laid it in her hands.

She was not only vengeance.

She was deliverance.

Her purpose was older than memory, carried on the wind, rooted in bone, woven into the sorrow of the land.

Tonight, it would be fulfilled.

She stepped into the furrows; her shadow drew long, and the prayers grew louder.

In the paling east, the stables lifted from the darkness, timbers familiar as a scar. Inside, she heard the shifting of hooves in straw, the muffled snort of a restless horse. Stepping through the wide doorway, air pressed close around her, musky with the sweet scent of hay and warm with breath.

She paused. This place had known her pain.

She walked the stalls, palm trailing the boards.

The dragging.

The switch.

The cold laughter of the man she had burned to the ground.

Her fingers curled against the wood. The shadows thickened. Movement in the far corner caught her attention. A man rose from the straw, broad shoulders blocking the faint light seeping through the boards.

Clem.

For a long breath, they simply looked at each other. Her black eyes met his steady gaze. He did not flinch.

He had heard the strange cries in the forest, seen lights that moved without fire. He had always known there were older forces here than any white man's law.

Seeing her, dark hair tangled with leaves, her skin pale as river stone, he understood. The whispers were true. The land had chosen Esther, and she had given everything.

His throat tightened.

His thoughts flickered to the others; Levi's quiet steadiness; Nora's fierce care; Milly, frail as a bird, how once he'd carried her fevered and hot, wrapped beneath her sister's shawl. He had crept through these fields with them, hearts hammering with the hope of freedom.

But the slave catchers had caught him before the first county line. Now, looking into Esther's black eyes, he knew. They were gone. He didn't ask how. Her unspoken sorrow told him more than words. He bowed his head, for respect, and mourning. They were not forgotten.

Not by her.

Not by him.

Not by the land.

When he lifted his gaze to hers, the silence between them had changed, not cold, not hollow, but heavy with truth.

"I see you, Esther," he said, voice rough with reverence.

Connection moved through her, fragile and whole, something that had survived what she'd become. Clem stepped forward. He didn't touch her. He didn't need to. The promise was plain.

He would walk beside her.

Whatever lay ahead, she would not walk it alone.

Thirty-Six

Promises Carried

"I have called thee by thy name; thou art mine."

- Isaiah 43:1

Clem went with Esther to see Eustace and Eliza before dawn had broke the heavens. Snow fell soft and soundless, blanketing the quarters in a hush that felt almost holy.

They paused before the small cabin.

The wood was worn, boards gapped wide with weather and time, but still they held fast. Esther stood beside the low lintel, cold settling heavy on her shoulders like judgment. The timber seemed to breathe around her, as if the house remembered her footfall and welcomed her home.

Clem said nothing. He only watched her, the night's weight showed heavy in his eyes.

Inside, the air changed.

Eustace looked up first. He blinked once, then again, staring toward the door. "Eliza," he whispered, not turning. "She's here."

His blanket slipped from his thin shoulders. For a heartbeat he braced to flee, ready to hide from the monster the stories had promised. Then he saw her face.

Pale. Strange. Not wholly human.

Yet somehow, still hers.

Something in his chest opened. He took a step, the board beneath his foot creaking. "Esther?" he breathed.

His small hand lifted and trembled, hovering, as if touch might send her back into the darkness. Esther did not speak; her old voice wouldn't come. She bent until their faces were level, and in the softening of her black eyes he knew.

She had changed. But she had never stopped being his.

Snowflakes clung to her tangled hair and in the thin light of dawn, she looked carved from winter, but the way she held his gaze, steady and patient, was the same as it had always been.

A stillness settled over the room. Eliza pressed a hand to her mouth; her breath hitched; tears slid down her cheek. She stepped closer, then stopped, letting the moment belong to the two of them. Behind them, Clem eased back a pace into the doorway's shadow, granting what privacy he could.

Eustace laid his palm to her cheek, light as a prayer. Her skin was as cold as the river, but he did not flinch. For a long breath, neither of them moved, his thumb brushing a fleck of ash from her cheekbone. He could feel, without words, what she had given up to return to him. How much she had carried to stand here now.

"I knew you'd come," he whispered, voice breaking.

Esther lowered her head until their foreheads touched. The simple contact was everything. She closed her eyes; fury and hunger thinned to a distant shore. There was only this; the boy she had rocked to sleep, the child she had promised would know freedom, the heart she had never stopped carrying.

Eustace drew a shuddering breath.

"I was so scared," he murmured. "I thought that I was always going to be alone."

Her hand rose to the back of his head and held him steady in the storm. When she finally spoke, her voice was low and strained, but it was hers.

"Never."

He pressed his face onto her shoulder. For the first time in longer than she could remember, a small warmth stirred within her chest.

Atchen had claimed her. The dark had remade her.

But this boy, her boy, still knew her name.

And in his touch, she was still Esther.

Thirty-Seven

First Light

"There is a day when the burden breaks, and the wind blows only for the free."

Clem stood beside Esther under the great oak, its bare limbs stretched broad above them. Dawn climbed slowly, painting the frost-kissed fields in shades of amber and gold. Smoke curled faintly from the smoldering ruins of the plantation house behind them, rising like a final breath, wispy and fading against the new-born sky. The bitter stench of scorched wood clung to the breeze, but it was met now by the sweet crispness of freshly fallen snow, like the world was trying to wash itself clean.

Around them, the people gathered, quiet, uncertain, reverent. Men and women with blistered hands and bowed backs, their children blinking against the light, cheeks raw from cold. The old ones, their memories bearing the weight of generations, stood wrapped in torn shawls. Their faces were tired, but their eyes were wide with something new.

Hope.

Clem stepped forward, worn boots crunching in the frost. He stood sure as a preacher delivering his sermon on a Sunday morning. His voice carried clear and steady, rolling across the yard like a church bell ringing for the first time in a long while.

"This is the morning you prayed for."

A deeper hush settled.

There was fear and wonder in their eyes.

"You have seen her," he said, turning slightly toward Esther. "You have seen what she done, how the land moved with her. You know it deep in your bones. She was chosen to end your suffering."

Heads began to nod. Murmurs swelled. Others lowered their gaze and simply wept.

Auntie Bet pressed her hand to her mouth, eyes brimming. Mose, her and Old Amos's boy, grown and steady, stood braced at her side, one hand gentle at her elbow, the other ready for his father if he faltered. He was corn-tall and weather-strong, his jaw set with the work of keeping sorrow from its knees. The three of them made a small, stubborn knot in the crowd. Auntie Bet bowed her head and let the prayer rise through her like warmth.

Isaac pinched his burnt pipestem between finger and thumb, then let it fall to the dirt. He set his hat back on his head the way a man settles a burden, then planted his feet. Old field scars ridged his knuckles; tobacco stain darkened his fingertips. He lifted his chin, looking past the smoke of ruin to the woman who had walked them into morning. "Lawd, have mercy," he said, not a whisper this time, but a low declaration that carried, and a few voices answered, "Amen." His gaze found the Barrow boys and, for a breath, the iron in him softened. He gave a small nod that said what needed saying: babies are babies, no matter who they born to.

Near the front, Mabel had come early and taken her place beside Eliza. She'd found her before the gathering, voice low, asking her help with the Master's boys. Now, Eliza stood with Henry in her arms, a pale, flax-haired babe of only a year, blue eyes wide to the morning, while John Junior, fair as his mother and no more than five, clutched her skirt and peered out from behind. Flora pressed up against Mabel's hip, curls sleep-tangled, watching Esther without blinking. The boys did not cling like strangers; they settled into these women the way a sapling leans against a fence that once kept it upright. For all of Mary's fine nursery talk, it had been enslaved hands that fed and washed and hushed them, and the small boys went quiet now, certain they were in the only softness they knew.

A ripple went through the crowd as folks recognized the children, Barrow's blood made small. A whisper passed from mouth to mouth, questions hitching on the cold.

"Why they here? Who brought them?" Until Auntie Bet's fingers fluttered for quiet and the murmurs softened into breath.

"She burned the Master's house and all its wickedness," Clem said. "She buried the whip in the ash. She broke the chains, so the innocent won't have to drag them no more."

Clara sobbed aloud, baby Ruth bundled in her arms; Thomas gripped her skirt and stared with a grave solemnity beyond his years. Isaac drew Martha in, his hand firm at her waist, holding her steady against the tremor of disbelief. Green stood at the back like a post set true, eyes on the road beyond the yard, tears slipping clean down his cheeks even as he kept watch. Eliza bent her head to kiss Henry's crown; John Junior pressed closer to her leg; thumb tucked in his mouth.

Esther stood silent beside Clem, her silhouette etched in light. The sun caught in the wild coils of her hair, dusted now with snow. Her skin gleamed pale as limestone; her eyes were fathomless and still. She looked made of earth and sky, terrible and holy.

And yet they did not fear her.

They looked on her the way one looks on the stars, not with dread, but awe.

She was a testament to the suffering they had endured, a reflection of their own pain and their own unbreakable will. The monsters who had enslaved them had broken their bodies; they had not broken their souls. Those souls had been forged into something stronger.

A hush fell, deeper than any silence that had come before.

In that hush, understanding bloomed.

They would rise from these chains.

They would carry the memory of every sorrow and every act of defiance.

They would move forward, one step at a time.

Clem's gaze swept over them, steady and full of quiet strength. At the far edge of the crowd, three strangers kept to the fence line. Samuel stood with his hands shoved deep in his pockets. Cora's hands were folded in prayer, pressed tight beneath her chin. Leander held the fence post like a man holding fast to a cliff, eyes on Esther, unblinking. Their clothes were wrong for them, mismatched and sagging, hems dragging, sleeves too short or too long, pinched from the clothesline, still holding the stiff crease of sun-dried cotton and the faint scent of lye and woodsmoke. All three were hesitant to join the crowd. They hovered in the frost like shadows, undecided, faces turned toward the oak but feet rooted to the furrows. Clem marked them with a quick nod, an unspoken welcome; when they did not move, he let them be and found his thread again.

"You're free now," Clem said. "As free as the birds that fly in the air. Free to leave, free to stay. Free to live and dream and speak as you please."

There were gasps. Soft sobs. Hands clasped tight. Preacher Jonas went to his knees as if the earth had reached up and taken him by the shoulders. Mercy lifted both palms to the sky; her little boy, Franklin, breathed "Mama," and clung to her dress, curiosity shining bright as a spark in his eyes. Eliza tipped her face into the wind and let it wash her tears away, Henry warm and heavy against her breast; at her knee John Junior loosened his grip on her skirt just enough to clap once, startled by his own boldness.

From somewhere in the crowd, a single voice rose, Old Amos. Cracked and wavering, raw from age and sorrow, yet still strong enough to carry over the frost-bitten morning.

"Wade in the water..."

"Wade in the water, children..."

The sound quivered on the crisp morning air. Auntie Bet found the alto line beneath him, steady as a hand at a back.

Other voices joined, uncertain at first, then swelling into a consonant harmony.

Mabel's voice trembled, but she sang; with one arm she drew Flora closer, palm spread over the child's curls. Martha and Isaac laced fingers, knuckles chafed and sure. Mose closed his eyes and beat the time against his thigh, keeping his parents upright with the other hand. Even Green sang, hoarse, raw, eyes on the tree line as if to keep watch and worship both. Samuel's thin thread of melody came rough at first, a man remembering how to sing; beside him, Cora's quiet hum strengthened, one breath after another, until it held. Leander stood, jaw tight, mouth shaping the words without sound, as if the song had to fight its way through.

Children clapped off-beat, too full of joy to care. Old women who hadn't stood straight in years rose to their feet. Men who had carried their burdens for so long bent their heads and let the tears come. They sang as if pouring centuries of sorrow into the sky to make room for joy.

Clem threw back his head and let out a loud whoop, full of joy and grief.

Esther stood in the center of it all, her shadow long across the snow-whitened earth. Eustace pressed close at her side, his small hand tucked tightly into hers, eyes wide and gleaming and fixed on her, as if by looking he could stitch this moment to his heart and never lose it again.

"I knew you'd come back," he said quietly, voice trembling. "I knew you wouldn't leave me behind." He swallowed. "I remember your singin' over the wash pot," he said, almost to himself. "When I heard the wind in the trees, it sounded jus' like that. I think that's how God told me you was comin' back."

She looked down at him, this child who had once clung to her like a lifeline, and something softened within her chest, a deep ache blooming into warmth. Atchen's hunger quieted, settled. A calm moved through her like the land sighing after a spring rain.

The ancient one did not speak. Did not stir.

But Esther felt her satisfaction. This, too, had been the purpose, not only vengeance, not only ruin, but deliverance.

She squeezed Eustace's hand, and though her mouth did not move, the message passed between them like blood through a vein. *You are safe now.*

In his small, tear-stained face she saw something more powerful than all the fury she had conjured.

Love.

Not fear. Not wonder. But love, undimmed by all she had become.

The song rose around them, jubilant and unashamed, lifting to meet the pale dawn. "God's gon' a trouble the water…"

The sun climbed higher, gilding every upturned face. Snowflakes caught the light and sparked like stars, melting warm on skin that had known cold for far too long.

She had given them this, a morning of joy, not sorrow.

In that moment they were not slaves.

Not ghosts or whispers or nameless scars.

They were free.

Thirty-Eight

Beneath the Soil

*"Child, the ground you stand on is made of more than dirt.
It's made of the people who could not leave it."*

Throughout that afternoon, the joyous celebration continued. Their prayers for freedom had finally been answered, and for the first time, their voices rose unafraid into the open sky.

They sang spirituals that had carried them through countless nights of sorrow. They embraced one another, laughing and weeping in the same breath. Children ran through trampled fields, red-toed and laughing, as if they'd discovered flight.

But amid the rejoicing, there was grief as well, old wounds that no freedom could erase.

Some drifted away from the gathering to visit, perhaps for the last time, the burial sites of those they had lost.

Mothers knelt on the frozen earth, their hands resting on rough wooden markers carved with names no ledger had ever recorded. They whispered tearful farewells, words too sorrowful for any ear but God's.

They left offerings, small tokens pressed into the soil, a scrap of cloth, a braid of hair, a stone worn smooth from years in a pocket.

[184]

At the far edge of the cemetery, where the shadows kept their hold, Preacher Jonas stood alone before a modest grave. He said nothing, only took off his hat and bowed his head. The snow clung to his shoulders and the folds of his coat, melting dark into the thin cloth. His breath rose in a cold mist, then faded.

 Before him was a simple marker of rough stone, the edges softened by time and weather. No letters carved, only a crude cross, scratched shallow into its surface. The world around him fell into hush; only the small crunch of snow under his boots, and a crow cawing from the pines.

His wife, Maggie, had died long ago, giving birth to a child they had both prayed for, a beautiful baby girl, taken by sickness not long after. Neither mother nor child was given a proper burial, and neither lived to see a day when humanity would have let them be free. Now, he stood in a world where chains had been broken. And yet, sorrow sat with him, heavy and real.

He knelt, placing a red cardinal feather at the base of the marker. Maggie had always loved their flash of color in the gray of winter. His lips moved in silence, prayer or promise, perhaps both.

Behind him, the hymns still rose, sacred and rich with life. But here, where the soil remembered every sorrow, the quiet was holy.

Not far from where Preacher Jonas knelt, Elias stood alone, his shoulders hunched against the cold. Before him lay the grave of his mother, a simple mound of earth marked by a flat stone.

He crouched down, brushing away the thin crust of snow until the stone's rough surface showed through.

"Mama," he said softly, the word catching in his throat, his breath hung white in the air. "I come to tell you… Levi's gone."

From his pocket, Elias pulled a short, smooth branch he had carved before the sun had risen. On it, he'd scratched his brother's name, as best he could. The letters were crooked and shallow, but they were his. He pressed the little marker into the earth beside their mother's stone. His fingers lingered in the cold soil, and for a moment he remembered the warm, loamy scent it carried in summer, when she would kneel in her garden, humming while she worked. That scent had always meant home.

Now it was hard and frozen beneath his hand.

"I figured you'd want him near you," he murmured. "So you can both rest easy."

He stayed crouched for a long while, the cold biting through his thin trousers, his lips moving in a silent eulogy.

At the far corner of the cemetery, Esther stood beside Clem, watching in silence. When her gaze found Elias, kneeling at his mother's grave, a sharp breath caught in her throat, the cold air burning as it filled her. Snow settled on her lashes, melting slow and cold, against her skin. The sight of Elias, kneeling there, his shoulders shaking, carved a deep ache into her chest.

She felt the weight of it, that Levi's name would never be called in freedom. And for the first time that morning, amid all the singing and new hope, the sorrow of what could not be returned pressed hard against her ribs.

Clem glanced at her but said nothing. The silence between them was its own kind of mourning.

Elias rose at last, his hand lingering on the new marker before he stepped away. When he turned toward the others, Esther lowered her bottomless gaze, as if to carry his grief with her, unspoken but felt all the same.

The wind stirred the snow, and the earth seemed to breathe beneath it.

Their freedom had come with a price.

And the land would remember every soul who'd paid it.

These people had been born into bondage. Every day of their lives measured by another man's profit. Every hope crushed beneath the heel of cruelty.

Now, they were free, and freedom was a stranger they did not yet know how to greet.

The old ones, Amos and Auntie Bet, stood apart from the bustle of those preparing to leave. Broadlawn had been their home since youth, its fields, cabins, and very soil written into their bones.

They remembered their wedding day, hand in hand, jumping the broom while kin and friends gathered close, laughter and song folding in around them like sunlight. The warm summer soil had smelled rich and sweet beneath their bare feet, the earth seeming to bless their union.

Within those same four walls they brought their son, Mose, into the world; caught his first cry, swaddled him against winter drafts, marked his height in faint scratches on the doorframe, and watched him lengthen like a young poplar. Here, they fought with their whole selves to keep their small family safe and whole, to make of three beating hearts something the ledger could not claim.

Now, the thought of leaving pressed heavy on their chests. Beyond the ridges and rivers they had always known lay only uncertainty. To step away from this place felt like stepping into a void.

They said little, only turned their heads away as others gathered their meager belongings.

But Mose would not leave them behind. He spoke gently, his large hands resting on their shoulders, telling them the world past Broadlawn was worth seeing, that the time for fear had ended.

It took a long while, and much convincing, but at last Amos and Auntie Bet agreed. Not because they trusted the road ahead, but because they trusted their son, and the woman who had burned the Master's house to the ground.

Hesitantly, they began to bundle what little they owned; a battered skillet, Mose's patched baby blanket, a worn Bible, its spine broken from so many hands passing it back and forth in secret.

Eustace had only one thing to carry.

He clutched his fiddle to his narrow chest as if it were a piece of his heart.

Esther watched him, remembering the nights she had held him close, humming the same songs he now played in the open air.

It was a bitter-sweet leaving.

This land had given them nothing but suffering, yet it was all they had ever known. Believing in freedom had always been an abstract prayer, something so far away it felt like a story you told to keep the cold out of your bones.

Now it was real, and many did not know how to trust it.

So, they moved carefully, as if one wrong step might wake them from this fragile dream. But the sun kept climbing in the sky, and no overseer came to call them back.

By the time the first stars began to glimmer in the blue-night, some of them had begun to believe without fear.

The wind moved through the tobacco fields, curling low over the graves, the cabins, the paths worn into the earth by generations of bare feet.

The soil remembered the hands that had sown and reaped, the blood it had taken, the tears it had drunk.

And now it felt the ache of three more souls. Sometime after dawn, Mercy found them shivering behind the drying barn, thin bodies hunched against the boards, bare feet blue with cold. She did not ask their names at first. She only lifted a hand and beckoned, and they followed her into the low warmth of her cabin, where the fire spoke soft and steady.

She shared what little she had, half a heel of cornbread, a ladle of water, a threadbare shawl unfolded from the trunk. "Eat," she said, and sent Franklin to fetch another pail.

The men, Samuel, careful-eyed and carrying old hurt in his shoulders, and Leander, younger, all tendon and wire, murmured their thanks without looking up.

Cora said nothing at all. Silence held her like a bridle; her throat worked but no sound came. They were all scarred and hollowed by hunger, but Leander's wounds ran deeper than flesh.

Mercy saw it in his stare; it frightened her like a set trap waiting to spring. She asked few questions. The answers were written on their bodies, rope-burn dark on wrists, welts like withered vines across backs, a tremor in the hands not born of cold alone. Mercy laid a quilt at their feet and pressed a scrap of fatback into the skillet, because a little grease can sometimes quiet a shaking soul.

By dusk, Samuel had found a quiet corner near the door, Cora a place by the hearth, and Leander the darkest wall, watchful eyes on the ember's edge, turning a small loop of twine between his fingers while the others dozed. Some griefs heal into scars. Leander's had not. It festered, sharp and patient, the way coal waits under ash.

Outside, wind moved through the rows. The soil, keeper of grief, drinker of tears, took note of these three as it had taken note of all the others.

And now, at last, it would remember their leaving.

Thirty-Nine

Quiet Exodus

"Let the earth keep what it must; let the living go free."

In the first light of morning, Esther walked to the stables. Frost silvered the trampled yard, each blade of grass stiff and white, crunching faintly beneath her feet. Smoke still drifted from the blackened bones of the Barrow house, curling upward in thin, weary threads that frayed into the pale sky. The burnt ruins smelled faintly of ash and scorched pine, carried on the wind like the last ghosts of what had been.

Nearing the threshold, the air hung heavy with warm hay and the faint, sweet musk of the horses themselves. Beneath it lingered an acrid bite of smoke, a reminder that something in this place had been ended, and something else had begun.

The horses stirred as she stepped inside. Warm breath steamed from their nostrils, curling into the cold air. Hooves shifted softly against the straw. A tail swished. An ear flicked toward her. The air here was warmer, heavier, the quiet broken only by their slow, steady breathing. They did not shy away.

She moved down the row, brushing her hand over the worn wood of each stall, pausing at every door. One by one, she lifted the latches. Iron hinges groaned in the quiet. She swung each door wide. For a moment, none of them moved. They stood at the threshold, nostrils flaring, dark eyes catching the faint light, just as her people had stood on that first morning, at the lip of a road none of them had ever traveled, weighing the hard safety of the known against the wide, cold question of freedom. The stall had its cruelties, but it was familiar; the pasture was a kind of silence they had never met. The hardest step is the first; one foot in the old pain, the other reaching into what might yet be mercy.

Then the first, a young colt, with a ragged forelock, stepped forward, it's head low, tasting the air. The others followed, spilling slowly into the dawn.

They blinked against the brightness, ears swiveling, manes stirring in the wind. A chestnut tossed his head sharply, a breath bursting from him in a white cloud that hung like smoke before vanishing. The old gray mare limped as she walked, her stride uneven but unhurried, as though she knew there would be no yoke waiting for her in the next field.

Their shadows stretched long over the frost-crusted yard, trailing them toward the open pasture rimmed in low mist. When they crossed the fence line, hooves darkened the pale grass, leaving a map of their passing in the white. Then, as if something in the wind called to them, they broke into a run. Manes streamed, tails lifted, and for a heartbeat they seemed weightless.

Esther stood still, watching them vanish into the silver distance. The ache in her chest was sharp and unexpected, a wound of letting go. They were free now. And like her people, they had left their chains behind; they would never return.

Esther knew the price of freedom.

They deserved it as much as any soul that had toiled under another's hand.

She turned back into the quiet of the stable, her steps carrying her toward the far corner where the light dimmed and the air grew heavier. Here, the smell shifted, the odor of musk, urine-damp straw, and the sharp tang of blood lingered.

The cages stood in shadow, iron bars black with rust in places, slick with excrement in others. Inside, the hounds stirred at the sound of her approach. Yellow eyes found her in the dim light. Their bodies were taut, every muscle coiled, as if expecting the chase. Low growls rolled from deep in their throats, vibrating through the stillness.

They knew her.

They had been fed on the scent of blood, their hunger shar-pened by the screams of the hunted. They had run her people down in the dark, teeth tearing flesh from bone, mouths slobbering with the thrill of the catch.

A memory surfaced unbidden, moonlight flashing off wet leaves, Eustace's hand slipping from hers, the pounding of her own heart as the baying drew closer. She had seen him stumbling into the brush, swallowed by shadows, while the hounds surged past her. Their voices had split the night, the sound so sharp it had haun-ted her bones for miles.

Her jaw clenched. Her hands curled into fists, nails pressing hard into her palms. The growls in front of her seemed to carry the echoes of that night, and for a moment it was as though the cold air was thick with the past.

Esther stepped closer, her shadow spilling across the straw. The growls deepened. Paws scraped the bars. Breath steamed from their nostrils, carrying the heat of their bodies into the cold air.

She did not speak. It was done quickly.

When she walked back into the morning, the frost seemed brighter, the air sharper. Behind her, the kennel was silent at last. And in that silence, she thought of Eustace, safe now, beyond the reach of teeth and chains.

Out in the distance, the wind lifted across the fields, carrying the scent of clean snow and turned earth.

The freed horses were only specks on the horizon now, running like living shadows against the pale light. She let her gaze follow them until they disappeared, and for a moment, the emptiness they left behind ached like a wound. But it was a wound born of freedom; one she was willing to carry.

She turned toward the yard and found Clem already at work.

He stood with an axe at the base of the Elder Tree, the old gallows of the yard, its black limbs clawing at a colorless sky. Wood chips lay sharp as bone around his boots. He had been at it all night, his shoulders were slick with sweat despite the cold, his breath a steady engine in the dawn. A great wedge bit deep where the trunk flared from the ground; pale heartwood showed like exposed tendon.

Esther halted a few paces off. No words passed between them. Clem set his jaw and swung. The axe struck a clean bite; the tree answered with a long, tired creak. Another swing. Another. Fibers tore like sinew. The wind fell still.

"Come on," Clem growled low, not to the wood, but to the hanging seasons this tree had kept, to the names caught in its rings.

The Elder shuddered. For a heartbeat it seemed to hesitate, as if deciding whether to stay and haunt or finally let go. Then the last holding fibers parted with a rough, ripping sigh, and the trunk began to go, slow at first, gathering weight, gathering memory.

It fell with a rolling thunder that shook the yard, a sound like souls fleeing, like ropes slackening, like breath released at last. A storm of frozen twigs rattled the ground; a dry burst of old leaves lifted and settled. The stump steamed in the cold. Clem lowered the axe and bowed his head.

A few folks who had gathered in the distance paused and raised their faces to the heavens.

From the far edge of the yard, Mercy, who had stood watching him all morning with her arms wrapped hard around herself, dropped to her knees. The sob that broke from her was raw and grateful and terrible at once. Last winter her husband, Cecil, had been whipped and strung from that Elder; he hung for five days until the cold finished what the lash began. Barrow left him five more, frost glazing his face, before the men were ordered to cut him down and hide him in the poor ground. Now the gallows were only wood again. Mercy pressed her forehead to the frost and wept for him, and for the part of herself that could finally breathe.

The tree lay in the frost like a felled shadow. Its black branches no longer reached for anything.

The land, scrubbed of its hunters and freed of its gallows, seemed to breathe easier for it.

When Esther began to move, the people moved with her. She did not call out. No words were needed. There was just a loosening, a lean in the same direction, as if a current had taken hold beneath their feet. They stepped out of the yard and into the rutted lane, bodies wrapped in shawls too thin for the cold, coats borrowed and buttonless, quilts thrown over shoulders like small, stubborn banners. Frost crackled under bare toes and split shoes. A tin cup clattered against a skillet in someone's bundle. Breath lifted in pale ribbons and faded into the sky.

Eliza walked near the front, Henry fussing against her collarbone, his small face flushed from the cold air. She hushed him with her cheek and a warm palm at the back of his head, rocking her stride to keep him quieted. Eustace was where he had always been, inside the reach of Esther's shadow, his fiddle strapped tight across his chest, eyes fixed on her back as if the lay of her shoulders were a map. A few paces behind, John Junior matched Eustace's steps, a wary little echo. Now and then he strayed to test the world, two, three steps off the path, then glanced over a shoulder and slipped back into the line, satisfied that the space would not swallow him.

Children began to forget themselves in inches. Thomas darted to kick a tuft of frozen grass and returned; Franklin edged beside Flora instead of clutching Mercy's skirt. Their mamas let them have that distance and did not call them back. The air between them held.

Old Amos and Auntie Bet kept a steady, small pace, the way a clock keeps time, Amos with a worn quilt bound tight across his chest, Auntie Bet with her eyes locked on the road ahead. Mose walked with them, a good son, one hand light at his father's elbow, the other ready if his mother's step faltered. Since his wife, Annie, was sold away the previous spring, he tended to worry too much; they were what he had left, and he guarded them like glass guards a flame.

They shouldered what could be carried, an iron pot swinging from a rope, a Bible wrapped in cloth, a single broom laid across a bundle like a promise that there would be a floor to sweep some-where else. Mercy kept Cora between herself and Samuel, folding them into the line with easy talk of supper and the road ahead, but her eyes never stopped counting Franklin's steps, smoothing his cowlick with her thumb as he trotted, always keeping him close enough to touch.

Leander drifted the far margin, a watchful figure at the line's edge. He kept his own counsel, silence honed thin as a blade; he'd made no friends and wanted none either. He traveled with them but not among them, pulled forward less by hope than by the emp-tiness behind him, as if the road itself had him by the collar and nowhere else would take him in.

They passed the split-rail fence and the last familiar tree, and still no one looked back. The ruined house smoked behind them like a bad dream fading in daylight. Ahead, the world lifted in dark folds, ridges blue with distance, the quiet hollows of the mountains waiting like a mouth not yet opened. They did not know where she would lead them, yet their heads were held high, their faces turned toward the rising sun. They knew she was their deliverance.

Esther led them, her hair loose around her shoulders, her black eyes catching the light. Freedom burned there, dark and steady, as she began the long march south and east toward the deep shadow of the Cumberland Mountains. She had never seen those ridges, had never set foot on their slopes, but Atchen guided her steps as surely as breath filled her lungs. The hush that followed was so complete it felt as if the earth was listening as they stitched a new path across the frost.

The journey ahead would not be easy. Hunger would walk with them. Cold would ask its price. But her people did not break. Drawn by something larger than fear, like iron to a lodestone, toward the possibility of a life not measured by another man's hand.

And so, they went together, against all odds, into the unknown that had finally, mercifully, opened itself to them.

Forty

Promises Kept

"The earth keeps what love entrusts to it."

By the end of the first week, folks began to grow weary. Their feet blistered and their limbs ached with every mile. The old ones spoke to their knees and backs as if to wayward kin, "Settle, we almost there, almost."

At night, the little ones cried in shivers and starts, and their mothers soothed them with warm hands and low songs, promises whispered in the dark, "There's a place coming, child. Green fields belonging only to us. A home where we will all be safe and warm."

Hunger settled deep in their bellies like a small, wakeful animal. What little they ate; they coaxed from the woods. But the land provided.

Eliza took the little ones into the trees at dawn, Henry bound to her chest with a strip of shawl, his tiny fists kneading at the cloth when the cold bit. John Junior's hand fit inside hers; Thomas trotted close by; even Franklin toddled behind on small feet. Clem walked a pace off, pointing with two fingers, naming what would keep them and what would hurt them. "Not that, see the milky sap? Burns your belly." He knelt to show them lamb's quarters hiding under last year's leaf-litter, wood sorrel green as a katydid and the tight fists of wild onion pushing up through frost. The children leaned in, noses chilled, breath fogging the air, and came back grinning with armfuls of bitter greens and onion tops that smelled like spring under the cold.

Elias wandered ahead with a length of wire and quiet steps learned from hard years. Samuel asked to go with him and kept his weight soft on the ground, learning where to set snares and how to breathe through stillness. By full light they'd return, when lucky, with a rabbit, sometimes two, ears still warm, apology in their eyes even as they handed them over.

Martha and Auntie Bet, who had fed whole households from scraps in Barrow's kitchen, made a miracle of it; greens and onion, a knob of fat saved for luck, a shake of salt from a pocket twist, the rabbits jointed clean. Cora, wordless and shy at first, slipped into the work as if her hands remembered, rinsing the greens, minding the fire, tipping a gourd just so, to let broth breathe without boiling away. She tied Flora's curls back with a strip of cloth, tucked the quilt tighter around John Junior, and when Ruth's cry climbed thin and high, she took her from Clara and rocked her with a slow, certain rhythm until her breath grew round again. She never spoke, but the mothering instincts lived in her; the steadying palm, the small, selfless kindness.

They set the pot low and let it whisper on the coals while the forest breathed around them, steam lifting into the pines, broth smelling of onion and iron and hope.

Before any hand lifted a cup, Preacher Jonas rose and took off his hat. The circle gathered itself close. His voice went soft and reverent, the way water talks over stone. "Lord, we thank You for this little plenty, for fire to warm it and hands to share it. Bless the path behind us and the one we've yet to walk. Remember the ones who could not follow; those taken, those fallen, those still bound and let their souls be safe with You. Keep our feet from snares, our hearts from hardening, our faces set toward the country You promised."

He paused, the silence deep and clean. "Make us worthy of the freedom we are learning."

A low "Amen" moved around the circle like a tide.

They ate from tin cups and dried gourds, palms wrapped to hold the heat, their heads bent over the steam. No one wasted a word. Between sips, voices threaded soft through the dark; Mose dreaming of land he could turn with his own hands; Mabel hoping Flora might learn her letters where no whip could reach; Old Amos murmuring that he'd like to sleep a whole night and not wake up to picking. Eliza tipped a gourd to Henry's lips, let him mouth the rim and taste the steam; he settled, warm against her chest.

They did not boast, and they did not plan out loud. They just shared their small dreams and let them rise with the steam, as if the trees might keep them safe until evening. And when the pot scraped empty, they tucked the children into beds of pine needles and settled their backs to the roots, bellies warmed, quiet and grateful, the taste of onion and wild greens still rich on their tongues.

Leander did not join the circle. He kept to the shadows, a figure half-turned away, eyes moving, mouth working in a murmur only he could hear. At times his jaw locked, then loosened, as if arguing with something no one else could see. His thumb worried the rope-burn at his wrist, testing a shackle that was no longer there. What had been done to him hadn't ended; it paced inside him, patient as a wolf. His grief had festered, and the old hunger in it prowled the corners of his mind, scratching to be let out.

Esther moved ahead of them, her strange, pale form gliding through the trees. She vanished into shadow and returned hours later, her black eyes dark with knowing. No one asked how she chose the path she took. They only knew the woods felt different after she passed, quieter, as if a held breath had finally been let go. Sometimes, far off, a lantern winked out and did not rise again. A hound's bay cut short. By dusk, a musket might lie abandoned in the frost, a patrol fire left to die on its own ash. Esther left no trace but the stillness that followed. Atchen fed her hunger and settled inside her like coals banked deep; warm, watchful, satisfied for a while.

They mostly traveled by night, slipping through hollows and thickets by starlight, easing over old wagon ruts and the frozen furrows of abandoned fields. At dawn, they hid where the world was thickest, a tumbledown barn heavy with hay, the deep breath of a limestone cave, a stand of pines so dense no torchlight could pierce it. And when they moved again, the way was open.

Now and again, the land told a different story: a ragged meadow stamped flat, cartridge paper curled like shed skins, blue and gray cloth gone the color of earth. Buttons winked cold in the moonlight. Men lay where they had fallen, faces turned to frost and sky, boys mostly, their mouths still open, as if calling for their mamas. The freed passed soft-footed, and no one spoke. Freedom had a price for all kinds of men; here it was tallied in bone and tin and winter breath. "Lord, remember," Jonas murmured, and the wind carried it. They walked on, careful not to disturb the fallen.

Sometimes, as the company moved, figures emerged from the trees behind them, faces hollow-eyed and soot-streaked, clutching bundles of rags. The newly freed. A woman with an infant bound to her breast. An old man who could barely walk but would not be left behind. A boy with a brand still raw on his shoulder. They joined without a word, drawn by the same promise. And so, the company grew, one weary soul at a time. When the wind hissed through the canebrakes and the sky bruised toward evening, the freed lifted their eyes to the tall figure at the front. Whatever she was, woman or spirit or something between, they trusted her. Because in her dark, silent presence, they had seen what was possible. And they believed she would see them home.

They stopped on a low ridge where the pines shouldered the wind. Frost crunched underfoot. Clem tested the air with his palm and nodded toward a curve of trunk. "Leeward's here. We'll bed in close."

Elias was already moving, quiet as a fox, thin as a sapling, and so like Levi in the tilt of his head when listening, the nick in his left brow, the long-lashed steadiness, that it caught at Clem's throat. "Lay 'em crosswise," Clem said.

"Yes, sir," Elias answered, weaving boughs in a clean herringbone that would lift bodies off the cold.

Eustace fetched armfuls of needles, shaking them loose like rain; Clem ruffled his hair and said, "Good boy, now mind your fingers." Elias watched him with that careful little brother-look he hadn't unlearned since Levi and set another bough in place. Clem shifted, making room at his side like he'd always had the boys there; Eustace pressed the needles into Elias's hands and grinned. The three of them worked at an easy rhythm, a small family taking shape without anybody needing to say the word.

Clara wrapped Thomas and Ruth together beneath a patched quilt. "Hush now," she murmured, tucking the corners, "the wind can't find you here." Thomas peeked out, solemn, and Ruth made a small, satisfied sound and burrowed deeper.

Old Amos rubbed his knees and gave them a rueful look. "These old bones forgot their manners."

Mose was there at once, a steadying hand under his father's elbow. "Sit, Papa. I got you."

Auntie Bet eased down beside him with a soft groan and caught Mose's sleeve, drawing him close. Her whisper was low as pine pitch. "That boy, Leander, I don't trust him. There's a turn in his eye I don't like."

Mose angled his shoulder against the wind and glanced at the tree line where Leander paced. "I seen it," he said. "Don't fret, Mama. I'll keep him in sight."

"Mm." She patted his wrist; be careful, be sure. Old Amos, not catching the words, only sighed and leaned back into the trunk, the hurt in his knees easing.

"Bet, sing us that ol' hymn," Amos whispered, and she did, the tune from home laying a thin warmth over the frost.

On his way back from settling his parents, Mose paused where Clara wrestled the quilt's edge against a sly draft. He knelt without a word and tucked the hem beneath Thomas's heels so the wind couldn't lift it. "There," he said, quiet. He fished a small stone from his pocket, warmed earlier at the coals, and slipped it, wrapped in cloth, near Ruth's feet. "Keeps the chill off."

Clara's shoulders loosened. "Thank you, Mose," she said, meeting his eyes for a heartbeat longer than courtesy required.

"Ain't nothing," he answered, but he checked the tuck once more, making sure the little ones were snug. Thomas watched him with grave approval; Ruth found his finger and squeezed before sleep took her hand again.

Mose stood and stepped back toward his parents, then hesitated and set a fallen branch across the windward side of the bedding, a small windbreak. "If it lifts, call me," he said.

"We will," Clara replied. Her voice carried warmth. Behind them Auntie Bet's low song found its third line, and Mose, already turning, joined in under his breath, the notes threading the space between them like something had begun.

Preacher Jonas set his hat beside the trunk and bowed his head. "Bless this small windbreak and the ones it keeps," he said to the dusk, words falling gentle as needles.

"Here," Clem said, sliding a thicker layer where the old ones would lie. He beat the boughs flat with his forearm; the resin lifted sharp and clean, like medicine. "That'll hold the cold down."

No one asked where Esther had gone. They could see her at a distance, tall and spare against the trees, kneeling at the base of a great pine with both palms to the ground as if feeling for a pulse. Then she began to dig.

Her bare hands worked through the crusted soil, past the web of roots and stone. The tree's breath rose sweet as pitch in the cold air. She dug until the earth gave up what it had kept for her, then stood and slipped back down the slope with an otherworldly stillness, something small and yellow cradled in her arms.

She stopped before Eustace.

The bundle was a scarf, faded marigold, frayed at the corners, the one their mama used to tie around her hair on Sundays. Esther placed it in his hands without a word.

He sat back on his heels and unwrapped it slowly, as if the cloth might tear under his fingers. Inside lay a shell ring, smoothed by years of touch, the one daddy had given their mama before he was sold south. Beside it rested a small Bible, the leather cracked, his own initials scratched crooked in the flyleaf. He had pressed it on Esther the night they ran, breathless and shaking in the dark. Keep it, he'd said. For safety. For God. For me.

The memories rose like a tide. Eustace held the scarf to his face and breathed in the faint ghost of his mama, soap, smoke, summer. His shoulders shook. Then he slipped the ring onto a strip of cloth and tied it at his throat, the shell resting cold against his heart. The Bible he held flat in his palm, thumb running along the broken spine, before tucking it safe inside his shirt.

Eliza's hand flew to her mouth. "Lord," she breathed, eyes shining, her love for Esther rising so fierce it near took her breath. She remembered the night behind the smokehouse, the hurried vow whispered into her ear, "I will come back for you." Against all odds, across fire and winter and miles of fear, Esther had kept that promise. Now, with Henry sleeping heavy against her chest, his cheek glossy with broth, life had found its way back to her; warm and weighty as a sleeping child.

Auntie Bet nodded, slow and certain, as if to say, this is how we carry our dead.

Esther's fingers brushed the back of Eustace's head, the same small circle she'd made when he was little and fevered. Her voice, when it came, was low as wind through needles. "For you."

He looked up at her then, the firelight catching the tears in his lashes. "Thank you. I knew God would give you back." he said, shy and earnest, as if the words had been pulled from the deepest part of him. "Is it true what you said, 'bout the Promised Land, it's a place where little boys can run in grass and climb trees and nobody come callin' with a whip?"

"It's true," she said.

He nodded hard, touching the ring at his throat. "Then I'll keep this safe till we get there."

Something eased inside her. Whatever darkness she carried went still. Her love for this boy kept her in the world of breath and touch; he was her warmth and her daylight, the small, steadfast sun by which she still knew her way. He was her purpose.

At the rim of the firelight, Leander's murmuring continued, low and agitated, as though he were speaking to someone who stood just beyond the trees. Esther's knowing gaze slid to him and held. Atchen lifted her head inside that silence, listening, hungry.

Around them the pines kept their slow counsel, resin and cold thick in the air. The people settled onto beds of needles and thin blankets, the ridge holding them like a cupped hand. In the hush, the marigold scarf lay warm against Eustace's chest, a small sun he could carry into the night.

Forty-One

The Vanishing

"Night keeps what it can. The rest it returns with thunder."

Dusk pressed down like a shroud. The ridge took the last light and kept it. Beneath the pines the camp began to stir, blankets shaken free of frost, small fires coaxed from dying coals, children roused with soft hands and low words.

Eliza woke with a start.

Henry was warm against her chest, his breath damp on her collarbone. The quilt at her hip lay flat where a small body should have been.

"Junior?" she whispered.

No answer. She pushed up to her knees, one hand already sweeping the ground, searching for the heat a sleeping child leaves behind. She found only cold. She looked left, right, under the bent bough where Clara had tucked the others, past the stacked gourds and the tied bundles. No flaxen hair. No blue eyes.

"John Junior?" Eliza's voice lifted, shaking with fear.

Faces turned. The children went still, as if the sound itself had told them to hush. In the space where Esther usually stood at the edge of the trees, there was only dark. She had gone out after the camp had quieted, to clear the path and had not returned yet.

"Leander?" Mercy called, softer, to the tree line.

No answer.

Mercy's eyes found Cora's in the twilight. "Did you see him go?" she breathed.

Cora shook her head, puzzled and grave, her mouth parting in a small, helpless no.

A dozen thoughts fell at once, hard and breathless. Maybe Junior wandered back down the slope to look for twigs. Maybe he was playing soldiers in the scrub. Maybe a catamount had scented camp. Maybe, God forbid, he had turned his face toward the plantation and started walking.

Fear held the camp in a tightening grip.

Clem moved before the panic found its feet. "Fires out," he said, low and steady. "No flame in the open. Martha, Mabel, make shelter. Use the quilts and that fallen limb. Keep the children close and dry. Mercy, you stay with Eliza and Clara." He nodded toward the men. "With me. Elias, Samuel. Mose, Green. We sweep north and east. Slow. Eyes up."

He turned once more. "Jonas, Isaac, see to the old ones. Bank the coals, one small flame near the children. If we call, answer once and hush."

The wind came hard out of the hollows, cold and damp, smelling of iron and rain. Somewhere beyond the ridge a loon called, long and solitary, a sound like grief you can't lay down. The first growl of thunder rolled the pine tops. Lightning cracked a thin white seam far off, then dark settled again.

The women worked by feel and memory. Quilts slung over a sturdy branch. A wall of boughs leaned into the wind. Eliza tucked Henry deep into the crook of her arm, his small cry rising with every gust. "Hush now," she breathed into his hair. "Hush."

Mabel pressed John Junior's cap, left behind, into Eliza's shaking hand. "We'll find him," she said, though her voice trembled.

Flora held the edge of the quilt with both fists; her eyes set like a grown woman's.

Clem and the others slipped into the trees.

The woods closed around them, trunks crowding close, briars knitting low, the dark made tight and thick by the coming rain. Lightning flashed nearer, blue and stark, and showed them for a blink; boots lifting, breath ghosting, the quick turn of a head at any sound. They moved in a line, no man more than an arm's length from the next, the storm laying its hand over their mouths.

"John!" Clem called, quiet-sharp. "John Junior!"

Only the wind, rattling needles and rustling dry leaves.

They pushed through laurel, wet leaves slapping their cheeks, and crossed a trickle of water gone black in the lightless understory. The thunder settled into a steady grumble, the sky taking its time.

"Hold." Elias lifted a hand.

They stood and let the forest talk. For a moment there was only the slow complaint of branches. Then, under the thunder's belly, a sound threaded through, thin and frail, a broken breath that hitched and fell and hitched again.

Sobbing.

"This way," Elias whispered, already moving.

They found him where the roots of a great oak clenched the hill like a fist. John Junior crouched in the tree's cradle, knees to his chest, hair pasted wet to his forehead. He had tried to be brave and failed, the way small boys do. He sobbed into his hands, not loud but all the way from the bottom of him. "Mama."

Eliza's name rose in Clem's throat and stayed there. He knelt instead. "Boy," he said gently. "You're all right." He reached, slow as winter coming. John flinched at the touch, then folded into the hollow between Clem's arms, shivering with relief as much as cold.

Lightning tore the sky wide.

Samuel turned at the flash and froze.

Ten paces off, half-hidden by a tangle of rhododendrons, a man sat slumped against a trunk, legs splayed, chin dropped to his chest. Rain had begun, fat drops knocking through needles, ticking on leaves. In the flash of the next bolt Samuel saw the face clearly.

Leander.

The bark at his back was lighter where no rain had fallen. His hands lay open on his thighs. His eyes were closed; lashes slick with rain. He had the look of a man emptied of heat, of fight, of the last thin wire that kept him bound to this world.

Samuel took a step, then another, and stopped. He did not call out. He did not lay hands on the body. He knew.

The storm came nearer. Thunder walked through the trees.

And with it came Leander's last hours, jagged and sharp as lightning behind the eyes: The auction yard in Lexington, mud up to the ankles, men and women raised on planks like meat on a shelf. A pale lady in silk under a pink parasol, eyes flat as coins, pointing with the tip of her glove. *Those three.*

A wagon. Rope through iron rings. The road long enough to forget your name and be given a new one.

Attic heat under a roof that never cooled. A sack pulled over the head. The clink of metal and the smell of charred flesh. Days with no measure but pain and thirst. The world made of breathing burlap and the scrape of footsteps you learned like a discipline.

Night that did not end. The mind making doors where none existed, then finding them bricked up. Words breaking apart until even prayer was just breath.

Freedom like a trick of light. The ropes cut. The sack gone. A woman with black eyes bending and saying; *Go.* Nightmares that never stopped replaying. The body still shaking as if the tormenter's hands remained.

Today, near dusk, the camp asleep, the black-eyed woman gone to clear the way. The small pale of a child's scalp in half-light. The brain, traitor quick, making one face be another. *Mistress Mary. Mary. Mary.* The old heat rising like bile. Hands moving before the man inside them could speak. A palm pressed to a small mouth to stifle the cry. Feet finding the dark path.

The land leaning in, hungry for any violence, offering itself as witness the way it always had.

A wriggle. A heel kicked sharp to the shin. A gasp that was not an evil woman's curse but a small boy's sob. The world snapping back into place, the hand snatching away, horror flooding in to fill all the space fury had left. The body set down. The boy stumbling into root-shadows, not yet screaming, no longer sleeping.

Silence under the trees.

A sharpened branch to the throat, the only door left.

Samuel closed his eyes and let the rain run over his face.

"Clem," he called softly.

Clem looked once and looked away, the boy tight to his chest. "We take the child back," he said. "We don't bring the storm with us."

They moved like one body, the forest flashing and darkening around them. Elias led, light on his feet; Green covered the rear, face set hard as a plank. Samuel stayed, not far, just enough space to keep the others from the worst of it. He knelt in the rain and set his palms to the earth.

"I'm sorry, brother," he said, not to excuse, not to judge. Only to acknowledge what Leander's life had been turned into.

He worked with what he had, hands, a flat stone, the blade he carried for skinning rabbits. The soil gave, stoney at first, then easier where the roots let it go. Rain beat a slow rhythm on his shoulders. When the shallow place was ready, he lifted Leander gentle as he could and laid him on the cold bed, straightened a leg that had fallen crooked and set his hands together. He pulled his own shawl from his back and spread it over Leander's stillness.

"Rest," he said. "May the land be kinder than men were."

He covered the grave until it was only a wet mound under the leaves. He found a fieldstone and set it; *We saw you. You were here.*

The thunder rolled away into the distance.

The loon called from somewhere in the dark.

Back at the shelter, the children crowded under the quilts, steam puffing from their mouths when they spoke. Eliza took John Junior from Clem and crushed him to her, swaying without moving her feet, the way a woman rocks a child even when he is too big to be rocked. "You scared me," she said into his hair, the words half sob, half relief. He clung to her, shaking with the last of it, and then, exhausted, he slept.

Cora sat with her back to the quilt, Henry tucked tight against her chest, one arm cradling his small body. His fingers found her hair and tangled there; she let them, eyes fixed on the tree line. Her mouth was set like a woman keeping a cry from frightening a child. Leander's absence pulsed in her; whatever else he was, he'd been someone who had walked the landscape of her nightmares.

She rocked once, twice, that old, silent sway, and bent her cheek to Henry's soft crown as if his warmth could pin her to the living. Mercy drew the quilt higher over them all, snugging the edge beneath Cora's elbow, as if cloth alone could turn aside the rain and the night's demons, while her other hand rested on Franklin's head, counting the small, steady breaths that meant they were still here.

Samuel came out of the dark, his head lowered, with only the storm on his shoulders and the smell of turned earth on his shirt. He met Clem's gaze and gave the smallest nod. Clem slowly bowed his head.

No one asked how. The how wore too many faces already.

They ate what was left of the broth, each without complaint. Preacher Jonas's voice rose a little over the rain, not sermon, not song, just a line from somewhere deep, "God be a fence."

Auntie Bet answered "*amen*," under her breath.

The wind shifted. The pines sighed like the end of a long cry. Along the ridge a single lantern flared and died, one of the patrol fires catching the storm and giving up.

Esther did not return before the moon rose high. But in the trees beyond the last circle of shelter, something in the land eased and lay quiet, as if a thirst had been slaked, as if a small, bitter debt had been paid. The living were gathered close. The dead were not alone.

When the thunder moved on and the rain thinned to a fine mist, the camp breathed again. It was a tired breath, and a hurting one. But it was theirs.

Forty-Two

Quiet Mercy

*"Be not forgetful to entertain strangers: for thereby some
have entertained angels unawares."*

-Hebrews 13:2

The darkness was alive with sound; the long winter-bare scrape of branches overhead, an owl's deep hoot, the soft crackle of frost settling into the ruts of old wagon tracks. Somewhere hidden in the trees, a lone fox screamed, sharp and shrill as tin. Around them their breath plumed white, then disappeared into the night.

The woods had been kind to Esther's people. For days they'd walked without hounds behind them, without the quick, sharp lantern-light that signaled the presence of men. Moonlight laid a thin blade across the path, bright enough to walk by, bright enough to make their shadows seem like separate souls.

At the edge of a broad cornfield, they halted. The stalks were long gone, scythed to stubble that rose from the frozen earth like a field of broken bones. Frost silvered each jagged stem; every step crunched faintly in the cold air.

Across the dark acres, a low barn slumped against the sky. Its roof sagged in the middle, patched in places with mismatched shingles, but the walls still held tight against the wind. Esther lifted her hand, and the line of travelers moved as one across the open ground, heads bowed, bundles clutched close.

Inside was warmer than hope. Heaps of dry cornstalks filled the corners, sweet with that sun-cured smell of late harvest. Dust hung in the beam of the moonlight cutting through a knothole, slow swirling like pollen on a spring breeze. Up in the loft, a barn owl watched with unbeaten patience, round head swiveling, then still again. Mice rustled beneath the straw and went the other way.

For the first time in days, it felt almost like peace.

Blankets unfurled with the soft sound of cloth over wood. Men and women slid down the walls until their spines met the boards; shoulders loosened; faces shed the hard shine of flight. The old ones tucked their hands into their sleeves. Auntie Bet warmed her fingers with a breath, before she gathered Flora beneath her shawl. She bent close and began, voice soft as worn leather, she told a tale older than the rows, of ancestors who could fly, who hid their wings when they were sold, and how, on a day when chains grew too heavy and the road too long, they unfurled those beautiful wings and rose, all together, into the open sky.

The barn quieted to listen. Thomas and Franklin lifted their fingers from playing in the dust and came near, eyes wide. Mose shook out two quilts and made a small island for the children to sit, then eased down behind them, hands folded, as Auntie Bet's words feathered through the rafters like soft-winged birds.

Eustace slid his fiddle from its cloth and set it in the cradle of his knees. Cross-legged near Esther, he drew the bow soft across the strings until a thread of sound lifted, low and wandering, the shape of a river remembered from a dream. Notes leaned into one another and swayed, old as a work-song, tender as a mother's hum. Esther felt it pass through the barn boards and into the ground, into her. Atchen lay quiet inside, listening the way the trees listen to the rustle of leaves.

In the shadowed corner, Eliza and Clem spoke with their heads bent close, their voices no louder than breath. Eliza shifted

Henry higher against her shoulder, the baby's sweet breath warm at her throat, one tiny fist tucked in her collar. Clem's knuckles brushed the child's heel as he nodded once, twice, his mouth a firm line, his eyes soft. John Junior kept to Eliza's side, bending a blade of straw into the shape of a star, his gaze slipping to the door and back again; when the melody turned gentle, he inched nearer, a small knee pressed to her skirt.

Esther closed her eyes. The music threaded the hush; bodies breathed in time. The owl shifted and folded its head beneath a wing. Straw ticked as it settled. Cold tucked itself into the cracks. For a little while, the barn held them like a cupped hand, and there was only sound; bow on string, the slow tide of sleeping, the small, contented sigh the earth makes when it is no longer afraid.

Then the barn door slowly swung open, creaking on winter-stiff hinges. A blast of cold swept through the barn.

The lantern's flame swung in the doorway, throwing a yellow spill across the straw. Two figures stood framed in the moonlight, men in rough, mud-dark overalls; the taller man carried the light, a shotgun slung across his shoulder. Frost-mist feathered from their mouths in the glow.

Everything inside became still. Eustace's bow hung in the air; the last note thinned to silence. Auntie Bet drew Flora into the deeper shadow of her shawl. Mose rose from his haunches by the wall, hands empty but ready; in two quiet strides he put himself between the door and the little ones. Clara scrambled across the straw with Ruth in her arms, breathing sharply; Mose reached back without looking and scooped Thomas to his hip, the boy's fingers knotting in his shirt. The children disappeared into the safety of their elders as the lantern wavered and the cold cut farther in.

For a long breath, no one spoke. The men in the doorway looked as startled as the freed folk pressed into the dim. Two worlds regarded each other across a narrow river of lamplight.

The older man cleared his throat. Broad-shouldered, his beard grizzled with ash-gray, knuckles winter-chapped; the leather on his shotgun strap creaked when he shifted. "Lord above," he said hoarsely. "Didn't expect to find anyone here."

Clem pushed himself to his feet with slow care; palms open at his sides. Behind him the women cinched their little ones close; John Junior peered around Eliza's skirt, eyes wide and wet with rising tears.

The younger man, no older than seventeen, held steady. He didn't reach for the shotgun on his father's back. His gaze skated over the nest of blankets, the straw beds, the fiddle on Eustace's lap, compassion and fear fighting in his face.

Esther stepped forward.

She didn't speak.

The lantern light climbed her tall form, ragged dress, pale skin, eyes black as the river, and stopped there like it had struck stone. When her dark gaze met the old farmer's, something passed between them, a measure taken, a silent understanding.

The lamp hissed, then steadied.

The man drew a slow breath and let it out through his nose. "Name's Nathaniel Weaver," he said, voice dropping as if not to wake the barn. "Friends call me Nathan. This here's my boy, Judd."

He angled his chin toward the black field beyond, where a small house sat with a single window lit, a square of gold trembling on the frost. "My wife, Eve, is in the kitchen." He hesitated, eyes flicking to Esther again and then to the faces along the walls. "Saw some movement out here in the barn; thought I better check it out." He took a breath. "We… we've had a spot of trouble lately."

Clem's voice came even, careful. "What kind of trouble, sir?"

Nathan's mouth worked. The lantern showed the field-cut into his palms, the tired slope of his shoulders, the way his jaw sawed like a man chewing on words he didn't want to say. In that moment, he looked older than his years, as if the night itself had been riding his back.

"Confederate soldiers been coming through," he said at last. "Taking our corn. Our pigs. Say it's for the army." He shifted the lantern, its light crawling over the faces watching him from the shadows. "Truth is, we ain't got enough corn left to see the winter through."

He hesitated, eyes flicking, briefly, bravely, to Esther.

The flame flickered and steadied.

"I reckon… if you'd stay here awhile, help us keep what's ours when they come back…," He swallowed. "Well, we'd share with you what little we have."

Silence settled like snow.

Clem looked to Esther.

In her black eyes there was no judgment, only the fathomless patience of one who chooses to listen and then consider. The barn seemed to lean toward her answer. She inclined her head. Inside, Atchen began to crawl.

Elias let out a long breath. It wasn't freedom as he'd pictured it. But it was shelter. And for this night, that was enough. He looked at Nathan's hands, cracked and work-worn; something in him squared. He thought of Levi, the quiet way his brother would plant himself in a doorway when trouble breathed. He saw a shadow of that in Judd's narrow shoulders, a son standing close to his father. Under Clem's glance he straightened, usefulness settling around him like a coat that fit.

"I can keep first watch," he murmured.

Nathan studied him a beat, then tipped his hat. "Thank you, son, but no need. Tonight, we rest. Come morning, I'll be obliged to take you up on that offer." He rested a hand on Elias's shoulder, brief and steady. "Let's get some warmth in you."

He turned to his boy and tugged his sleeve. "C'mon, Judd." Father and son stepped back into the cold. Their lantern bobbed across the stubbled field toward the small house where a single window burned like a square of honey in the dark.

The barn held its hush. Esther stayed near the door, a tall, un-moving shadow. She had known too many broken promises to trust easily. Atchen lay quiet inside, watchful as an animal in winter, listening for hoofbeats that did not come.

Then baby Henry's cry split the stillness, shrill and fierce, a pane cracking in the frost. Shoulders jerked; someone sucked in a shuddering breath. Eliza gathered him tighter, palm warm on his back, "Hush now, hush," rocking until the wail fell to hiccups against her collarbone. Small murmurs rose, the human sounds of comfort and answer, and the barn remembered to breathe.

Lantern light returned, quick-footed on the frost. Nathan and Judd shouldered through the barn door with armfuls of bundles wrapped in clean cloth. They set them on an upturned crate. When the cloth opened, the smell lifted warm and startling into the cold, oven baked bread and rendered fat, a breath of apple from corked jars. The barn seemed to breathe it in.

No one moved at first. Franklin edged forward, bare feet whispering over dirt. He reached out one small hand and touched a biscuit, as if it might vanish or bite, and felt it's heat melt into his palm, grease shining along the crust.

Nathan's mouth softened. "My Eve, was up before first light baking," he said, voice low, the way people talk in church. "Figured folks with a long road behind 'em might need a bite to set things right." The last word cracked like thin ice.

Clem swallowed hard. "Thank you," he said, thick with emotion. "You don't know what this means."

Nathan nodded once. "I think maybe I do."

They went among the people, father and son, hands careful, offering without hurry, biscuits still warm in the center, bacon grease brushed over the tops to shine them; jars of cider the color of amber, catching the lamplight like trapped sun. Tin cups clinked softly. Steam curled into the cold and drifted toward the rafters where the owl watched, unblinking.

At first, they reached with wary fingers. But hunger outweighed caution. Mabel cracked a biscuit and tipped the larger half into Flora's small hands. Beside her, Clara touched a shine of grease to Ruth's lip; the baby's breath lengthened and went warm against her wrist. Samuel went along on his knees, passing cups down the line. "Careful, it's mighty hot," he murmured, and the cider moved hand to hand. Two folks over, Martha and Auntie Bet sipped and without meaning to, closed their eyes at the same time: the sweetness chasing the iron taste from their mouths.

Eustace cupped his tin with both palms; his eyes fixed on the steam wreathing his fingers. He raised it and drank slowly, as if he could hold the moment in his mouth. It was the best thing he had ever tasted. He looked up at Esther, as if to be sure this was real.

They ate in silence, the heat of the freshly baked bread sinking into their hollowed bellies.

Beyond the door, the moon rode low and white over the cut field. Inside, in the gentle noise of chewing and breath and the faint creak of beams, the barn felt, for a little while, like a world that could last. And beneath it all, Esther stood, still and watching, the ancient spirit in her quieted for now by warmth given freely and bellies fed, while the hunger she saved for wicked men waited its turn.

Nathan and Judd didn't leave when the food was gone. They stayed. They folded themselves onto the straw like kin at a kitchen table, hats in their laps, boots dusty, asking nothing. Nathan spoke first, weather talk, planting talk, the kind of talk that lives in a man's hands, late frosts that bit the peach buds brown, a spring so wet the mule sank to the hocks, a good year for apples if the bees held. Judd, shy at the edges, told how a sow learned to lift the latch with her snout and raided the turnip patch every dusk until he outsmarted her with a rock and a length of twine.

Elias lifted his cup and, with a sheepish grin, told how he'd once tried to gentle a wild colt, "Had a look in his eye like the devil's own cousin" and how the next thing he knew the animal sent him sailing clean over the fence to land flat on his back in the mud. He showed the flight with his hands, the slap, the flail, and the splatter; laughter rippled warm around the barn. "Levi was there," he added, the grin softening. "Leanin' on the rails, laughin' low 'til he saw I'd sunk near to my ears. He laid a board across that muck like a little bridge and said, 'Crawl, little crawdad,' then hauled me out by the scruff and wiped my eyes with his sleeve." The laughter was gentle. Elias's gaze, weighed down with memory, drifted to the door where Esther stood in the half-light; she was the closest thing left to his brother. Her dark eyes met his for a breath, then she let her lids fall, not in sorrow but in something like rest, the peace of the moment settled over her like the warmth of the sun.

Eve came in after a while, apron dusted with flour, cheeks flushed from the stove. She pressed more cider into cold hands, touching each wrist gently as she passed, counting children with her eyes the way a mother does. "Drink," she murmured. "Warm yourselves." She tucked a quilt corner higher over baby Ruth and smoothed Thomas's hair without thinking twice.

Lantern light honeyed the straw. Breath steamed and faded. The owl settled. Eustace picked a few shy notes, a tune too small to scare the peace away. And in that rough old barn, for the first time anyone could remember, no one was property. No one was a price marked in a ledger. They were simply people, tired and doubtful and human, sharing heat and bread while the moon hung white over the silvered fields.

Esther remained near the door, a stillness at the edge of the circle. Atchen lay quiet within her, sated for now, as if even the old hunger knew to let this gentleness live.

In the soft afterward, as voices thinned to whispers and the children slid toward sleep, a new belief took root, small, stubborn, bright as an ember. That beyond whips and patrols and winter's lean hand, the world might yet hold more good hearts than any of them had dared to hope.

Forty-Three

The Warmth of Kindness

"In the blue hour, even the axe rang like a hymn."

The next day dawned crisp and clear, the kind of blue morning that makes every edge look sharpened. Frost rimed the fence rails and stitched white veins across the churned yard; each breath left a small cloud that drifted and tore in the sun. From the stovepipe on the Weaver house, a thin column of smoke climbed straight up, sweet with hickory and bacon, and that morning set down some- thing rare among them: a hush of mercy, a simple belonging. The air did not carry the sound of a whistle or the baying of dogs. No orders. No hunt. Only a rooster's late complaint and the far off, conversational caw of crows in the sycamores.

Before the day's work began, Nathan placed a hand on Clem's shoulder and steered him toward the north pasture. A bay gelding stood there with his head over the fence, breath feathering white, ears flicking at their steps.

"Good heart on this one," Nathan said, slipping the reins into Clem's hands. "Name's Jasper. You ride?"

Clem's palm smoothed the horse's neck, feeling the warm, living weight beneath his winter coat. "I been tending to horses my whole life," he said, the truth following close behind, "but I ain't been allowed to ride one in a long while."

Leather creaked. The gelding blew soft, as if answering. Clem set a foot to the lower rail and swung up bareback, easy as remembering his own name. Jasper shifted and settled under him, and they moved off along the edge of the field, first at a walk, then an easy trot. Frost cracked under hoof; sun glanced off the gelding's shoulders. Clem's laugh; quick, surprised, young, broke loose and floated back across the stubble.

Nathan hooked his thumbs in his belt and grinned, watching like a man pleased to offer a gift that costs nothing and returns double. When Clem climbed down, they stood eye to eye. Nathan clapped his shoulder. "Horse knows a decent hand."

Clem nodded. "And a man knows when he been treated decent." They shared a look without rank in it, then turned back toward the yard together. After that, the day took up its work.

Nathan offered, and the men took it with grateful hands. Clem and Mose shouldered axes and set to the woodpile behind the house. The first swing bit clean; sap bled sticky at the heartwood of the log. They fell into a steady cadence, lift, breathe, strike, iron ringing the crisp morning air. Chips flew and stuck to their pant legs; the smell of fresh-cut oak rose green and sharp. Old Amos sat awhile on an overturned bucket, rubbing heat into his knee, then joined them to stack the split rounds, his good eye narrowed in pleasure at the neat, rising cords. Elias knelt aside with his pocket-knife, shaving kindling to fine curls that fell like pale ribbons at his boots. Eustace ferried armloads of sticks to Eve's wood box, his fiddle tucked safely back in its cloth, his small face beaming with the usefulness of the task.

By the barn, Preacher Jonas worked shoulder to shoulder with Judd, mending the warped door. Jonas held the plank straight while Judd set the nail; the hammer spoke in calm, measured blows. They shared the slow language of making, test the swing, check the hang, plane what binds. When the last hinge pin dropped, the door rolled true along its track with a satisfying hush. The scent of fresh pine lifted in the cold air. The two men stood a moment in the pale light, hats pushed back, admiring what their hands had set right. Judd tipped the brim of his hat and grinned, sudden and boyish; Jonas's mouth softened into plain pride.

The door held, true and square.

Near the side porch, the women gathered with Eve. Baskets yawned open at their feet, mounded with ears of corn. The husks rasped and whispered as they worked, silk clinging to their fingers like fine hair. Martha's laugh rose, round and warm, as she twisted an ear clean in one pull and showed John Junior how to braid the silk into a little rope to keep busy hands from trouble. Auntie Bet hummed a work tune under her breath, the melody settling every-one into the same easy rhythm. Flora and Thomas sat cross-legged on the step, turning fallen husks into dolls with pinched waists and flared skirts; little Franklin copied them, his first attempt lopsided and beloved. From time-to-time Eve came along the line with a ladle and tin cups, passing warm broth that steamed in the cold; onion, a scrap of ham bone, black pepper, and a hunk of bread for each pair of hands. Every small offering unknotted another thread of fear from someone's shoulders. Eliza cupped her portion, eyes closed as she drank; when she opened them, the tightness at their corners had eased. When Isaac passed with a board on his shoulder, Martha tipped him a wink and a grin, tucked a heel of bread into his pocket, "for later", then went back to the husks, quick and sure.

To the east, a thin ray of sun caught on the breath of morning, creating a small prism in the winter sky. Under the hedge, chickens scratched, turning frost to dust. Inside Esther, Atchen lay like heat without flame, watchful, quieted by the honest weight of morning labor and the simple abundance of shared food. The yard filled with human sounds that did not bruise, the thunk of the axe, the rasp of a plane, the soft talk and softer laughter of people whose names were their own. For a little while, the day felt like a Sabbath bor-rowed from some kinder world, and the ground beneath their feet seemed to hold them up instead of hold them down.

Inside, the kitchen swelled with the smell of supper, onion and fatback softening in the pot, bay and pepper riding the steam, cornbread hissing where batter met hot iron. Eve moved between hearth and table with practiced grace, the hem of her skirt whispering the floorboards, her wooden spoon tapping the rim like a heartbeat. Eve had made a little nest beside the stove, two baskets pulled close to the warm bricks. Ruth slept open-mouthed, one hand splayed like a star, while Henry breathed in small, certain puffs, milk-sweet and soft. The iron ticked as it cooled; neither child stirred. Eliza stood a moment in the doorway, listening to that even rise and fall, then let the door ease shut on its latch.

Out in the yard, the children found Buster, the Weavers' old hound, asleep by the woodpile. At first, they kept their distance, eyes darting, hands half-raised as if to fend off teeth. They had only known dogs as weapons; mouths taught to punish and return them to chains. Buster lifted his gray head, blinked his wise, amber eyes, and thumped his tail. He stood and came forward slowly, offering his muzzle, humble as a handshake.

Eustace went to his knees first. He held out his palm, flat and careful, just as Eve had taught. Buster leaned in and sniffed him, warm and hay-scented, then pressed his nose against the boy's fingers. The laugh that broke from Eustace, small, disbelieving, was enough to draw tears from Eliza's eyes where she stood in the doorway. Flora edged close next, then Junior, then little Franklin with both hands buried in the dog's ruff as if anchoring himself to a friendly world. Soon there were sticks sailing and soft shouts skimming the cold air, Buster loping and returning, tongue out, tail flagging high.

"Come on then," Nathan called after a moment, tipping his hat toward the back yard. "Got something more to show you." He led a trailing ribbon of children to the second barn, the low one that kept the tools and feed. He lifted the latch and pushed through the dim into a small pen lined with fresh straw. The smell met them first, milk-warm, sweet and animal. In the nesting box at the center, a speckled bitch lay dozing, her sides rising slow, while a tumble of puppies kneaded and nuzzled, eyes still drowsy, paws no bigger than the whorl of a thumb.

They gathered in a hush, as if before a miracle.

Eustace knelt, hands on his knees, and the smallest of the litter, half-white with one ear the color of river mud, wriggled sideways until it found his palm and, without ceremony, fell asleep there. The boy's mouth opened; nothing came out but breath.

Nathan scratched his grizzled jaw. "Buster's gettin' on," he said softly. "But he still throws good pups. If you've a mind to take one when you go, that little fella looks to have chosen you first."

Eustace looked up at Eliza. She searched his face, the cautious hope of it, the old hurt gone soft around the edges, and nodded. "All right," she said, voice steady. "But you carry him proper and mind him like he's kin."

"I will," Eustace whispered low, gathering the warm weight against his chest. The pup yawned, a pink crescent, and tucked its head under his chin.

Dusk drew down blue and close. Nathan and Judd stacked a small bonfire in the side yard; Clem set flint to it, and the dry tinder took like it had been waiting. Sparks joined the first stars, and the circle around the flames pulled tighter. A jar went hand to hand, Nathan's winter whiskey, cedar-scented from the stave, men taking small sips that spread heat through cold ribs. Preacher Jonas tipped the mouth to his lips and passed it on without drink, eyes smiling faint at the foolishness of joy. The women talked low, shawls drawn close, trading recipes and birth stories and the names of neighbors they might never see again. Eve handed around cups of cider with a knob of butter melting on top, and the sheen of it made every mouth shine.

Eustace set his fiddle under his chin; his bow found a tune that felt like walking, steady, lilting, with a catch in it where the heart remembers to be grateful. The puppy slept in his lap, rising and falling to the measure. Buster stretched on his side by the fire, one ear cocked toward the lane, content and watchful. Now and again, John Junior slipped from the gathering to the porch, peeking through the cracked door to where the babies lay in baskets by the stove. Seeing Henry's blanket lift and fall, seeing Ruth's hand twitch in sleep, he came back to the fire and sat near Eliza, the worry gone from his small face.

A little way apart, where the light thinned to amber, Samuel and Cora sat shoulder to shoulder on a split log, close enough to feel the heat, far enough to keep their shadows to themselves. Samuel's hands cupped a tin of cider; now and then his thumb ran the old rope-groove on his wrist the way a man checks the weather in a scar. Cora turned her cup slowly, learning how to hold warmth again. She had no words, but when a knot in the fire popped, she didn't flinch, she breathed through it, eyes on the flame until it was only wood again. Their silence wasn't empty; it was a stitch, tight and neat, holding two torn edges together. When Samuel slid half his biscuit into her palm, she didn't protest, only met his glance and gave the smallest nod, something like thanks, something like we're still here. They ate, and their hands steadied.

Esther stood just beyond the light, where the fire's edge feathered into darkness. The glow drew a copper rim along her cheek and left her eyes starless. Inside, Atchen lay quiet. Yet something in the far distance ticked against that calm, a taste in the wind of tallow and iron, of horse-sweat and wet wool. Somewhere, beyond the ridge a crow flew hard and straight, cawing into the crisp night sky. Buster's ear lifted higher; his chest rumbled with a low, uncertain sound before sinking back to peace.

The fire popped again. Laughter rose and fell. A squirrel chittered its name along the fence line. And under the easy talk and the lingering scent of woodsmoke and corn cakes, a quiet knowing drifted through the yard, the road ahead would not be gentle. But for this one night, they had warmth, and full bellies, and the simple, unremarkable grace of a hound asleep at a child's feet.

Forty-Four

Broken Solitude

"He that stealeth a man… shall surely be put to death."

-Exodus 21:16

The morning carried the sound of marching boots.

At first, it was only a faint quiver under the frozen lane, a tremor that found the crockery on Eve's shelf and set a spoon to ticking in its cup. Then it gathered itself into rhythm, boot, boot, boot, the measured tramp of men who believed the road belonged only to them.

Nathan stepped onto the porch, pulling his coat tight against a pale sun that offered no heat. Frost filmed the porch rail beneath his palm. In the yard, Buster lifted his graying head and gave a low, uneasy whine, one ear pinned to the lane.

They came out of the sycamores' shadow in a long gray line. Overcoats the color of ash, cuffs frayed, belts shiny with tallow, their faces raw with cold and certainty. Horse breath steamed like ghosts. Saddle leather creaked. A small guidon snapped in the brittle air and then hung slack.

At their head rode an officer with a yellow sash tied neat at his waist, hat cocked, lip curled in a smile that had never had to earn itself. He did not dismount. He let his horse stamp on Nathan's hard-packed yard and looked down on the front porch as if it were a stage laid for him.

Nathan didn't flinch.

He crossed his arms over his broad chest as the officer's mount came up to the steps. Two privates peeled off toward the smokehouse without being ordered. Another drifted toward the back lot with a practiced eye, as if he could smell hidden sacks of corn.

"Sir," Nathan said evenly, voice carrying without shout. "I told you boys the last time you came round, our winter supplies are running low. If you take any more of my pigs, my family won't make it through the cold."

The officer's gaze slid past Nathan over the porch to the single window where a curtain fluttered and stilled. His eyes weighed the doorway, not just the pantry and the smokehouse, but what else the house might owe if he chose to call it debt. His gloved hand rested easy on the butt of his pistol, not gripping it so much as enjoying that it was there.

"I told you, Mr. Weaver," he drawled, slow as syrup and twice as thick, "these supplies are being commandeered to support the Southern troops." His smile lifted a fraction. "And that is exactly what my men intend to do."

From the house came the quick hush of Eve's breath. She stepped into the doorway, flour still dusting her forearms, a dishrag twisted in her hands like rope. Behind her a cluster of small faces pressed to her skirts before she eased them back, one by one.

"Sir," she said, quiet but clear, "we ain't got as much as you think."

"Ma'am," the officer tipped his hat without warmth. He flicked two fingers, the men at the smokehouse kicked the latch and disappeared inside. His gaze slid back to Eve and lingered a beat too long, traveling down and up again like a hand. One of the privates, young and sharp with hunger of another sort, hitched his belt and smirked. "Reckon there's provisions in the house we ought to inventory," he said, eyes never leaving her. "Some things folks hide better 'n corn."

Nathan shifted, squaring himself between the door and the yard. The dishrag twisted tighter in Eve's hands.

Clem stood just inside the side yard fence, hands empty, eyes trained on the soldiers. Mose was a step behind him, jaw set tightly. Jonas had drifted to the corner of the house and bowed his head, which looked like prayer but was also counting rifles, counting men.

Without lifting his chin, Jonas murmured, "Where's Elias?"

"Back barn with the tools," Clem said, low.

"I'll fetch him," Mose breathed, already angling a shoulder.

Clem's hand found his sleeve and held. "No. Let the boy stay where the noise can't find him. You know what they'll do to Nathan if they learn he's keepin' folk that ain't his."

Mose swallowed, heat riding his breath, but he stilled. The old anger in him wanted to move; the good sense did not. Jonas's fingers traced the brim of his hat, steadying himself. "Then we hold," he said, soft as an amen. "Keep 'em out of sight and keep this man's house standing."

Judd came around from the barn at a trot, breath fogging, hammer still in his fist. He pulled up short when he saw the line of gray, the yellow sashes. He slowly set the hammer down without being told and straightened, shoulders squaring, hands high.

The officer turned his horse just enough to look the boy over. Something pleased him.

"How old are you, son?"

Judd swallowed. "Seventeen, sir."

"Fine age." The officer's smile showed a glint of tooth. "The Commonwealth is calling her sons. You'll come along with us and do your duty."

Nathan stepped down one stair, then another, until he stood at the bottom, level with the horse's chest. "He's not a soldier," he said. "He is just a boy."

"Then he'll do you proud." The officer didn't bother to look at Nathan as he said it. His greedy eyes drifted past, toward the doorway where Eve stood bracing the frame with her small body.

"You'll not have him." The words were flat as a board laid over a ditch.

The officer finally turned his head. Whatever was soft in his mouth went out. "This is not a petition, Mr. Weaver. It is a levy." He nodded once. Two men broke from the line and moved toward Judd, rifles slung across their shoulders, hands already reaching. A third set his boot on the porch step and drew the back of his glove slow along the jamb beside Eve's shoulder, testing the grain, testing the house. "We'll be having a look indoors, too," he said, not bothering to raise his voice. "If the lady takes to fussin', we'll sort that as well."

Buster came forward, hackles lifting, a warning rippling up from his chest. A soldier swung the butt of his rifle in a lazy arc; striking him square in the muzzle, the old hound skittered back, whimpering, humiliated.

"Sir," Eve said, one hand fluttering at her throat now, the other turned outward in a plea she could not swallow. "Please."

Nathan put himself between the soldiers and his son. The officer raised his free hand. "I'll ask you to step aside, sir."

"No." Nathan's voice didn't rise, but something in it deepened until the porch boards seemed to hear it. "You'll not take my boy." He did not look away from the officer, but his stance covered Eve as if he were two men wide.

It happened quickly after that. A shoulder slammed into Nathan's ribs. The officer's horse sidestepped, iron edge of its shoe gouging the yard. A rifle stock came down like a mallet; wood met bone with a sound that drew a cry from Eve. Nathan folded to his knees and then to his hands, breath gone, eyes watering. Judd lurched, caught one of the men by the sleeve, and got a fist across the mouth for his trouble. Blood sprang quick and red on his lip. The men had him under the arms then, hauling him, boy and burden both, toward the line. The third soldier's hand had already found the tie of Eve's apron, fingers rubbing the knot, as if considering whether it ought to come loose.

Eve moved without thinking. She caught Judd's sleeve and held tightly; a soldier wrenched her wrist until she cried out and let go. Clem took a step he shouldn't have, and Mose's hand clamped down hard on his forearm. Not yet, that grip said. Not like this.

Inside the barn, the freed souls had gone to ground. A hush like held breath settled among the cornstalk heaps. Children's fingers clutched at their mama's skirts. In that close straw-sweet dark, the air tasted suddenly of fear and a coming storm.

Out beyond the yard fence, under the gray flank of the sycamore, Esther stood where the light thinned to shadow. The cold made no claim on her. The yellow of the officer's sash burned like a brand in her sight. The horses felt her before the men did, ears tipping, whites showing, breath chopping shorter. A caped crow let go of its branch and arrowed away, calling out, as if to warn the next ridge.

Inside, Atchen woke. Her hunger uncoiled, slow and exacting, sharpening every edge of the morning. The world narrowed to the boy's blood on his lip. To the soldier's glove grazing Eve's apron and the smile it dragged across his mouth. To the tremor in Eve's hand after he let go. To the hard, satisfied crinkle at the corner of the officer's eye.

The two soldiers had Judd in the lane now, his boots scraping furrows in the frost. Nathan pushed to his feet, staggered, lunged again. The officer barely sighed. "Teach the gentleman manners," he said, and a rifle stock lifted for a second blow.

The wind, which had been nothing all morning, rose and went shivering through the pines. The sun walked behind a thin cloud. Somewhere down in the holler a coyote yipped, another answered from farther off in the distance.

Esther stepped forward, out of the shadow and into the pale, pitiless light.

Forty-Five

The Taken

*"What is stolen in a cold morning,
will be repaid double in the long dark."*

They took Judd at noon, dust rising in pale ghosts under the soldiers' boots. By early afternoon the lane had swallowed their noise, only the groove of wheels and a dark ribbon of hoofprints told where they'd gone.

Esther did not follow them then.

She stood patient in the shadow of the sycamore, still as bark. The yard held its breath around her, the clatter of a dropped pail, Eve's muffled sob, Nathan's ragged curse snatched by the wind, she let it pass through her without moving. Atchen paced inside her like a caged beast, testing the metal of her bones.

When twilight bled down the field and the frost began to find the ruts, she slipped from the fence line and into the trees.

The evening smelled of rust and leaf mold, woodsmoke far off, horse-sweat closer. Bats cut their tight seams through the dusk. She moved faster than shadows, quiet as a falling ash, following the broken shape the men had left behind them, a scuffed root, a bent reed, a shred of yellow thread snagged on briar where the officer's sash brushed the world.

Night drew its veil.

She found the camp where the lane shouldered into a stand of young pines. A cook-fire had been beaten to coals, red as a heartbeat under ash. Canvas pup tents slouched. Tin rattled somewhere in the night. Men slept in rags of gray, mouths open to the cold, breath turning to ghosts and back again. Their boots ringed the fire like offerings. Rifles leaned in a neat triangle against a stump. Judd was tied to a wheel, hat lost, lip split, eyes shut tight as if sleep might offer the mind a brief escape.

The horses sensed her; heads came up, ears cut like knives. A bay mare whinnied and then was still.

She went among the tents like winter fever. Canvas sighed. A hand twitched. A snore clipped short. Where she passed, breath failed and did not return. The cold in her touched throats and ribs and made the small, breaking sounds that men do not live through. Blood sang against canvas. A boot kicked at nothing and lay still. Some never woke up. One unfortunate soul did; his eyes opened on her face, he thought it was the moon gone black, terror found him first, and then pain followed, slow and deliberate, before the world erased itself.

Atchen rose within her, the old hunger taking shape, teeth in the dark, a cold joy in the unmaking. She gave these men back their commerce in fear, returned it measure for measure, then more, until the pines swallowed their cries and the earth took their heat. She marked them with silence, but not quickly; the demon in her was patient, and she let their hearts learn what death weighs when it sits on the chest and will not move.

She saved the officer for last. He lay with his hat over his face; his sash looped carelessly round his fist. When she took the hat away, his hand reached for a pistol that wasn't there. He saw her and remembered the mother's hand he had bent back, the boy he'd claimed like a pig from a pen.

"Do not take what is not yours," she said, and the voice in her was pain and fury.

Her hand moved and something in his chest *gave*; a deep, awful collapse that stole the breath from his body and the fight from his eyes. Blood painted her cheeks; her black eyes reflected only red. His pride thinned to pleading and then to nothing. When she was done, he lay folded in on himself, uniform dark and ruined, the tent holding only the quiet she had come to claim. Outside, the camp made small noises of cooling. The pines put their breath back. The wind went on about its business. And Atchen, satisfied, lay like a cat curled at the hearth.

Judd woke to gentle fingers working on the knot at his wrist. He flinched before he knew who held him. "It's me," Clem whispered from the dark. The rope loosened as if it had been waiting to fall. They walked the lane without lamp or a word. Frost glittered in the ditch like a field of low stars.

In the deepening twilight, Nathan met them at the fence.

No words passed between them.

Clem felt the grip of Nathan's hand on his shoulder, brief, full, remarkable in its simplicity. In all his life no white man had ever put a hand on him without laying claim.

Eve took Judd's face in both palms, kissed his split brow, as if it were a sacrament, and tucked his head beneath her chin. The boy shuddered then calmed, as if he could breathe again for the first time since morning.

For a long moment, the yard was only breath and the creak of the gate on its hinge. The field kept their secret; the sky kept the rest.

When night fell fully, Esther knew it was time.

She stood at the edge of the clearing, turning toward the black hem of the ridges lifting in the east. The mountains called like a low note struck inside her body, an old, insistent thread pulling taut.

Nathan and his family came to the barn to see them off. Eve's arm stayed firm around Judd's shoulders; worry and gratitude braided together on her face. Nathan's hat was in his hands. Buster lay with his chin on his paws and watched, tail thumping, as if to say he understood.

There were no speeches.

Only the frost whispering into the corn stubble, the old barn sighing as it gave its heat back to the night, the river, far off, talking to itself under thin ice.

Eliza clasped Eve's hands, eyes wet but steady. "You showed us more kindness than we ever knew the world could hold," she said, voice low.

Eve shook her head. "You're good people. You deserved it all along."

Nathan cleared his throat, then stepped past the gate with a lead-rope in his fist. Jasper came behind him, ears pricked, the same bay Clem had ridden at first light the previous morning. The horse wore a blanket and a sawbuck saddle strung with bundles: a sack of meal and dried beans; a hunk of salt pork; a small hatchet and flint; an awl, needles, and thread in a tin; two extra quilts; a laying hen in a small wooden cage; a coil of rope; a kerchief of apples gone sweet with keeping.

"He knows your hand," Nathan said, and pressed the reins into Clem's palm. "He'll carry better than most men. He's yours now, take him."

Clem set his jaw and tried to give them back. "We can't take him; he belong to you."

"You can," Nathan answered, not unkindly. "Winter's long in those mountains. Let a good horse do his share."

Their eyes held and Clem nodded, the kind that seals a promise. He stroked Jasper's neck; the bay breathed him in and stood silent.

Eustace lingered on the step, fiddle under one arm, a warm bundle of pup under the other. He crouched and wrapped both arms around Buster's old neck. "Mr. Buster," he whispered into the hound's ear, "don't you worry. I'm gon' take good care of your ba-by. Promise." Buster huffed, as if sealing the deal.

The children were quiet with the solemnity of leaving, bundles knotted tight. Happiness and sorrow drank from the same cup. Leaving this place meant leaving the first kindness they had known.

But the mountains waited.

And freedom, though it had already rooted in them, still lay ahead like high ground after a flood.

Esther stepped onto the rutted track. She did not call. She did not turn. They fell in behind her without a word, feet finding the lane by memory and faith. The moon shouldered over the far trees and poured a silver road across the stubble and frost.

With weary bones and hearts that still dared to hope, they went into the night, Jasper's steady footfall, the faint rattle of tin against the saddle, the soft cluck of a hen at his flanks, and the last part of their journey began.

Forty-Six

The Promised Land

"Every seed must break before it can grow."

The morning came full and bright; a blanket of light laid along the ridge. Esther moved directly, with great purpose. The pull in her grew stronger, an unspoken promise that the journey, at last, was nearing its end. Atchen told her they were close. But it was the land that steered her feet. With each step the air changed, it took on a sweetness she had not breathed in years, cool water, crushed fern, the first green thought of spring.

They entered the foothills.

Here the trees rose taller than any tree they had ever seen. Great chestnuts thrust skyward in columns of living green. White pines lifted their dark spires through a silver mist. The wilderness was old here, older than any planter's map, the ground soft with centuries of leaf-fall, stones furred with moss, the creeks speaking in a clear, quick tongue. Rhododendron thickets shouldered the trail; laurel leaves clicked softly in the wind. A pair of wild turkeys ghosted across their path, bronze backs flashing. While, high above a red-tailed hawk turned, drawing slow circles in the clouds.

Esther climbed, her bare feet silent on damp rock. Below, her people paused and lifted their faces to watch, Clem steady as an oak, leading Jasper by the rein. The bay's ears pricked to the mountain wind, while the bundles on his saddle swayed in time with Clem's stride. Something had shifted in the man; his back was straighter, his brow set calm. He carried himself like a freeman who owned a good horse and the ground beneath his feet.

Eliza walked just behind him, Henry warm against her hip, John Junior close at her skirts. She had never thought the world would give her motherhood, yet here it was, one fair head tucked to her shoulder, one small hand claiming her hem, as if it were a lifeline. Eustace kept to Esther's shadow, the puppy tucked against his chest, quiet as breath. Mose and Elias came on with the weight of tools and quilts across their shoulders; Mabel held Flora tight to her side. Even the puppy, feeling the strangeness of this sweet air, went still.

On the crest, the wind met her cool and sweet, like water rushing through a mountain stream. She turned and looked down. Spread before them lay a hidden valley, cupped like a palm between the verdant arms of the mountains. Mist lay low along a lush meadow where the creek unspooled in flickering bends, shaded by alders and sycamores. Dark hemlock guarded the far slope; on the near, redbuds were beaded with tight, wine-colored buds; a single dogwood held white stars like a small constellation remembered. The south face was already soft with spring, skunk cabbage spears pushing through the seep, chickadees stitching the quiet with their clear two-note song. Water beetles spun ripples into a pool where trout dimpled, then vanished. No road. No fences. No smoke but the valley's own breath lifting from the warmed earth.

For a long moment, no one breathed. This place belonged to them alone.

Old Amos took off his hat, pressed it flat to his chest and breathed deep. Beside him, Auntie Bet let her hands ease open at her side, and in that unclosing there was a kind of surrender, like laying down a burden you'd forgotten had weight.

Atchen went quiet, not gone, but watchful. You brought them, the ancient one said, and what moved in her was no longer hunger so much as kinship. She had been born of want and ruin: starved until her bones rang hollow, taken and used, then burned by her own, to live or not in the dark. Esther had known the same furnace, yet her people did not cast her out. They gathered her back and she spent herself for them, piece by piece, until there was almost nothing left but the keeping. To a spirit born of abandonment, this refusal to forsake was a revelation. And in that knowing, something shifted: the world was no longer only debt to be collected or flesh to be reckoned with. Atchen named these people not as spoil or sentence but as *ours*. And she named Esther, who had carried her through fire without letting go, *sister*.

The land answered that truth in a small way; a red wolf slipped from the laurel and stood before them unafraid. Then, loped off on long, easy legs, its tawny coat catching the light like burnished copper. Amongst Atchen's people, the red wolf was Grandfather, keeper of the world's balance. She took its appearance as a sign; they had found *Nekawaya*, the land that listens, and it would provide for Esther's people.

Esther's throat tightened. The thread that had been pulling her since the river loosened and unraveled into the open air. She felt Levi rise in her like a warm current and pass, tender as a hand smoothing her hair. She felt her mother in the rich, loam smell coming off the meadow, in the hush beneath the big trees. All that grief did not leave her. But it changed shape.

"This is it," Clem said softly, as if afraid to bruise the view. "This is it, Miss Esther."

No one called her an angel now. No one called her a monster. They called her Esther and simply stood with her, seeing what she saw.

Eustace stepped forward until he stood beside her hip. He didn't speak. He didn't need to. The yellow scarf she had given him warmed his neck; Mama's shell ring touched his sternum with every breath. He lifted her Bible in both hands and held it to his chest. The new pup nosed his wrist and sighed.

Esther raised her hand, slow as a blessing, and the group began to move, careful, down through the switchbacks, feet finding the old deer paths that braided the slope. Their steps grew less cautious as the last of their fear slipped away. At each turn the valley opened a little more; a hidden bench perfect for growing beans, a tumble of flat stones that would make a hearth, a dry ledge under rock where children could pretend to be birds. By the time they reached the creek, the sun had found the spine of the day and laid a brilliant spark on every ripple.

They knelt to drink. Cold, mineral-crisp water stung their tongues and woke them from the long night. Auntie Bet cupped both hands and let the creek run over her fingers like a baptism. Beside her, Old Amos washed his face and laughed, a sound nobody had heard from him since the tobacco was high, then flicked a bright handful at her wrists. She squealed and with a quickness that belonged to a younger woman, splashed him back. For a heartbeat the years slid off them; they were two sweethearts in summer water, grinning like thieves. Clem caught Eliza by the waist and spun her in a wide circle, her laughter ringing out like a bell; Henry squealed and batted at the glittering water; John Junior dipped a careful hand and grinned, this was a world he could trust. Clem glanced at the old ones and then at Eliza, a soft promise passing between them without a word, that love might live long enough to grow old and playful here, too.

Esther stood with her feet in the water, the current combing over her toes. Atchen's voice was a low rustle, flowing like dark waters through her thoughts.

"We will build," Clem said, and the way he said it made the word bigger than timber and nails.

Eliza glanced at Esther. "Will we be safe?"

Esther lifted her gaze to the rim of the mountains. The air brought her only water, green, and the clean, faint musk of deer. No powder. No tallow. No iron. "Safer than we have ever been," she said, and though her voice was still rough as an old scar, it held no tremor.

In the meadow's middle, a bare patch of earth waited where a garden might go. Eustace went there first and set his fiddle down like a claim. The children ran and fell and rose and ran again; the puppy chased the creek's light and bit at his own reflection. Mose and Elias began to gather deadfall; Martha and Clara spoke of stones for a bread oven; out of old habit, Mabel counted little faces that need not be counted. They were safe.

Esther watched, and the watching filled her.

The valley did not promise there would be no hunger, no winter, no work that bent the back. It promised only that the work and the hunger and the winter would be theirs. The cost of every breath would be paid to no one.

High on the ridge, a wind lifted out of the pines and ran down through the dogwoods, across the grass, and into their clothes and hair. It smelled of thaw. It smelled of beginnings.

Esther closed her raven eyes and let it pass through her. When she opened them again, the world was not the same. Behind them, the long road lay like a shed skin. Before them, the land opened its hand.

They stepped into it.

They had reached the Promised Land, a cradle of green held safe in the mountain's hands.

Esther stood a moment longer and watched them spill into it, Clem guiding Jasper straight to the creek to drink, Thomas kneeling to touch a snail hidden under damp moss, Clara pressing both hands to her chest, as if steadying a heart that had finally found room to beat. Eustace stood very still, pup tucked under his chin, eyes roaming as if memorizing every tree.

With every beat of their hearts, they had known so much sorrow. The memory of awful days moved through them like weather, but here it thinned under the warmth of the sun. In this place their scars would heal, and their lives would bloom.

She felt Atchen listening inside her, full of old wrath and older memory, yet what rose from the roots was gentler, leaf-soft, river-cool. In this hidden hollow the land would take them in. It would bare its teeth at their hunters and open its arms for them.

Because they had suffered enough.

At last, she allowed herself to rest.

She sank at the base of a towering white oak, its bark ridged like a map, its limbs arched high and spare against the pale sky. The smell of loam lifted, clean and dark; sunlight came thin through the branches and painted her hands in shifting lace. She let her back find the rough, living spine of the tree and closed her eyes. The sweet sounds of the valley gathered around her, the creek talking over stones, mourning doves cooing in the quiet, a soft breeze combing the meadow until the grass lay one way, then shifted the other.

She was so tired. The kind of tired that lives in the bones, older than sleep. Her breath slowed and evened. Her fingers loosened on her torn skirts. A single dogwood petal, shaken loose out of season, drifted down and clung to the dark curl at her temple.

Time went thin and long.

Then the small weight of a hand found her shoulder.

"Esther," Eustace whispered.

She did not move.

"Esther…" His voice cracked on the second syllable. He dropped to his knees in the leaf-litter and clutched her arm with both hands, the shell ring at his throat knocking softly against her sleeve. "Oh Lord, no. Please, not my Esther," he sobbed, the pup pressed between his body and hers, trembling and small.

It was not the Lord who answered. It was the land.

The ground beneath her let out a slow, deep exhale, a hush that carried something ancient and solemn. The oak's weight hummed through her spine. The creek's voice steadied.

Esther had given tribute. The dark, bloody soil had accepted her sacrifice.

Her head turned slightly, like a leaf shifting in a breeze.

Eustace's breath caught; his hands stilled. Her eyelids fluttered open, not to light, but to the shape of a face she would have known with her eyes closed. As ever, her sightless gaze found him unerringly. A tired smile curved her lips. "My sweet boy," she whispered, the words worn smooth with use, polished on every night she'd ever tucked him close.

They were the last words she ever spoke.

Around them the valley went on being a valley, water glistening stones, a red-tailed hawk keening high over the ridge, the wind setting the meadow in slow motion. But those near enough to see; Eliza's hand over her mouth, Clem's jaw locked and shining with tears he would not let fall, Preacher Jonas stepping out of his prayer and into silence, felt the world tilt and set again on a different axis.

For her people's salvation, Esther had traded many things. Her eyes would not see their houses rise or watch the dogwood break into constellations. Her legs would never carry her along the deer paths or up into the blackberry tangle come summer. Atchen had taken her price, the last untouched sliver of what the world had left her. And yet mercy ran through the loss like a silver thread.

Her breath had stayed. Her pulse lifted and lowered, sure and small at her throat. When Eustace slid his palm into hers, her fingers answered with the faintest pressure, tucking one loose curl behind his ear the way she had done every night as she sung him into sleep. The puppy nosed her wrist and settled, sighing. The oak held her up as if she belonged to it.

"She's still with us," Eliza said hoarsely, falling to her knees at Eustace's side. "She is with us."

Clem took off his hat and bowed his head, then pressed it to his chest with both scarred hands. He had walked beside her since the first dark mile, through ash and winter and the hard silence of choosing, and he knew what it had cost to bring them to this green valley of mercy. He stood as if keeping watch, not for enemies now but for the debt he meant to shoulder from this day on. A hum rose in him, unforced and low, the kind a father makes without thinking when a child finally sleeps; it moved through the gathered like a warm breeze and settled around Esther soft as a blanket. Jonas set his hand to the oak and closed his eyes, blessing in a language older than any he'd spoken from a pulpit.

Eustace laid his forehead gently against Esther's. His shoulders shook, and then the shaking eased. He lifted his head and with hands that did not tremble, he took out his fiddle and set the instrument beneath his chin. He played for her a ballad that she felt through the earth, through the roots, through the very air she breathed. It was a song of love and gratitude and a promise that he would carry her for the rest of his days.

Together they would build. They would learn the turns of the weather here and where the creek ran low in drought and which hollow held frost the longest. Children would grow into the timbre of their own voices. The old would lay down to rest and not be counted as a burden.

Esther would not walk among them. But each morning, when the light came thin through the white oak's branches, it would find her warm and comfortable in her bed, surrounded by those she loved with her entire heart. She had carried her people to freedom, and for her sacrifice they would love and honor her for the rest of her days.

And each night, when Eustace drew his bow and the music went out over the water, it would pass through her, and the trees, and the earth that had taken so much and, at last, given back.

Somewhere in the forest, Atchen quietly watched.

She had given Esther back to her boy.

And he knew freedom.

Forty-Seven

Freedom

"They that sow in tears shall reap in joy."

-Psalm 126:5

In Esther's hollow, her people found home.

In the years that followed, they made the land their own.

During the first spring, they raised modest cabins from the timber of trees, green-scented poplar and straight chestnut laid true, chinked with moss and clay. Smoke billowed from new chimneys in thick white curls, and the warm aroma of wood and fat and fresh-cut boards settled into everything like a benediction. They split rails, fenced gardens, and turned dark earth with tools passed hand to hand. In its rich soil they planted oats and corn and wheat. From its creeks they took ramps and brook trout, bronze-bright from riffled water. In the fall they shook wild apples from limbs and filled their aprons with walnuts and chestnuts sweet as milk. The wilderness that had once seemed vast and mysterious became a sanctuary and a promise, a country that kept faith.

They were strong people, made so by what the world had required of them, and strength turned to gentleness when it was at last their own. Men and women formed families and spoke vows under the white oak, fingers woven together, faces open to the sky. Babies were born into hands that would never be sold. Children learned their given names without whispering. No overseer's whistle cut the morning. No hound traced fear through the night. The only calls were those of birds and mothers and the creek telling its endless story against stone.

Eliza and Clem jumped the broom there, too, Eustace set the tune, Elias hummed under it, and Fiddle, his rough-coated pup, barked an amen. Clem lifted her hand, and they stepped together, clean over the bristles and into a life no master could touch.

Eustace and Elias settled into their new life, as if it had been waiting for them all along; they moved around the little cabin like brothers born to the same mama, trading shirts, arguing soft over nothing, sleeping head-to-foot when storms rattled the roof, each reaching for the other in the dark without thinking. Clem showed them how to dress a hoof and set a gate true; Eustace taught Henry a fiddle lullaby one note at a time, while Elias took John Junior down to the creek to learn a snare and the names of fish. More than once, Eliza looked up from the hearth to see all five of them crossing the yard together, Clem with his easy stride, Eustace carrying the milk pail careful, Elias balancing Henry high upon his shoulders, John Junior trotting between, and her heart knew the gratitude of family.

Their boys grew straight as young poplar; John Junior, quick with figures and gentle with colts; Henry, fleet as a trout and laughing like creek-water over stone, both boys were full of pure silliness and joy. Some evenings Eliza would sit on the threshold while the boys slept and the lamp burned low, and she would remember that night behind the smokehouse, Esther's breath close, squeezing her fingers hard enough to leave a mark. *I will come back for you.* Those words were the iron they tempered themselves on, the crucible that held through winter and hunger and all the miles between. "She kept it," Eliza would whisper into the quiet, pressing her palm to the floorboards grown from their own trees. "She kept it, and we're here, together." And Clem, listening from the table with his tools laid out neat, would look at his boys, all of them, and smile the quiet, proud smile of a man who has what he set his back against the world to win.

Eustace grew tall and quick, all elbows and laughter, running barefoot through moss that remembered only the weight of deer. Fiddle, now long-legged and serious, shadowed him from ridge to water's edge. He learned his letters as if they were a new kind of freedom, one you could carry inside your mouth and never lose. In the evenings, he sat beside Esther beneath the great white oak, his voice sure and proud as he sounded his way through words that once lived only in other men's houses. When the light went thin and gold, he would braid her hair, fingers gentle, weaving a tapestry of turkey feathers and autumn leaves through her dark curls, talking on as he worked.

He told stories of golden mornings and heavy harvests, of cabins built so tight that even January could not slip a breath between the logs, of weddings where the whole hollow sang, and of the children who would come after them and never learn the language of chains. Esther listened, her face warm with joy. Though her sight was gone and her limbs quiet, she bore witness as her family grew, as the valley filled with voices that would never again be silenced.

Sometimes he played, bow drawing sweetness from the fiddle he had carried through the long road to freedom, and the valley shifted to hear it, owls pausing mid-call, the creek gathering itself to a hush. On soft evenings, he would lift Esther in his arms and carry her to the front porch, settling her in a chair with quilts tucked warm at her sides, the white oak's shadow laid gently across her feet.

And when the last hint of orange drained from the evening sky and the lanterns came up in the doorways, Esther would follow that music backward through time, Saturday nights kindled out of memory. She felt Levi's hand at the small of her back, the scuff of their bare feet in the dirt, the two of them turning slowly in a circle while the stars spun overhead. Lanterns swung from branches; little ones darted between skirts with molasses chews stuck to their teeth. She saw Solomon and Clem laughing low, talking of horses and wide fields they swore they'd ride one day with no hounds at their backs. And Mama, oh Mama, sipping sweet tea, eyes shining with laughter. Saturday nights were made for music, and in those songs, Esther felt freedom long before she could touch it.

Though her eyes would never open on the world again and her legs would not carry her another step, Esther lived her life through the joy of her kin. The people honored her sacrifice. They wove quilts and tucked them around her when snow sifted down out of a slate sky. They washed and brushed her hair and tied it back with Mama's marigold scarf on feast days. They left first-fruits, a persimmon warm from the tree, a sheaf of wheat, a handful of chestnuts, on her bedside table.

Children learned to climb the low limbs of the great white oak where she first rested and sit quietly, listening to the tree's slow speech. When storms shouldered over the ridge and threw white fire from cloud to spine, they gathered close beneath Esther's oak and felt the ground take the thunder for them.

At the borders of the hollow, something old kept watch. Not hunger now but keeping. Atchen's fire glowed low and steady, a coal beneath ash, present in the prickle before a stranger's step, in the way crows gathered, flying hard and straight to the ridge and sat there, cawing their warning. Word passed through roots, mycelium, and creek light. These are ours. More than once, riders turned back at the gap without knowing why. The land had learned their names and would not give them up.

Seasons threaded themselves into years. Wheat stood like brass and fell under clean scythes. Corn silked and tasseled. Snow made every cabin a small mountain in moonlight. They sang hymns as they buried their dead and marked the ground with stones. They bore their young and danced until the lamp oil was gone and then kept dancing by firelight. They taught their daughters to laugh full-throated and their sons to bake bread and mend harnesses and hum over a sleeping child.

They made a church of air and water and woodsmoke and, some Sabbaths, of four walls and a roof they had raised together, where Preacher Jonas spoke softly about a God who had walked them out of Egypt by way the map could not show.

Eustace's voice changed and settled; he read faster and farther, then read back to Esther the lines he loved best. Sometimes, he set the book aside and told her what was not printed anywhere, the way the wind lifted the wheat into waves, the taste of a chestnut roasted in coals until it burst, the way Fiddle had learned to fetch without chewing the stick. And always, when words were done, he lifted the fiddle and played the valley's day into evening, so that everything that lived inside their circle could find its way home to her by the sound.

As the years passed, they tended Esther as they tended the springhouse and the smokehouse and the seed corn, with reverence and daily hands. She lived long in that hollow, through many winters and springs, her bed kept warm, her hair brushed, stories poured into her like light, Eustace never far from her side. And when at last her breath thinned and went, it left her not alone but ringed by the ones she had carried into freedom, their hands on her, their tears on her quilt, their gratitude spoken plain. Somewhere in the ridges, the Mother of Hunger wept, soft as wind through pine, grieving a sister who had carried her into daylight.

They spoke her name when they taught a child to read, when a woman quickened, and when a man laid down his tools at dusk and found he had worked a whole day without fear. They told the story right, not as a whisper of terror but as a lit path: the girl who stepped into the dark and returned with her people unchained.

On winter nights, when the wind slipped a knife between flock and fleece and the chestnut shells rattled in their baskets, the children gathered close and asked for it again. They sat cross-legged, backs to warm boards, eyes big and solemn in the lamplight. And someone, Eliza, or Clem, or Eustace himself with Fiddle's gray muzzle on his knee, would begin: of Broadlawn, and fire, and a river that ran red and then ran clean again; of a woman with eyes like the first night and hands steady enough to lift a people, of a mountain that opened and said, *This is the way*. The story of Esther, the one who had crossed the hills and walked through darkness. The one who delivered her people to freedom. The telling always ended the same: She brought us here. We brought each other the rest of the way.

In the gentle hush that followed, the little ones lifted their faces toward the ridge, where the moon laid a narrow road along the snow and the oak's crown tossed its dark prayers against the stars. They believed, with all the solemn certainty of children, that no power on this earth would ever take their freedom again.

And if the wind sometimes carried a low hum through the laurel, half river, half song, they knew it was only the land remembering their names.

HALLOWED GROUND

Nancy Buchewicz is an artist and writer who keeps her bags near the doorway and her eyes on the nearest ridgeline. A multi-disciplinary artist working in oil, acrylic, and textiles, Nancy also teaches art workshops and has raised four children while moving among small mountain towns across the United States. Her fiction is rooted in landscape, memory, and human resilience, written at the crossroads of history and imagination. *Hallowed Ground*, her debut novel, grew from time in mountain archives and years spent walking old roads, listening to the trees tell their tales.

Visit Nancy online at www.nancybuchewicz.com